STUART

belly
up

SIMON & SCHUSTER BOOKS FOR YOUNG READERS
An imprint of Simon & Schuster Children's Publishing Division
1230 Avenue of the Americas, New York, New York 10020
This book is a work of fiction. Any references to historical events, real people, or real locales are used fictitiously. Other names, characters, places, and incidents are products of the author's imagination, and any resemblance to actual events or locales or persons, living or dead, is entirely coincidental.

SIMON & SCHUSTER BOOKS FOR YOUNG READERS is a trademark of Simon & Schuster, Inc.
For information about special discounts for bulk purchases, please contact Simon & Schuster Special Sales at 1-866-506-1949 or business@simonandschuster.com.
The Simon & Schuster Speakers Bureau can bring authors to your live event. For more information or to book an event, contact the Simon & Schuster Speakers Bureau at 1-866-248-3049 or visit our website at www.simonspeakers.com.
Also available in a Simon & Schuster Books for Young Readers hardcover edition
Book design by Lucy Ruth Cummins
The text for this book is set in Garamond.
Manufactured in the United States of America
0515 OFF
First Simon & Schuster Books for Young Readers paperback edition July 2011
10 9
The Library of Congress has cataloged the hardcover edition as follows:
Gibbs, Stuart, 1969-
Belly up: murder at FunJungle / Stuart Gibbs.
p. cm
Summary: Twelve-year-old Teddy investigates when a popular Texas zoo's star attraction—Henry the hippopotamus—is murdered.
ISBN 978-1-4169-8731-4 (hc alk. paper)
[1. Mystery and detective stories. 2. Zoos—Fiction. 3. Zoo animals—Fiction. 4. Murder—Fiction.] I. Title.
PZ7.G339236Be 2010
[Fic]—dc22
2009034860
ISBN 978-1-4169-8732-1 (pbk)
ISBN 978-1-4424-0639-1 (eBook)

STUART GIBBS

belly up

A funjungle NOVEL

Simon & Schuster Books for Young Readers
New York London Toronto Sydney New Delhi

contents

For my children, Dashiell and Violet

I'd just been busted for giving the chimpanzees water balloons when I first heard something was wrong at Hippo River.

Large Marge was the one who caught me. No surprise there. Marge O'Malley was a security guard, but all she did most days was follow me around, waiting for me to cause trouble. I saw her slinking after me all the time. She'd always try to hide behind rocks and trees and stuff, but it was never hard to spot her, because Marge was built like a rhinoceros.

"You're in big trouble this time, Teddy," she snarled. She was making a big show of apprehending me in front of a crowd of tourists, shoving me up against the rail of the chimp exhibit and frisking me for weapons—like I was a mugger in some urban back alley instead of a twelve-year-old boy at FunJungle, the newest, most family-friendly theme park in the world.

"Why don't you arrest some *real* criminals for once?" I asked.

"Right now, you're the only person I see making trouble."

"That's just 'cause you're not paying attention." It was true. Half the park guests broke the rules. There were signs posted *everywhere* telling them not to feed the animals, or bang on the glass of their exhibits, or harass them in any way, but they all did it anyhow. Only ten feet from where Marge was patting me down, an entire family was pelting a baby chimp with peanuts. They weren't trying to feed it—which would have been bad enough. (The animals had very restricted diets to keep them from getting sick.) They were *laughing* every time they hit it.

"Watch this," said the dad. "I'll bet I can hit him right in the head."

Right as he was about to let fly, though, a huge red water balloon sailed out of the chimp exhibit and nailed him in the face. It exploded on contact, drenching him.

Before he could recover, another balloon hit him. And another. And another. The chimps were fighting back, just as I'd hoped. That's why I'd armed them. If the security guards weren't going to protect the animals, then I figured I ought to help the animals protect themselves. After all, how would *you* like it if someone banged on your windows and chucked peanuts at you all day?

Within seconds, the whole chimpanzee troop was lobbing balloons, howling with delight as they pelted the family from all sides. The family stumbled about, slipping in the water and spluttering for air—and now everyone was laughing at *them*.

Well, everyone but Large Marge, who was born without a sense of humor. She whipped out her radio and alerted headquarters. "HQ, this is O'Malley. We have a water-balloon situation at Monkey Mountain. I've apprehended the perpetrator, Mr. Theodore Fitzroy, but I need backup." Marge always spoke like she'd seen way too many cop movies.

"Never mind that," the dispatcher responded. "Get over to Hippo River. We're getting reports that something's wrong there."

Marge frowned, though not out of concern for the hippos; she was annoyed her request for backup had been ignored. "I don't think you appreciate the magnitude of the situation here. . . ."

"This is coming straight from Buck," the dispatcher said, meaning Buck Grassley, the chief of FunJungle's security. "Hippo River is a Code Red. If you're at Monkey Mountain, you're the closest to the scene. So get over there *now*."

Marge snapped upright and jammed her radio back

in its holster. The idea that there was an actual emergency had stirred something inside her. She grabbed my ear and dragged me toward the exit. "Don't think this saves your bacon, mister. You're still in trouble for what you did to that poor family."

"That family ought to thank me," I told her. "If I hadn't given the chimps water balloons, they'd have thrown *poop*."

I wasn't making that up. I'd seen chimps defend themselves in the wild by throwing their own feces. But as usual, trying to explain anything to Marge was useless.

"Watch your language or I'll wash your mouth with soap," she snapped.

The family that had been bombarded with balloons stormed out of Monkey Mountain right behind us, so soaked that their shoes sloshed. "See if we ever come to this park again!" the mother announced indignantly.

Good riddance, I thought, stifling a smile.

The truth was, except for Marge's vice-grip on my ear, I was happy to be heading to Hippo River. I wasn't sure what a Code Red meant, but it promised to be interesting. Maybe some clumsy tourist had fallen into the exhibit and needed to be rescued. Technically, that was probably a bad thing to hope for: Most people don't realize that hippos are actually the second most dangerous African animals. (Water buffalo are the first.) They're mean, they're unpredictable, and they have razor-sharp teeth a foot long. In the wild, they've been known to stomp lions to death and bite crocodiles in half. If someone fell into the hippos' territory, they'd be screwed. But after a few weeks at FunJungle, I was bored out of my skull and willing to take excitement anywhere I could find it.

That might seem pretty surprising, given that I spent every day at a place that claimed to be "America's Most Exciting Family Vacation Destination." FunJungle was the biggest, most elaborate zoo ever built and it had been jam-packed since it had opened two weeks before. But unlike the thousands of other kids who visited every day, I didn't go home when they closed the park at night. I *was* home.

Both my parents worked there. My mom was a famous gorilla researcher. My dad was a renowned wildlife photographer. (They'd met when *National Geographic* had sent him to photograph Mom's gorillas.) Now Mom oversaw the care and research of all FunJungle's primates while Dad worked for the publicity department, taking glamour shots of the animals for websites and magazines.

FunJungle had been built way out in Texas Hill Country, where land was cheap; the closest city, San Antonio, was more than half an hour away. So the park had provided housing for my family and a few other animal specialists who'd come to work there: Our mobile homes sat just beyond the back fence. None of the other specialists had children, though, which meant I was the only kid for thirty miles in any direction.

Now, don't go thinking I was bored because I don't like animals. I do. In fact, I bet I know more about animals than any twelve-year-old you've met. I spent the first decade of my life living in a tent in the African Congo. I didn't see a TV until I was six; instead, I watched animals—and Mom and Dad taught me everything they knew. I learned how to track elephants, communicate with chimps, and defend myself against a hungry leopard. Heck, I learned about animals you've probably never even heard of: bongos, hammerkops, Gaboon vipers, guenons. My first friend was a gorilla my age named Mfuzi. I *loved* being around animals every day.

I was bored because, until not long before, I'd had an amazingly exciting life. Living in the Congo was one incredible experience after another—and when I *did* leave the jungle, it was always to visit fascinating places with my father on his assignments. Dad was a real adrenaline junkie and he encouraged me to embrace adventure: We'd rappelled into caves to find giant bats in Mexico, stalked tigers in Uttar Pradesh, and even snorkeled with blue whales off Fiji.

But then, right after I turned ten, a civil war broke out in the Congo and my parents decided it was no longer safe to raise me there. (If not for me, they probably would have risked their lives to stay with the gorillas.) Mom grabbed the first job she could find back in the States, a research position at Emory Primate Labs in Atlanta, but that was a bust. None of us was happy in Georgia; we all missed Africa terribly. So when my folks were offered work at FunJungle, which billed itself as "the closest you can get in America to being on safari," we figured living there might be more fun for all of us.

And for a while, it was. FunJungle was by far the best zoo in the world. All the reviews said so. It was three times larger than the next biggest zoo, its exhibits were innovative and there was plenty to do. But it still wasn't the Congo. After a few weeks, to keep myself amused, I'd had to resort to playing practical jokes, like giving the chimps water balloons—or switching the signs on the men's and women's restrooms—or replacing all the black jellybeans in Large Marge's lunch with rabbit poop.

That's why I was fine with letting myself be dragged along to Hippo River. I was only hoping for a little excitement.

It never occurred to me that Henry would be dead.

It didn't occur to Marge either. She shoved through the crowd at Mbuko Hippo Overlook, still dragging me by my ear, flashing her little tin badge—and suddenly, there Henry was, lying in the shallow water of his enclosure, all four legs pointing straight at the sky.

Most of Henry—and there was about 4,000 pounds of him—was underwater, resting on the bottom of his pool. I couldn't see his body, since the water was clouded with hippo poop, as usual. Only his feet were visible, jutting above the surface, pale white now that the blood had drained from them. They were thick and stubby, looking like giant, moldy marshmallows floating in day-old hot chocolate.

"Isn't that cute?" a mother asked her children. "Henry's sleeping upside down!"

Marge's grip finally relaxed on my ear. She was so stunned, she'd forgotten about me. Instead, she stared at Henry vacantly, not knowing what to do.

She wasn't the only one. There was always a crowd at Mbuko Hippo Overlook, but today it was more packed than usual. Maybe word had got out that Henry had kicked the bucket and some folks had come running to see, but most of the visitors appeared to have been caught by surprise. They just stood there, gaping at those feet, unable to believe Henry the Hippo was dead.

I admit I was pretty shocked myself. Since FunJungle had more than five thousand animals on display, you expected things would go wrong now and then. Every day, dozens of animals got sick; maybe even one or two would die. But for

Henry to go belly-up . . . that was pretty much the worst-case scenario, given that he was the park's mascot.

FunJungle had been advertising all over the world for a year before it opened, and every one of those ads—every TV commercial, radio spot, and billboard—featured Henry. Well, not the actual Henry, but a cartoon version of him who said corny things like "Come visit FunJungle! It's more fun than a barrel of monkeys . . . and I ought to know!" Cartoon Henry didn't look much like the real Henry—he was skinny, purple, and friendly, while the real Henry was fat, gray, and mean—but that didn't seem to bother the tourists. Henry was famous, so they flocked to see him. It was bizarre. There was a far more interesting hippo, Hildegard, in the exhibit right next to Henry's, but most guests didn't give her a second glance. Hildegard could've done backflips and everyone would still be packed ten deep to watch Henry nap.

"Wake up, Henry! It's time to get up!" a little boy near me yelled. Several other boys decided this was a good idea and joined in.

Their parents looked at one another blankly. Cartoon Henry had told them all that a day at FunJungle was supposed to be "nonstop family fun"; explaining the circle of life and death threatened to be quite the opposite.

"Johnny, please," said one mother. Her son was happily proving he could chant the loudest. "I don't think Henry is going to wake up. Hippos are very sound sleepers."

"That's right," a queasy-looking father added. "Plus, his ears are underwater."

Hippo River was the most popular exhibit at FunJungle, though this wasn't only because of Henry. It was right by the main entrance—the first thing visitors saw as they came through the front gates—and it was pretty spectacular. (As it should have been. I heard FunJungle had spent more than thirty million dollars on it.) The exhibit took up ten acres— and once you entered it, it was really like being in Africa. You started at a thundering 150-foot waterfall, then hiked through a jungle filled with birds and monkeys, visiting scenic viewpoints from which you could see flocks of flamingos, huge Nile crocodiles—and, of course, the hippos. Each viewpoint had a quaint name that had been designed by a computer to sound African, even though they meant absolutely nothing: Ngodongo Gorge, Lallabasi Basin, Wullumon Camp.

The *real* draw at Hippo River, however, was the underwater viewing areas: places where you could watch the hippos through huge glass walls. This wasn't a revolutionary idea: Lots of zoos had similar exhibits for viewing polar bears—and a few even had ones for hippos. But no one had anything on the scale that FunJungle did.

The folks who'd designed FunJungle were actually pretty

smart about animals; they knew hippopotamuses were far more interesting below water than they were above it. Heck, a lot of the time (and I know this from experience) you can watch the surface for hours and never even see a hippo; they need to breathe only once every ten minutes, and even then, they usually just poke their nostrils out. But underwater, it's a whole different story. Hippos swim, play, eat, give birth, and nurse their young on river bottoms. (Mom told me they also make baby hippos down there, but FunJungle kept Henry and Hildegard separated during visiting hours to make sure this didn't happen in front of the guests.) Plus, while hippos look like big, lazy sacks of fat on land, they're surprisingly graceful in the water. So FunJungle had eight gigantic windows to view them through—and even a pricey restaurant where the prime tables were right against the glass; guests could have a fourteen-dollar hamburger and watch hippos swim past a foot away. You can't do *that* in Africa.

Unfortunately, there had been a few glitches with the exhibit. Most obviously, the water filtration system wasn't strong enough. Henry ate nearly a hundred pounds of food a day and sent most of it straight through his digestive tract, clouding the water faster than the filters could clean it. If Henry stayed near the windows, where the water flow was better, you could get a decent, if somewhat hazy, view of him. But Henry preferred to spend his time in a small backwater of his enclosure, wallowing in his own filth. This rendered the underwater viewing areas all but useless. Restaurant patrons ended up eating their fourteen-dollar burgers with nothing to see except sewage.

Of course, this was now a relatively minor problem.

It was June in Texas, which meant it was ninety-eight degrees in the shade. Under the harsh glare of the sun, Henry was starting to smell worse than usual—which was really saying something. Hippos are naturally quite flatulent, but Henry was the worst I'd ever encountered; he could emit odors powerful enough to make you nauseated fifty feet away.

"He's not sleeping," a little girl said, wrinkling her nose in disgust. "He's dead!"

Other parents' eyes widened. The girl's parents immediately shriveled under everyone's gaze. "No, he isn't," her mother said hopefully. "Hippos don't die like that. When hippos die, they float to the top, like goldfish."

"He's dead," the little girl announced again.

"Let's go see the elephants," said her father.

All the parents thought this was a wonderful idea. ("Maybe *they're* still alive," another father said under his breath.) None of the kids wanted to leave, though. Those who thought Henry was sleeping were intent on waking him. Those who suspected he was dead were fascinated.

Know how kids sometimes can't help staring at something they're disgusted by, like roadkill? Well, imagine how captivating roadkill the size of a minivan would be.

The parents who didn't look squeamish were growing annoyed. Many turned to Marge, expecting that, as the only person in the vicinity wearing a FunJungle uniform, she should be doing *something* to address the Henry situation. But Marge just kept staring, slack-jawed, at Henry's corpse. Marge wasn't the best decision-maker on normal days; I'd seen her take ten minutes to decide whether to have the fried chicken bucket or the triple nachos grande for lunch. (For the record, she'd ultimately opted for both.) Faced with an actual crisis, her brain had apparently overloaded and shut down.

Nearby, a teenager dressed in a Henry Hippo costume paced nervously, unsure what to do. His job usually didn't require much thinking; he was essentially supposed to stand still, wave hello, and let tourists take his picture. Mbuko Overlook had been selected as the best place for this because it offered the most shade. The Henry costume was thick and heavy and had poor ventilation; in the direct Texas sun, it could quickly get to over a hundred and twenty degrees inside. On the first few days the park was open, the Henry portrayers had mistakenly been stationed at unshaded Mulumbo Point. Two had passed out from dehydration, collapsing on small children.

The actors only had hour-long shifts, because they had to drink a ton of water to survive in the suit and would inevitably have to pee. However, their job orders stated that during that hour, they were never to leave their posts, no matter what. The Henry on duty now obviously felt he shouldn't be there, lurking around the dead hippo like his ghost, but he didn't want to get in trouble, either.

An excited family came along, unaware that the real Henry lay dead just around the corner, and positioned their children at the fake Henry's feet for a photo. The worried actor fidgeted so nervously that the mother had to steady his hands twice.

It seemed someone should take care of this, but since Marge was a basket case, that left me. Once the family had taken their pictures, I approached the actor and told him, "You should probably get out of here."

"Are you from Administration?" Henry asked, contorting to get a look at me. The costume had been designed so the actor inside could only see through some gauze in Henry's open mouth, which was angled downward. It was well suited to prevent the actors from stepping on children, but not for looking people in the face or, as had been proved on several occasions, avoiding low-hanging tree branches. Since I was standing outside his range of sight, the actor had no way to tell I was only twelve.

"Yes," I said. "Now move it before you freak anyone else out."

"Yes, sir!" The actor hurried away so quickly he forgot to watch his feet, stumbled over a bench, and face-planted in the landscaping.

I shook my head in disgust. Some people have *way* too much respect for authority.

Henry staggered to his feet and reeled away drunkenly, scaring a few guests.

A hand clamped on my shoulder. I spun around to find Martin del Gato glaring at me.

Martin was the director of operations at FunJungle, which was an odd choice, because he hated children and animals. Dad said he was supposed to be some hotshot business genius, though. I could usually spot him coming from a mile away, because in a park crowded with T-shirt–clad tourists, he was always the only person wearing a three-piece suit. Martin was perpetually overworked and constantly appeared to be five seconds from a heart attack, but he somehow still found time every day to chastise me for doing something wrong. "Who gave *you* permission to dismiss my employees?" he demanded.

"I figured *someone* needed to do something," I replied. "Seeing as Marge has gone brain-dead."

Martin gave me a glare so hot I could imagine eggs frying

on his bald head. "Why would anyone need to dismiss the actors?" He scowled.

"Because of what happened to Henry," I said.

Martin looked at me blankly—and I realized, to my surprise, that he didn't know about Henry yet. He turned toward Mbuko Overlook and took in the stunned crowd. I guess, in his haste to reprimand me, he hadn't noticed them. His anger was quickly replaced by concern. "What's wrong with Henry?" he asked.

I'd been reading about Ancient Rome the night before; apparently, they used to kill messengers who brought bad news. "You should probably see for yourself," I told him.

Keeping his hand locked on my shoulder, Martin shoved through the crowd. When Marge saw him, she finally snapped out of her comatose state and pretended she was doing something important. Martin blew right past her— and caught his first glimpse of Henry.

He said something in Spanish. I didn't know what it meant, but I'll bet a hundred dollars it was something for which I'd have been sent to my room for saying in English.

For maybe half a second, Martin seemed truly saddened by Henry's death—and then his inner administrator kicked in. He immediately went into Damage Control Mode. "Go find Doc," he told me. "Wherever he is. Tell him to get over here ASAP."

I considered pointing out it was a bit too late for the head vet to help Henry, but decided against it. Martin probably wanted to get rid of me as much as he wanted to locate Doc. Meanwhile, his attention was already on other things. He instructed Marge to get all the tourists out of there, then started barking orders into his radio.

I knew better than to stick around after Martin had essentially told me to scram, but I felt compelled to take one last look at Henry. I'd seen plenty of deaths in Africa, so I wasn't that freaked out by animal corpses, but something really bothered me about this one. I'd been at Hippo River the day before and Henry had been in a rare good mood, prancing about on the river bottom, putting on a great show for the tourists. He was only twenty, which was young for a hippo, and he'd certainly looked healthy. It didn't make sense for him to be dead.

Suddenly, Marge grabbed me by the collar, yanking me away from the overlook. "What are you still doing here?" she growled.

"Trying to guess who's bigger: Henry or you."

Marge's eyes narrowed in anger, but I wrenched free of her grasp before she could do anything. Then I raced off into FunJungle, leaving the corpse of the world's most famous hippopotamus behind.

2 · DAMAGE CONTROL

I found Doc out in SafariLand, trying to lance a boil on a warthog.

This would have been a pretty easy procedure if his patient had been human. A boil's really just a big pus-filled sac on the skin, sort of like a giant zit, only a lot more painful. Lancing it means popping it with a sterile needle so the pus can run out and the swelling can go down. It takes only a few seconds. But you can't explain that to a warthog. You can't say, "If you hold still for a moment, I'll make you feel better." All the warthog knew was it was in pain, it was angry, and the last thing it wanted to see was some guy coming at it with a giant needle.

For this reason, a lot of zoo vets would have just darted the warthog with sedative, waited for it to fall asleep, and then done the job nice and easy. But Doc wasn't like that. Mom and Dad both said he was one of the top vets in the country, maybe even the best; he'd run the veterinary hospital at the prestigious Bronx Zoo before FunJungle had lured him away. Doc hated using sedatives, because it was tricky to get the dosage exactly right. If you gave the animal too little, it might wake up in the middle of the procedure and attack you—so most people tried to err on the side of caution. The problem there was, if you gave the animal too much sedative, it might fall asleep and never wake up again. Doc didn't like people a whole lot, but he really cared about animals. He hated the thought of one of them dying for no good reason. So rather than take that chance, he and two of the biggest zookeepers he could find were out in the broiling sun, trying to pin down the pissed-off warthog and lance it without being gored by its tusks.

It didn't look like the best time to inform Doc that Henry was dead. The men had been trying to subdue the warthog for a while with no success, and Doc was in a nasty mood. But then, Doc tended to be in a nasty mood most of the time anyhow, so I figured maybe he'd be too distracted by the warthog to get angry with me for bringing bad news.

Doc had just backed the warthog into a corner of its paddock when I arrived. He was a tall man, well-muscled from years of overpowering animals and baked brown from long days in the sun, with a mustache so thick it looked like a wooly bear caterpillar had fallen asleep on his upper lip. He groaned when he saw me, though I didn't take it personally. Doc pretty much groaned in response to *anyone* approaching him. The only person he actually seemed to like was my mom. (They'd met fifteen years earlier when she'd done a gorilla-research apprenticeship at the Bronx Zoo.) "Beat it, Teddy," he snapped. "I'm busy."

I'm not sure what I'd ever done to earn Doc's distaste. I think merely being human was enough.

"Martin told me to come get you," I said.

Doc's reaction proved he liked Martin even less than me. "Go tell Martin to go jump in a lake."

"Henry's dead," I told him.

Doc and the keepers were surprised enough to take their eyes off the angry warthog. They all glanced at me for a moment to confirm I wasn't making a bad joke, then quickly returned their attention to their patient before he could make a run for it.

"For how long?" Doc asked.

"I don't know. . . ."

"Well, guess."

I checked my watch. It had taken me almost twenty minutes to track Doc down. First I'd been told he was in The Swamp, then Amazon Adventure, and finally SafariLand. I'd run myself ragged looking for him. "Forty-five minutes. An hour, maybe."

"Any idea why the old bastard croaked?"

"I think that's what Martin wanted to talk to you about. He wants to see you ASAP."

"Why? Henry's dead. It's not like he can get worse."

"I don't know why. He just said to find you. . . ."

"Tell Martin to find a place for an autopsy and I'll be along when I can."

"An autopsy? For Henry? Martin's not going to like that."

Doc smiled for what was probably the first time that day. "No, I suspect he won't like it at all."

If it seems surprising that Doc wasn't upset by Henry's death, there was a perfectly good reason for this: Henry was the meanest zoo animal of all time. Hippos already have a reputation for being among the most foul-tempered members of the animal kingdom, but even keepers who had worked with hippos for years thought Henry was the nastiest one they'd ever come across. You couldn't have picked a worse animal to be the mascot of a multi-billion-dollar family theme park. His selection had been a colossal screw-up. To understand how it happened, though, you need to know how FunJungle came to be.

FunJungle had been built by the Texas billionaire J.J. McCracken. J.J. always admitted he didn't know much about animals, but he knew a heck of a lot about making money. He'd been born dirt-poor in a small town not far from where FunJungle now sat—and somehow managed to parlay a couple hundred dollars he'd won in a poker game into enough money to make him the third-richest man in America. The way J.J. spoke about this, it sounded like anyone could do it—but the fact was, he had a gift. Whatever he invested in always made money. Dad often said that if J.J. McCracken set his money on fire, the next day, burned dollars would be worth more than gold.

Despite being so rich, J.J. had a reputation as a friendly, folksy guy who'd never let having money go to his head. Instead of wearing fancy suits, he preferred blue jeans and sneakers. Rather than live in some Beverly Hills mansion, he had a ranch in Texas Hill Country near his hometown. He drove a pickup truck instead of riding in a limo and preferred BBQ to sushi. And whenever he was interviewed about how he'd thought up FunJungle, he inevitably gave all the credit to his thirteen-year-old daughter, Summer.

Summer had been only six when she'd given J.J. the idea. ("Planted the seed" was how he always put it.) Like most children, she'd loved animals, so when her dad had given her the choice of going anywhere in the world for vacation, she'd asked to go on safari in Africa. J.J. had agreed, but then learned no safari company would take anyone under age seven—no matter how much he was willing to pay. When he broke this news to Summer, she was devastated. Why wasn't there anyplace for children to go on safari in America? she'd asked. "Good question," her father had replied, and decided to build one.

Of course, J.J. McCracken wouldn't have built FunJungle merely to please his daughter. No, he smelled profit. His research staff quickly discovered that zoos and aquariums attracted more than five hundred million visitors in America each year—more than all sporting events combined. So then, J.J. reasoned, if he built a zoo impressive enough to siphon off only a fraction of those people, he'd make a mint.

To lure all those tourists, however, FunJungle had to be more than *just* a zoo. It had to be a theme park as well: a place people would be willing to cross the country to see; a place they'd visit for days on end; a place they'd want to come back to every year. J.J. declared that FunJungle should be a combination of the San Diego Wild Animal Park and Disney World—and then proceeded to steal ideas from each.

SafariLand, for example, was directly copied from San Diego: Several massive enclosures—each more than a square mile in size—held hundreds of animals living together in a facsimile of the wild. There were two ways to see it: You could take a thirty-minute monorail ride around the perimeter—or for an extra hundred dollars per person, you could take a personal safari *inside* the enclosures. You'd travel in a Land Rover with a guide and only a few other people. I'd gotten to do this for free with my parents before the park opened, and I have to admit, it was darn close to going on safari in Africa. Maybe even better, because at FunJungle, they let you feed the rhinos apples by hand.

FunJungle had all sorts of other attractions that other zoos didn't. There were souped-up animal exhibits like the Polar Pavilion—an indoor polar bear and penguin exhibit where it really snowed—or Blue Planet, the world's largest saltwater aquarium, featuring a man-made coral reef you could snorkel over and several pools where you could pay to swim with dolphins. There were shows where animals performed tricks, a sky ride, a carnival midway, water slides, two huge play areas for kids—Mom called them "jungle gyms on steroids"—and even a few vaguely educational thrill rides. My favorite was "Life of a Bee," which used a motion simulator to put riders through a harrowing five minutes of being attacked by everything from birds to flyswatters. It was awesome.

In addition to the park, J.J. also planned to make money from the hotels around it, which he owned. There were only two so far—although others were slated for construction—and they were unlike any other hotels in America. One was a safari lodge on the edge of SafariLand; the other was a "Caribbean resort" next to the Blue Planet snorkeling area. They were extremely well-designed; visiting each felt like going to a whole different country. Neither place was cheap, but both were booked solid more than a year in advance.

Finally, there was the merchandising.

To be really profitable, J.J. knew FunJungle had to keep making money long after people had visited it. To do this, he stole an idea from Disney: The park shouldn't just have animals. It should have *characters*. To most people, one hippo was exactly like any other. But if you created a personality—à la Henry the Hippo—people wouldn't simply want to see him: They'd buy anything with his picture on it.

Now, even if you didn't know Henry was a jerk, it still might have seemed like a bad idea to make a hippopotamus the cornerstone of a merchandising empire. After all, as mammals went, hippos were fat, dangerous, and not particularly attractive. But merchandising wasn't about selling reality. As J.J. often pointed out (incorrectly): "Mickey Mouse is just a rat in suspenders."

The real reason for selecting Henry as the mascot had far more to do with television than biology. J.J. knew all along that it would take years to build FunJungle, so he decided to create excitement about its inhabitants well ahead of time. He already owned a cable TV network, so he ordered the employees to develop an animated series called "FunJungle Friends." (Here, he was stealing another idea from Disney, which had used *The Wonderful World of Disney* to blatantly market Disneyland well before it opened. It was a good idea to steal, though; not only could J.J. plug his own theme park—but he got advertisers to pay *him* to do it.)

FunJungle Friends was originally about a bunch of zoo animals who'd slip out of their cages after the keepers went home and have all sorts of wacky adventures. Eleanor Elephant, Zelda Zebra, Larry the Lizard, and Uncle O-Rang were the stars. Henry Hippo was supposed to be only a minor character at first; he didn't even appear until the fourth episode. But for some reason, people loved him. Even the animators couldn't quite figure out why. Maybe children found Henry nonthreatening. Maybe he was just a particularly attractive shade of purple. Whatever the case, he was a hit. Henry Hippo merchandise began outselling that of all the other characters by a huge margin, and his cry of excitement—"Jinkies McPinkies!"—quickly became a national catchphrase.

J.J. was thrilled. *FunJungle Friends* quickly became *The Henry Hippo Show*, a series of Henry Hippo movies was greenlit—and Henry was named the FunJungle spokesperson. (Or rather, "spokesanimal.") The park was reconfigured to place Hippo River right by the front gates. The marketing department began slapping Henry's face on every piece of merchandise you could think of. On his show, Henry started imploring kids to visit him at FunJungle years before the park even opened. The effect was immediate; children across the country clamored for FunJungle vacations. Families came to Texas just to see the construction site. Henry was a phenomenon—and he made FunJungle a phenomenon along with him. Throughout it all, however, no one ever stopped to consider what a *real* hippopotamus was like. (Of course, anyone who knew a whit about hippos would have— but no animal specialists were hired at FunJungle until long after the decision to revere Henry had been made.)

The hardest thing about starting a zoo from scratch isn't building it; it's getting the animals. You can't walk into the closest pet store and ask for a couple hippos. A hundred years ago, when zoos were a new concept, they all used to simply capture animals in the wild—and when those animals died, they'd go back and get more. Today, most zoo animals are endangered, so regulations have been established to prevent taking them from their natural habitats. Instead, most animals are procured from other zoos or official breeding facilities. These places aren't like puppy farms, though, churning out new animals as fast as they can. Hippos only give birth to one or two young a year, tops. Hippo River had enclosures for four hippos, but it wasn't until construction was almost completed that anyone discovered procuring even *one* hippo might be difficult.

Naturally, J.J. McCracken wasn't pleased to hear this. (I heard he threw a chair through a plate-glass window.) Then he demanded his people better get him at least one hippopotamus—and do it fast. FunJungle *couldn't* open without a Henry. So the purchasing department scrambled to find a hippo. Any hippo. And in their haste, they ended up with the worst hippo in America.

Henry was originally named Brutus, and he'd already been in four different zoos before FunJungle got him. Each place couldn't wait to get rid of him. First of all, he was dangerous. In Boston, he'd bitten three keepers badly enough to send each to the hospital. And in Seattle, he'd squashed a keeper up against the side of his enclosure so hard that he cracked four of the man's ribs, then kept him pinioned there for half an hour until being coaxed away by a box of Twinkies.

Next, there was the mating problem. In order to increase their animal populations, zoos usually try to pair all their male animals with females. This had been attempted with Brutus every place he'd lived. His interaction with females had been limited to two emotions: complete disinterest and occasional bursts of inexplicable anger. The females would at first find him cold and aloof. (In Los Angeles, where they tended to psychoanalyze things a bit too much, one keeper had accused Brutus of giving the female he was paired with "a devastating case of low self esteem.") And then one day, for no particular reason, Brutus would turn against his partner: a full-force attack, biting, kicking, butting them with his head. On several occasions, Brutus had to be tranquilized before he mortally wounded his mate.

Finally, there'd been the poop.

In the wild, male hippopotamuses occasionally exhibit an extremely disgusting method of battling for dominance: They aim their butts at one another and fire streams of feces. This had rarely been documented in zoos, probably because male hippos are usually kept apart. And until Brutus arrived on the scene, it had never been witnessed in any situation other than dominance conflicts.

Brutus seemed to think it was funny.

He genuinely enjoyed shooting poop at people. There was no rhyme or reason to it, except that he was said to have an uncanny knack for knowing which zoo visitor was wearing the most expensive outfit. Without any warning, he'd hoist his rear out of the water and fire away. In the National Zoo in Washington D.C., where the walls around the hippo pit were unfortunately low, in the course of one week Brutus had sullied two senators, the secretary of state, the Swedish ambassador and the president's daughter, along with four of her Secret Service agents.

After that, even the conservation-minded National Zoo Association had given serious consideration to putting Brutus to sleep. Fortunately, a small circus had offered to buy him. They'd put up with him for only two months; he'd bitten three clowns and had taken to firing feces at the audience every time he was brought into the center ring. The circus's owners were ready to feed Brutus to the lions when they heard FunJungle was desperate for a hippopotamus. The owners quickly fudged Brutus's records, claimed he was an entirely different hippo, and didn't feed him for three days before the FunJungle purchasing department came to visit so that he couldn't soil them. The circus offered him for a song and FunJungle snatched him up in a second.

The hippo was renamed Henry and delivered to FunJungle with great fanfare. The Marketing Department turned Henry's journey across the country into a national media event. They made no secret that Henry had been bought—or rather, "rescued"—from a circus; it was a much better story that way. A specially designed semi with its own built-in pool was constructed to transport Henry. In each town he passed through, families lined the streets to see him. His arrival at FunJungle had been celebrated with a huge party. Even though the zoo wasn't open yet, thousands of people had come to get their first glimpse of Henry and consume a giant hippo-shaped cake.

The next morning, within the space of forty-five minutes, Henry bit one keeper and then showered none other than Martin del Gato himself with poop. It was at this point that Doc, who knew Brutus's reputation, determined that FunJungle had been hoodwinked.

Martin was livid. J.J. McCracken was even angrier. The entire animal purchasing department was fired on the spot and the marketing department began damage control. Plexiglas "just-in-case" shields were quickly installed along the walls of Henry's enclosure to protect the public from hippo poop. Hildegard, the only other hippo FunJungle had managed to acquire, was removed from Henry's enclosure. All keepers were given orders to stay the heck away from Henry unless armed with electric cattle prods, and even then, they were only to approach him at night, since he was on display during the day. A feeding system was designed to keep his contact with humans to a minimum. The emergency measures seemed to work; Henry still fired feces at visitors on occasion, but the shields protected them and the kids thought it was funny. (Still, in the name of good hygiene, cleaning crews were on call during park hours to clean up the messes as quickly as possible.)

In the meantime, Martin had his minions desperately combing the world for a new male hippo that could be secretly swapped out with Henry. After all, to humans, all hippos basically looked the same. People could *usually* tell the difference between a male and a female—which was why FunJungle's administration hadn't tried to pass Hildegard off as Henry (although, believe me, they'd thought about it)—but no one would really know if Henry had suddenly been replaced with another male. SeaWorld did it all the time with killer whales. Some of the parks were on their tenth Shamu already.

If the "new" Henry had already been found, the death of the old Henry probably wouldn't have bothered many people at the park. No one there had liked Henry, not even his keepers. But his death now, so shortly after the park had opened, was most likely going to be a public-relations disaster.

By the time I returned to Hippo River, damage control was well underway. Temporary fences had already been erected around Henry's paddock and signs were posted every ten feet announcing: SORRY. THIS ATTRACTION IS TEMPORARILY CLOSED TO IMPROVE YOUR ENJOYMENT. (Ironically, the only signs FunJungle had with this message featured Henry Hippo.) A phalanx of young employees had been deployed to allay any concerns guests might have. Any guest who asked about Henry was told he was "off display due to medical reasons." Any guest who complained he was dead was immediately refunded their entry fee and given a coupon for 10 percent off FunJungle merchandise to boot. Meanwhile, a crane was being brought over from one of the construction sites to hoist Henry's body out of his pool the moment the last visitor left for the day.

Martin was in the midst of everything, working two cell phones at once. He frowned when he saw me approaching alone. "Where's Doc?" he demanded.

"Doing surgery on a warthog."

"Now? Did you make it clear to him how urgent this situation is?"

"Yes, but he said Henry's not going to get any deader."

Martin glared at me a moment, then rubbed his temples. "Did Doc, by any chance, indicate *when* he might feel like joining us?"

"It shouldn't be too long. He's just lancing a boil." I hesitated a moment, then added, "He wants you to find him a place to do the autopsy."

As I feared, telling Martin this was like poking a cobra with a stick. His entire head turned red. "An autopsy?!" he snapped.

Everyone within earshot—including a lot of tourists—stopped in their tracks and turned toward us.

Martin mustered the best smile he could for them, then grabbed my arm and dragged me behind a stand of banana trees. "It's bad enough that our mascot is dead. Now that quack wants to cut him open? Where does he expect to do that?"

"The animal hospital?"

"Henry won't fit in the hospital! They don't make autopsy tables big enough for hippopotamuses!" Martin nervously ran his fingers through what was left of his hair, not so much talking to me as talking with me nearby. "I mean it's not like this is a human being. You could autopsy a human anywhere. This is a hippo, for Pete's sake! It's the size of a truck! And God knows what'll come out of him once Doc cuts him open. We'll have to sanitize the whole park." Martin paused and thought a moment, like he was adding up how much sanitizing the park would cost him. Then he turned to me and said, "I'm not doing it. I'm just burying Henry. Go tell Doc that. And then tell him to forget about the stupid warthog and get over here!"

I knew there was no point in arguing. So I ran all the way back across the park to talk to Doc again. FunJungle was over a mile from end to end and it was nasty hot out. I was pouring sweat by the time I got back to SafariLand.

Doc didn't look much better. He'd lanced the boil, but it obviously hadn't been easy. He was covered with dirt and sweat and there was a long, bleeding scrape on his shin where the warthog had tusked him. My reappearance—along with the news that Martin didn't want to do the autopsy—didn't help his mood at all.

"Go tell that knucklehead that an autopsy is standard operating procedure for any deceased zoo animal," he growled. "And tell him if we don't figure out why Henry died, it'll cost us money in the long run. That ought to get his attention."

"How will it cost money?"

"Suppose something toxic is leaking into Hippo River. The autopsy would tell us that and then we could fix it. But if we don't do the autopsy, then we don't find out about the toxic leak—and next thing you know, we're up to our necks in dead hippos. Ask Martin if he's comfortable with that."

I ran back to Hippo River. By now, FunJungle had closed for the night. The last guests had left. Usually, the stores by the entrance stayed open an extra hour to give the guests a chance to spend every last penny they had on FunJungle merchandise, but Martin had ordered everything shut down early that night. The crane had arrived and the strongest employees at the park had wrapped a huge metal sling around Henry. Now the hippo's massive, dripping corpse was being winched out and loaded onto a flatbed trailer.

The local news stations had gotten wind that something was up. News vans were parked right outside the front gates and park security was shooing camera crews away from trying to film the crane over the wall. I could see Large Marge up on a ladder, swatting a cameraman with a rolled-up newspaper.

I found Martin and told him Doc's argument. He grimaced at the thought of more dead hippos, then reluctantly conceded Doc was right. "Great," he muttered. "One more thing I have to deal with."

"I thought of some places big enough to autopsy Henry," I told him. I'd had plenty of time to mull it over while running back and forth across the park. "The employee cafeteria's huge. Plus the floor's linoleum, so it wouldn't be too hard to clean. . . ."

Martin shook his head violently. "No way. If the state health inspectors find out we've had a dead hippo anywhere near the food, they'll shut us down."

"Does it have to be indoors? We might be able to haul out some big lights and do it right in the entry plaza. . . ."

"Not a chance. It's only a matter of time before the news copters get here. I'm not letting them film it. Plus, we'll end up with every vulture in the state here by the time we're through." He pointed at the sky. There were already a staggering number of vultures wheeling overhead, lured by the smell of Henry's corpse. In the landscaping nearby, hidden from the TV cameras, members of the security team were trying to fend them off with BB guns, but it wasn't working.

"How about the Henry and Pals Theater, then?" I asked.

That was a big auditorium near the entrance where a musi-cal revue was performed five times a day, featuring actors dressed as Henry and other FunJungle characters. "It's got a big stage with a lot of lights, and since they have to move scenery in and out, there's these big doors that you could probably get Henry through. . . ."

Martin started to shake his head again—saying no to me was an automatic reflex for him—when it struck him that I'd had a good idea. He quickly dialed one of his phones and ordered whoever answered to start prepping the Henry and Pals Theater for an autopsy. Then he returned his attention to moving Henry's corpse. He didn't even bother to compli-ment me on a job well done or thank me for my help.

I'd been hoping that, in return for my assistance, Martin might allow me to watch Henry's autopsy. Sure, it would probably be disgusting, but it would be a heck of a lot more interesting than hanging around Monkey Mountain for the hundredth time, waiting for Mom to finish her work. Only, Martin made it clear he was done with me and I knew he wasn't going to change his mind; the whole Henry situation had put him in a fouler mood than usual.

I also knew I wouldn't do any better to ask Doc. Doc never let me watch anything—not even the birth of a baby wildebeest out in SafariLand, and I'd seen a thousand of those in Africa.

None of this meant I couldn't see the autopsy, though. It only meant I'd have to do it without permission. So while Martin was distracted, I slipped away and headed for the Henry and Pals Theater.

At the time, I was merely looking for some excitement. If I'd had any idea how much trouble sneaking into that autopsy would ultimately cause me—or how much danger I'd end up in—I never would have done it. Never in a million years.

Getting into the auditorium wasn't any trouble.
All the adults had their hands full moving Henry and the
doors were left unguarded for long stretches of time. There
was a big network of catwalks and lighting grids over the stage.
I scrambled up into it, found a spot where I could blend into
the shadows, and then sat down to watch the show.

Once the flatbed brought Henry to the theater, it took
half an hour for everyone to lug him up on stage and an
additional fifteen minutes for Martin to shoo everyone out;
plenty of adults wanted to watch the autopsy as much as I
did. But eventually, only Doc, Martin, and I were left in the
room with the dead hippo.

Doc turned on the stage lights to illuminate Henry. I'd
never realized how hot those things were. They burned so

brightly I could feel the heat from them five feet away—but they were also blinding to anyone on the stage, which allowed me to watch everything below with little fear of being spotted.

Henry had been laid on his back on a huge sheet of protective plastic; Martin didn't want bodily fluids leaking all over his new stage. As I stared down at the hippo, I realized I'd forgotten how big he was. Even as hippos went, Henry was enormous. Doc looked like a toy next to him, barely the size of his head.

Martin turned out to be one of the only park employees with no desire to watch the surgery. But then, as I said, Martin didn't like animals that were *alive*. A dead one was even more repulsive to him. So he found a seat in the back of the auditorium, as far as he could be from the body while still able to talk to Doc, then began texting feverishly on his phone.

Doc wheeled out a tray of gleaming scalpels, some of which were the size of meat cleavers. He pulled on a white smock, latex gloves, a face mask, and protective goggles, then took out a canister of clear goo and dabbed a bit under his nose. I wasn't sure what it was for—until Doc made his first incision into the body. Up till that point, I'd been worried that watching an autopsy might make me sick; it hadn't occurred to me that *smelling* it would. Henry's insides reeked worse than month-old diapers. The goo somehow masked the stench for Doc, but I caught it full-on, even from ten feet above. For a moment, I thought I was going to heave my lunch onto Henry. I had to clap my hand over my nose and wait a few minutes for the nausea to pass.

Eventually, I risked another look down. Doc had already made surprising progress, given the size of his patient. I should've expected as much. Doc had been a zoo vet for nearly thirty years; he'd done plenty of autopsies before. Still, it wasn't fast enough for Martin, who fidgeted in his seat.

"What's taking so long?" he asked.

"You do realize this is a hippopotamus I'm working on?" Doc shot back. "I have a wall of fat a foot thick to cut through here. It's like operating on an opera singer."

Someone knocked on the auditorium door. Martin opened it, then ushered Pete Thwacker inside.

Although I was trying to keep quiet, I couldn't help but let out a tiny groan.

As the head of public relations at FunJungle, Pete's job mainly appeared to be to look good on TV. He was handsome—all the women said so—and he knew it. He had blond hair with so much product in it that it wouldn't budge in a tornado, and teeth so white that a full smile could blind you. He always wore expensive suits and rarely passed a shiny surface without checking his reflection in it.

It was a joke that he worked for FunJungle, though. He'd been transferred from a detergent company J.J. McCracken owned. I guess he'd done a good job there, but that didn't mean he was prepared to work at a zoo. He knew less about animals than anyone I'd ever met and was constantly making bonehead statements. Only two days before, during a press conference, he'd said that gorillas were monkeys. So I'd corrected him, telling everyone that gorillas are *apes*. Although I'd been serious, the reporters thought it was hilarious. Pete didn't. He'd kept smiling in front of the adults, but after the conference he'd called my mom and claimed he'd seen me shoplifting at FunJungle Emporium. Then he suggested she should consider sending me to military school. Luckily, Mom had seen right through this; she wasn't a big fan of Pete Thwacker's either.

Neither was Doc, I discovered. I heard him groan in response to Pete's arrival too.

"Have any idea what killed him yet?" Pete yelled from the door. He wasn't interested in getting any closer to the dead hippo than Martin was.

"I think so," Doc said.

"Really? What?"

"Cigarettes. Did you know Henry was smoking six packs a day?"

It took Pete a little too long to realize this was a joke. "Ha-ha." He sneered. "I'd have hoped that you, of all people, would realize how serious this is. Every TV station in the country is calling me to find out what happened to Henry.

CNN says they're breaking the story at the top of the hour. That's twenty minutes from now. If I don't have an answer by then, they'll think we're hiding something. For all I know, they'll report Henry committed suicide."

"How on earth would a hippo commit suicide?" Doc snorted.

Pete paused to think about that. "He could hang himself. . . ."

"How? Hippos don't have rope. Or opposable thumbs to tie it with."

"Then he could throw himself into the crocodile pit. I don't know. Point is, I need a cause of death ASAP."

"I might not be able to give you one. This is going to take time to do right."

"Please. It's an *autopsy*." Pete sighed. "Just get it done. I mean, so what if you make a mistake? The hippo's already dead."

"If you want this to go faster, you're welcome to come up here and help."

Pete turned green at the thought of this. He was saved by the ring of his cell phone and headed to the farthest corner of the auditorium to answer it.

Doc returned to his work. He'd finally cut through the fat and reached Henry's internal organs. I leaned out a bit from the catwalk, angling for a better view. I'd seen plenty of dead bodies in Africa—even a couple dead hippos—but they were never exactly pristine. Nothing was dead in the wild for more than a minute before the scavengers descended on it. That was how you usually found a dead animal in the first place; there'd be a cloud of vultures hovering above it. By the time you got there—even if it was shortly after death—the carcass would be torn apart. First the lions would eat their fill, then the hyenas, and finally the vultures and jackals would move in. Within a day, even an elephant could be picked clean down to the bones. So I'd never had the chance to see what a dead animal looked like with all its organs still on the inside.

It was less disgusting than I'd expected. In fact, it wasn't really disgusting at all. There wasn't much blood and the organs didn't appear all that slimy. Inside his abdomen, Henry seemed to be mostly stomach. This wasn't a surprise; Henry had an insatiable appetite, even for a hippo. When he hadn't been sleeping, he'd usually been eating. Normal hippos ate about forty pounds of food each day. Henry ate *sixty*—and even that hadn't been enough for him. The one way he'd actually interacted with park guests was keeping his mouth wide open and letting people throw food into it. On several occasions, zookeepers had caught people tossing trash or pennies into his mouth as a joke.

Henry's lungs were huge as well. This made sense, as Henry could hold his breath for more than ten minutes. The heart was tough to find amidst the other organs and when it did show up, it looked tiny in comparison, even though it was the size of Doc's head.

Doc examined the heart carefully, feeling along the arteries and veins. "No sign of cardiac arrest," he reported, then turned his attention to the stomach.

The moment he sliced it open, a wave of putrid gas blew out. I had to fight to keep from retching again. This smell was the worst so far. Even Martin and Pete, all the way across the auditorium, looked like they might be sick.

"Whoa!" Doc gasped. "You *never* get used to that!"

He applied more of the smell-killing goo to his upper lip, then examined the contents of the stomach. It was mostly hay, along with some vegetables that had been swallowed whole— and a few assorted pieces of trash, mostly wrappers from Henry Hippo Happy Meals. Doc glanced over it all quickly— even he found rooting through partially digested hippo food nauseating—and moved on to the small intestine. This was as thick as a fire hose, purplish, and coiled in on itself like a rattlesnake ready to strike. Doc had barely begun examining it when he noticed something. "Hmm," he said.

Martin and Pete snapped to attention. I leaned out a bit farther on the catwalk, trying to peek over Doc's shoulder and see what had caught his eye.

"What've you got?" Martin asked.

"Peritonitis," Doc answered.

"What's that?" Pete asked.

Doc sighed, purposefully loud enough for Pete to hear. "It's an inflammation of the abdominal wall. In this case, it appears to have been caused by perforation of the duodenum."

"Could you repeat that in English?"

"That *was* English."

"I mean English that people who aren't doctors can understand."

"There are holes in Henry's small intestine. They're tiny, but they didn't have to be big to cause damage. Intestinal juices leaked out of them, which caused Henry to get sick. Want to see one?"

"Not really," Pete said, provoking another sigh from Doc.

Martin approached the stage, however. "What made these holes?"

"That's what I'd like to know." Doc pointed to his little tub of goo. "Rub some of that under your nose and put on some goggles."

Martin did so, then tentatively peered into the hippo's body, as though he was afraid something might jump out of it and bite him.

"Watch," Doc said. Then he squeezed the intestine.

A thin stream of fluid squirted out through a tiny hole.

"*That's* what killed him?" Martin asked. "That tiny little thing?"

"There's more than one. See . . . ?"

He reached for more intestine. Martin stepped back, blocking my view. So I grabbed a wire and leaned out as far as I could.

The catwalk shifted beneath me with a loud creak.

Doc and Martin immediately stopped what they were doing and looked around the auditorium.

I should've probably just held still, but before I could think it through, I reflexively ducked out of sight. The catwalk shifted and creaked again.

This time, Doc and Martin realized the sound had come from above. They shaded their eyes and stared up into the lighting grid. "Is someone up there?" Martin yelled.

I didn't dare answer. I didn't even dare breathe. I just stood as still as I could, hoping the catwalk and the bright lights were enough to shield me from their view.

The seconds crept by like hours. Finally, Doc said, "I don't see anything" and turned his eyes from the lights.

Martin stared up into the lighting grid a little longer before turning away. "Definitely sounded like something was up there," he said suspiciously.

"Has Bung gotten out again?" Doc asked.

"Not this week."

Bung was FunJungle's three-year-old orangutan. In zoos, orangs were notorious for getting out of their enclosures, and Bung had been no exception. He'd already escaped twice—though never during visitor hours. Luckily, he'd been quite easy to find both times, as he had a terrible sweet tooth and had gone directly to the ice cream stand near Monkey Mountain. The second time, he'd broken into the freezer and consumed five gallons of rocky road before the keepers could pry him away.

"Probably just a raccoon then," Doc said. "They've been getting into the vents at the hospital, too." He returned his attention to Henry.

I wanted to see what was going on, but was afraid to take any more chances. I stayed put on the catwalk, scared to move a muscle, which meant I couldn't see the autopsy worth a darn anymore. I could still *hear* everyone loud and clear, though.

"Look," Doc said, examining the intestine. "There's another hole. And another. And another!"

"And another over there," Martin added.

"It's getting close to time for the news," Pete called out. "Do we have an official cause of death? This perry-whatever?"

"Peritonitis," Martin corrected.

"Maybe not," Doc said.

"What are you talking about?" Martin sounded annoyed.

"It's obviously peritonitis. You said so yourself. . . ."

"I mean there might be something else going on here. There were five holes in only two inches of intestine. That's not normal. And look, here's two more."

"So the hippo's got a crummy intestine," Pete said. "What's the big deal?"

"The big deal is, I don't think anything natural could have perforated his intestine like this."

A moment passed. Then Martin grasped what Doc was saying. "You mean, you think somebody *did this* to Henry?"

"Maybe," Doc replied.

"How?"

"It'd be easy. You'd just have to take something small with a lot of sharp points—sharp enough to pierce Henry's intestine—then wad it up in some food and throw it into his mouth. In fact, given the number of holes—here's three more—someone probably tossed in a lot of these things."

"Wait a minute," said Pete. "Are you suggesting Henry was *murdered*?"

Doc hesitated a moment before answering. "Yes."

Despite the heat from the lamps all around me, I felt a chill go up my spine. The possibility that Henry had been murdered alarmed me—though I have to admit, there was something exciting about it too.

Martin wasn't nearly as shocked by the idea. Instead, he

seemed annoyed by it. "That's ridiculous," he huffed. "Why would anyone want to murder Henry?"

"I'm not saying it was done maliciously," Doc replied. "Quite likely, it was an accident. You've seen what our guests throw in Henry's mouth. They think it's funny. Maybe someone threw in this sharp thing—whatever it was—as a joke, not realizing it would kill him."

"So that's what you think I should tell the news?" Pete asked, incredulous. "That our beloved mascot was killed by one of our guests?"

"He wasn't exactly beloved. . . ."

Pete didn't even wait for Doc to finish the thought. "Forget about it. If I go out there and tell the press Henry was murdered, they'll think I'm insane."

"So don't use the word 'murdered.' If a guest did this to him, the public should know. They should understand that when they throw garbage into an animal's mouth, that animal could die. . . ."

"I think it's a bad idea," Martin said.

"Why?" Doc sounded incredulous.

"It makes us sound like we're running a shoddy zoo. It's bad enough Henry died so soon after our grand opening. If we say one of our own guests killed him, the animal-rights activists will go ballistic. They'll ask why we allowed people to throw things in his mouth. Why didn't we put up barriers to keep it from happening? We'll get accused of animal abuse. Or cutting corners to get the park open on time. . . ."

"You don't know that for sure."

"We can't take any chances." Martin turned to Pete. "Tell the press Henry died of natural causes. He'd had a rough life in the circus. We knew that when we brought him here, but we'd hoped he still had more years left in him. At least his final months were happy ones, though."

"You got it." Pete was out the door before Doc could protest.

After he was gone, there was a heavy silence. I stood as still as I could, astonished by everything I'd witnessed. It was shocking enough to hear that Henry had been killed. But Martin's desire to keep it a secret *really* stunned me. It was the first time I'd realized that FunJungle was being run like a corporation, rather than a zoo.

Finally, Doc said, "There's also the possibility that someone killed Henry on purpose."

"Why would someone want to do that?" Martin snapped.

"I think you know."

There was a long silence, as though Martin was carefully weighing what to say next. Meanwhile, I could barely contain myself. I wanted to shout at the top of my lungs, to ask who they thought killed Henry and why.

But I didn't. And to my disappointment, Martin didn't

take the bait. Instead, he snapped off his goggles and headed for the door. "That's preposterous. No one would be crazy enough to murder a hippo."

"People do lots of crazy things."

Martin tapped his foot rapidly, something I'd noticed he did when he got nervous. "Henry died of natural causes," he said finally. "That's what I want to see in your report. No accusations of murder. No crackpot conspiracy theories. 'Natural causes.' End of story."

I couldn't believe what I was hearing.

Neither could Doc. "Let me get this straight," he said. I could hear the aggravation in his voice. "Someone may have killed our mascot—the most famous animal in the entire country—and you want me to cover it up?"

"Yes, that's exactly what I want," said Martin.

"But that's—"

"A direct order. Do it—or there'll be consequences."

It was a long time before Doc said anything. Even though I couldn't see him, I could feel the tension in the room. I wasn't sure what consequences Martin had in mind, but Doc seemed troubled by them. When he finally spoke again, he sounded very tired.

"All right," he said. "I'll bury it."

It took Doc a lot longer to finish with Henry than I'd expected. Even though Martin remained in the auditorium, interrupting his phone calls now and then to prod Doc or complain about how much time he was taking, Doc still insisted upon doing his autopsy properly. He went through Henry's intestines inch by inch—and a full-grown hippo has more than sixty feet of intestine.

The whole time he was doing it, I had to stay up in the catwalk, trying to stay silent. My legs began to cramp terribly, although that was nothing compared to the pain I felt in my bladder. I'd drunk a lot of water before the autopsy and now it all wanted to get back out again. Of course, the more I tried to not think about it, the more I thought about it—until I ultimately felt like I was going to explode. It was torture.

Meanwhile, Doc just kept poking along, like examining hippo intestines was the greatest fun you could ever have. I couldn't tell for sure how many holes Doc found, but I knew from his occasional comments to himself that it was more than a hundred. To his annoyance, however, he never found what he was *really* looking for: the objects that made the holes. "C'mon, where are you?" he'd asked repeatedly, and ultimately grumbled, "Dang things must've gotten pooped back out."

By nine thirty, I'd been hiding for nearly three hours. I was just about to cry uncle and blow my cover when, to my incredible relief, Martin finally goaded Doc out of the auditorium. Doc still wanted to sift through the contents of Henry's stomach, but Martin convinced him it could wait until the next day—and I think even Doc was getting nauseous after rooting through Henry's innards for so long. The moment they were out the door, I scrambled down and booked for the exit. I'd really wanted to look into Henry's belly and see some of the perforated intestines up close, but I couldn't spare another second. The auditorium door automatically locked behind me as I dashed out.

I don't think a cheetah could have run to the nearest bathroom as fast as I did.

Once I'd taken care of my business, however, I still had some things to deal with. I was starving and my mother was surely ready to kill me for coming home late.

Mom always expected me home by eight for dinner. She didn't much care what I did before then; the park was so far from civilization she figured I couldn't get into a whole lot of trouble. Usually, I was home well before dinnertime. In fact, I'd never been late before.

So I ran back as fast as I could. At night, I could make much better time through the park because the crowds were gone. I had the wide promenades all to myself; it was like running through the streets of a ghost town. It wasn't quiet, though. Many animals are most active at dusk and early evening. In fact, normal zoo hours—right in the heat of the day—are practically the worst time to see animals in action; that's when they prefer to nap. Now, as I ran, I could hear animals all around. Calling, growling, roaring, chirping, croaking, trumpeting. The night was alive with noise.

There were still a few park employees about, mostly cleaning staff and groundskeepers. J.J. McCracken wanted his park spotless when the gates opened every morning. At night, every piece of trash got picked up, every railing polished, every hedge trimmed. I'd been around FunJungle long enough that all the cleaners knew me, so no one called security to report that a family had forgotten one of their children.

The trailer park where we lived was behind the back fence, right next to the employee parking lot. In the daytime, it was hideously ugly. Rather than being organized in any sensible fashion, all the trailers had been placed where the land was flattest; it looked like they'd been scattered by a passing tornado. At one time, some landscaping had been attempted and quickly forgotten; now only patches of crabgrass grew among prickly pear cactus and a few stubby cedar trees. The single amenity J.J. McCracken had provided us all with was a hot tub, which was totally useless, seeing as the temperature outside was often more than a hundred degrees.

At night, however, the trailer park was far more welcoming. Since the closest town was so far away, the mobile homes looked kind of like a tight frontier community in the midst of a vast wilderness. There was something comforting about the warm glow of light from their windows. The sky above was one of the few places left in the United States that was free of light pollution; on that moonless night, I could see millions of stars and the Milky Way was a bright slash across the sky.

We lived in the farthest trailer from FunJungle, right on the edge of the wilderness; white-tailed deer wandered past our home every day. A herd of six was grazing by the front steps as I returned, but they scattered at the sight of me.

I could hear the TV, which was surprising. Mom rarely turned it on. She was so used to living without one after all her time in Africa, she often forgot we even had one. She didn't like it much, calling it the "idiot box," preferring that we read or play games to pass the time instead.

It took a special kind of person to become a field biologist, and my mom was one of the best. I'm not just saying that; she'd won all sorts of awards from conservation organizations and anytime there was a magazine article about her, important scientists lined up to say how great she was. She was really smart, but also tough enough to deal with the hardships of living far from civilization. In the Congo, she'd faced hungry lions, rampaging elephants, blood-sucking leeches, and—most dangerous of all—poachers. She was incredibly patient; when she'd begun her research, she'd watched her gorillas twelve hours a day, every day, for an entire year until they finally began to accept her as one of their own. After spending so long out there, she felt the gorillas were her family. It wasn't like she was putting them in competition with me though; in fact, I thought it was nice. You couldn't find another biologist in the whole world who cared more about her subjects.

Given her adventurous background, it might seem surprising that Mom now enjoyed working at a zoo. But given the war, staying in the Congo wasn't an option—and besides, FunJungle wasn't merely a zoo. J.J. McCracken wanted it to be a world-class research facility too. (Dad claimed this wasn't because J.J. was interested in science, though; there were big tax breaks for research facilities.) J.J. had told Martin del Gato to recruit the best of the best, and where gorillas were concerned, that was Mom. Martin had offered to double what Mom was getting paid in Atlanta, but to his surprise, she wasn't that interested in money. Field biology doesn't pay much; she hadn't gone into it expecting to get rich. Instead, what she cared about was research—and the key to doing good research was an exceptional animal habitat.

So Mom had begun her work at FunJungle long before we moved there, serving as a technical consultant on the design of Monkey Mountain. Under her supervision, the exhibits were altered from mere viewing areas into dynamic living spaces where the animals could thrive. Mom knew what gorillas and other primates would enjoy in their new homes—and she knew what she and other scientists would need to study them. With her input, Monkey Mountain became the world's finest man-made habitat for gorillas—as well as chimpanzees, orang-utans, gibbons, colobus monkeys, and ring-tailed lemurs.

J.J. had cut similar deals with other scientists to bring them to FunJungle, allowing them to help design their exhibits as well. Therefore, our trailer park was a who's who of famous field biologists. One of the world's greatest elephant researchers lived on one side of us; a polar bear specialist lived on the other.

FunJungle had found one other incentive to lure Mom there: giving Dad a job too. That was great for all of us, as it meant that, for the first time in my life, Dad was around more often than he wasn't. And yet Dad still craved an adventure now and then, so his contract allowed him to do an occasional assignment for someone else. That's why only Mom was waiting for me at home that night. Dad was in China, taking pictures of giant pandas for *Outside Magazine*.

I banged through the front door. There was no point in trying to sneak in. Our trailer only had three rooms, and after so much time in the jungle, Mom had a highly attuned sense of hearing. She'd probably heard me crunching across the dry crabgrass from a hundred yards away.

That was another reason the TV being on was odd. Mom always said it was too noisy; it interfered with her ability to hear the world around her.

Once I came inside, I understood why it was on. It was tuned to the local news, which was all about Henry.

This wasn't much of a surprise. J.J. McCracken's decision to build FunJungle was the biggest news in that part of Texas since the Battle of the Alamo. The local TV stations had covered it nonstop from the moment it was announced. There were daily reports on how many tourists were coming, how well the park was running and how soon it would be until new attractions were opened or new hotels were built.

Anytime a new animal arrived, it was the lead story. I'd seen a newspaper survey that said Henry was the second-most recognized celebrity in the state, just behind J.J. McCracken but ahead of the quarterback for the Dallas Cowboys. So his death was huge news.

They weren't actually showing Henry when I came in. (That was fine with me. I'd seen plenty of Henry that day, inside and out.) Instead, they were interviewing Summer McCracken, J.J.'s daughter, about how she was handling Henry's death.

In the time since she'd given her father the idea for FunJungle, Summer—now thirteen years old—had become quite famous herself. I'd never really understood why. Sure, she was rich and lots of people said she was pretty, but she didn't really *do* anything except go to boarding school. And yet, everyone was still fascinated by her. At the supermarket checkout, there was always at least one magazine with her on the cover, claiming to have the latest details on what she was up to and who she was dating. Even the employees of FunJungle were crazy about her; I'd overheard several excitedly discussing rumors that Summer was home from school and might even deign to visit the park. It was ridiculous.

I watched the end of her interview. Summer had a lot of composure for someone only a year older than me— but maybe, if people had been interviewing *me* my whole life, I would have been like that too. Despite being obviously upset about Henry, Summer managed to be very well-spoken. "I think we're *all* really shocked by this," she told the reporter. "Not just my family, but all the people who work at FunJungle—and everyone who's ever come to see Henry here."

I wondered if Summer didn't know what Henry was really like—or if she was just faking the heartfelt stuff. If she was, she could have given Pete Thwacker a run for his money in the PR department.

"It's a terrible shame," Summer went on, "but I think it's important to note that the last months of Henry's life were happy ones. . . ."

"You were with Henry, weren't you?"

It always surprised me how Mom could sneak up on me so quietly, even within the confines of the trailer. She'd mastered moving silently during her years with the gorillas. I wheeled around to find her standing right behind me, arms crossed. She was wearing her standard work outfit: a khaki shirt and shorts.

I hesitated, trying to determine if it was worth lying, but finally decided it would be pointless. Mom could always see right through me. "How'd you know?"

"You smell like a dead hippo."

Of course. Mom had also honed her sense of smell in the Congo. When you spent a lot of time in the jungle, it paid to know when something dangerous was creeping up on you. The way most humans sensed danger was through sight—but the way most animals did was through hearing or smell, which were much more effective over long distances, especially at night. Dad said Mom could smell a lion from half a mile away—and even tell if it was male or female. He always claimed to be joking about this last part, but I think it might have been true.

I hadn't even been that close to the hippo. At the nearest, I'd still been ten feet away. But I guess the stench had stuck with me.

"Your dinner was ready an hour and a half ago," Mom said. "I was worried sick about you. Why didn't you call?"

"I couldn't."

"That's no excuse, Theodore. I was almost ready to call park security. . . ."

"I was watching the autopsy. Henry was murdered!"

That surprised Mom enough to silence her for a moment. She turned off the TV so as to give me her full attention, then asked, "What are you talking about?"

I told her the whole story. She listened straight through without interrupting. I'll bet most other mothers would have punished me the moment they heard I'd snuck into the autopsy, but Mom was different. She was naturally curious—and she loved animals even more than I did. If someone had done something to harm Henry, she wanted to know about it.

While she listened, she reheated my dinner and set it before me. I was so hungry, I dug right in. It took the whole meal for me to finish telling everything that happened.

Once I was done, Mom sat silently for a while. Finally, she said, "That's very interesting, but technically, you don't have any *proof* Henry was murdered."

"Doc *said* he was."

"Did he really? Or did he just suspect it?"

I had to think about that, going over the whole autopsy again in my mind. Finally, I admitted, "He just suspected it, I guess. But *something* had to make all those holes in Henry's intestine. . . ."

"True. But you have no way of knowing if someone fed it to Henry on purpose or not."

I frowned; this wasn't exactly the response I'd been hoping for. "I guess not."

Mom glanced at my empty plate, then nodded to the sink. I took all my dirty things over and cleaned them.

While I did, Mom cut me a slice of chocolate cake and poured a glass of milk. "Murder is a very serious charge," she said. "When you say that, you're insinuating that someone purposefully planned to kill Henry. Now, can you think of a reason anyone would want to do that?"

"Doc said he could."

Mom paused, ever so slightly, while putting the milk back in the fridge. I could tell she was surprised by this, but she didn't want me to know. "Did he say what that was?"

"No. But Martin seemed to know what he was talking about."

Mom set the cake on the table. "I think you must have misunderstood them. I can't think of any reason someone would want to murder an animal."

"People do it all the time. It's called hunting."

"I mean in a zoo."

"A lot of people here didn't like Henry."

"That doesn't mean they'd want to kill him."

I shrugged, but I knew Mom was right. I couldn't imagine anyone hating Henry so much that they'd murder him. But then, I couldn't understand why anyone would want to kill an animal with a gun, either. I'd seen what poachers could do in Africa, shooting an elephant just for its tusks, or a rhino for its horn. It was always unbelievably horrible and cruel. How could anyone think an elephant's tooth was beautiful, but not the elephant itself? And though I'd never seen the results of the war in the Congo, I'd heard more than enough about them. All I could figure was, adults were capable of a lot of bad behavior for reasons that were far beyond me.

So even though it didn't make sense that someone would

murder Henry, I still didn't doubt someone would do it. I tried to think of a way to explain this to Mom, but I couldn't. Besides, something in her demeanor told me she didn't want to hear it anyhow.

Finally I asked, "So you think it was just an accident?"

"I'm not saying someone didn't purposefully feed Henry something they shouldn't have," she told me. "People do lots of cruel and stupid things. When I was studying at the Bronx Zoo, there was a sea lion pool. People would throw coins into it all the time. The sea lions kept eating the coins and getting sick. So the zoo put up signs warning everyone not to do it. And people kept doing it anyhow. This wasn't garbage. This was *money*. Money they could use. There was no point to it, but they kept doing it, and eventually one of the sea lions got sick and died. The zoo ultimately had to post security guards to keep people from throwing their money away."

I'd eaten my cake quickly. Mom took my plate to the sink. She seemed saddened by the whole conversation. "So, yes, maybe someone killed Henry," she said. "But I don't think its murder. It's just what humans have always done to animals."

Before I could argue the point, she turned me toward the bathroom and said, "Now go take a shower. You're making the whole trailer smell like dead hippo."

Mom always went to sleep early and got up early. That was another habit left over from living in the Congo; there hadn't been much to do at night there and the gorillas were usually up an hour before dawn.

I lay in bed reading until I saw the light go out under her door. I waited another fifteen minutes to make sure she was asleep, then slipped out of bed, called the San Antonio police, and asked to talk to the homicide division.

I felt bad for sneaking around behind my mom's back, but I felt I had to do *something*. Mom hadn't been there for the whole autopsy. She hadn't heard the concern in Doc's voice when he told Martin about the holes in Henry's intestine. I had.

"Sergeant Tustin. How may I help you?"

"I'd like to report a murder," I said.

"Did you witness it, perform it, or simply find a body?" Sergeant Tustin sounded surprisingly bored.

"Um, the last one. Sort of."

"You *sort of* found a body? You mean you only found part of one?"

"No. I didn't find it. Someone else did. But I heard that the victim might have been murdered."

"How did you come by this information?"

"From the doctor who performed the autopsy."

"The coroner? If the coroner found evidence of a murder, he would have already reported it. . . ."

"No. It wasn't a coroner who did this."

"Then what kind of doctor did?"

"A veterinarian."

There was a pause at the other end. "Wait," Sergeant Tustin said, sounding annoyed. "This is about an *animal*?"

"Yes."

"You're calling the homicide division about an animal."

"Because homicide's murder, right?"

"What's your name, kid?"

I hesitated; this wasn't going the way I'd expected. "I'd rather not say."

"You wouldn't? Okay, then." There was some typing at the other end of the line; Tustin was using a computer. "You're calling from 512-555-2647?"

I gulped. "Uh . . ."

"Fitzroy residence," Tustin continued. "555 means you're out by FunJungle, so . . . Oh, no."

"What?"

"This isn't about that hippo? What's his name? Harry?"

"Henry. Yes. The vet thinks he might have been—"

"Listen, kid. We've got our hands full here investigating the murders of *people*. We don't investigate dead animals. I mean, animals kill each other all the time. That's what they do. That's why they're animals. Somebody finds their cat chewed in half by a dog, we don't go out and arrest the dog, you know."

"But this is different. Henry was famous."

"Really? Here's what I recommend. Drop by the lion cage. I understand, nine times out of ten, when a hippopotamus is murdered, it's the lions who have done it."

"I'm serious. . . ."

"Yeah, sure you are. This isn't funny any more. Keep it up, and I'll send a team of police over there . . ."

"Good!"

". . . for *you*."

"Oh." I didn't know what else to say except "Sorry. I didn't mean any trouble. . . ."

"Good-bye, Fitzroy." Sergeant Tustin hung up.

I put down the phone and realized my hand was trembling. My heart was hammering in my chest.

How had *that* happened?

I'd always thought calling the police to report a crime was the right thing to do. I'd assumed they would be eager to investigate crimes, like the policemen I'd seen in the movies. But Sergeant Tustin had seemed more interested in arresting *me*.

Outside the trailer, someone sneezed.

It wasn't that loud. If it had happened in the middle of the day at FunJungle, I probably wouldn't have noticed it. But in the stillness of the night, it might as well have been a gunshot.

I quickly lifted the window shade, peering into the darkness.

No one was there.

I listened carefully, picking up the faint sound of what might have been footsteps hurrying away.

Part of me wanted to run outside to see who'd been there—but a bigger part of me thought this was a bad idea. If someone was spying on me, chasing after them could be dangerous.

Had someone been spying on me, though? I wondered if I was being paranoid after my unsettling call with Sergeant Tustin. There were other reasons someone might have been outside our home, even though it was on the farthest edge of the trailer park. We had plenty of neighbors, many of whom worked odd hours and were comfortable in the outdoors. Any one of them might have been taking a circuitous route home to their trailer. Or someone might have stepped outside to do some stargazing. Or maybe someone was actually heading to the hot tub for once, but had been distracted by a possum or a deer.

Heck, maybe it had even been a possum or a deer. Animals sneezed on occasion. And they didn't sound any different from humans.

I made sure the trailer door was locked tight, just in case.

Then I slipped back into bed, trying to calm myself, thinking everything through.

I seemed to be the only person who wanted to know who'd killed Henry. Doc had hidden the proof. My own mother hadn't believed me. And the police thought I was just a prank caller.

But it seemed to me that, if someone really *had* murdered Henry, that was important. If the killer got away with the crime once, why wouldn't they do it again? What if more animals ended up dead because no one was doing anything to help them?

If there was a murderer, people needed to know. And if I couldn't convince anyone of that, then I'd have to find evidence that would.

I was going to have to investigate Henry's murder myself.

There was a fresh heel print in the ground near our trailer.

I found it in the morning. It was ten feet from our door, but I could clearly hear our radio through the trailer's flimsy walls. Whoever had stood there might have been able to hear me on the phone with the police; I thought I'd kept my voice down, but maybe, as I'd grown more upset, I'd gotten louder.

The print was a neat half circle, as though from the heel of a dress shoe. That made it unusual, as our neighbors all dressed casually for work. Like Mom, they wore sneakers or work boots. I wondered if any of them even owned dress shoes. Mom didn't.

I measured my shoe against it. The heel was considerably larger than mine. An adult. A pretty big adult, which most likely meant it was a man—although that wasn't 100 percent for sure. Large Marge wore shoes big enough for an orangutan.

The rest of the sole had been resting on rock, so it hadn't left a print. The ground around our trailer was extremely rocky, so I couldn't find any other prints, save for a skid mark in a patch of mud near the corner of our trailer, as though someone had slipped while hurrying away.

The heel print had definitely been made recently, though. There was a tiny ball of deer poop squashed beneath it.

I know my poop. I learned how to track animals in the Congo, and one of the keys to tracking something is knowing what kind of poop it leaves behind.

There was deer poop everywhere around our trailer. The ground was a minefield of little pellets. I think the smell of the larger carnivores wafting out of FunJungle scared off the coyotes, which were the only local predators big enough to take down a deer. So the deer were almost always around. They'd cropped the grass in the trailer park bare and turned it all into poop. It came out in scatterings of soft black balls, although after a day in the Texas sun, they'd bake into hard brown nuggets. The one squashed under the heel print was relatively fresh. And the heel was oriented to indicate that whoever had been standing there had been facing our trailer, not the woods.

I couldn't guarantee that the person had been listening to me, but the heel print made me nervous, just the same. First Sergeant Tustin, now this. Adults seemed more interested in keeping an eye on me than learning who'd killed Henry.

But I was still determined to find the murderer. If anything, finding the heel print made me *more* determined.

The obvious place to start was Hippo River.

As Doc had pointed out, the objects that had killed Henry were no longer in his digestive tract. So there was only one other place they could be. That was one advantage of investigating a dead zoo animal; I knew exactly where Henry had been every day for the last few months. The moment the park opened in the morning, I set off for Hippo River.

I'd expected to have the place to myself, but to my surprise, it was even *more* crowded than usual. Hundreds of Henry devotees had made a pilgrimage to see where he had died—and more were coming by the minute. The front gates were mobbed. Mourners streamed through the security metal detectors and sprinted for Hippo River.

Adding to the mayhem was a large animal-rights rally, right outside the park. The activists were from the Animal Liberation Front, an organization that believed all animals should live freely—and thus, zoos were "prisons." The ALF had targeted FunJungle since its opening day, though with poor results: Families who'd been eagerly anticipating a trip to FunJungle for months weren't about to turn away because some demonstrator handed them a pamphlet. The protests had dwindled over the past two weeks—the day before, only two people had shown up—but now Henry's death had galvanized the ALF. A huge group of protesters now rallied around an effigy of dead Henry—a stuffed hippo with its eyes Xed out—waving signs, blowing whistles, and trying to convince the tourists that Henry had died as a result of negligent care.

That really bugged me. A hundred years ago, some zoos might not have treated their animals well, but these days they all try to provide the best treatment possible. I wish the world didn't need zoos—and I'll bet most zookeepers do too—but right now, they're important. Zoos have prevented plenty of animals from going extinct—and Mom always says there wouldn't even be a conservation movement without them. Most people don't get to grow up in the Congo like I did. Instead, they come to care about gorillas or elephants or polar bears because they see them in zoos. When the ALF accused FunJungle of negligence, they were insulting every keeper there, my mom included.

So I did my best to ignore them, finding a spot as far from the protest as possible to scope out Hippo River. As I did, two problems with continuing my investigation came to mind.

The first was access. Henry's enclosure was now barricaded. The hastily-erected fence Martin del Gato had ordered the night before had now been replaced by sturdy plywood walls like the kind that surrounded construction sites. Even the windows in the underwater viewing areas were blocked off. The walls wouldn't have been hard to scale, but security guards were posted to prevent thrill-seekers from doing any such thing.

The rest of Hippo River was still open, however. ("Our guests ought to be allowed to see at least *one* fat aquatic mammal," J.J. McCracken had reportedly groused.) I wandered over to Umfundisi Scenic Viewpoint under the pretense of seeing Hildegard, thinking maybe I could dive into Henry's pool from there, but quickly found that wouldn't work. As annoying as the barricading of Henry's enclosure was to me, it was devastating to the tourists who'd come to mourn him. Since Umfundisi was now the only place anyone could get a glimpse of Henry's old home, it was a mob scene. Tourists were packed twenty deep, ignoring the live hippo nearby so they could stare at a tiny sliver of a dead hippo's empty enclosure. There was no way to dive into Henry's pool without a hundred people seeing me.

Even so, the second problem was even more daunting: Hippo poop.

Most likely, the objects that had killed Henry were in the

water. That was where hippos generally did their business. (In Africa, hippo poop was the primary fertilizer for most aquatic plants.) Which meant I'd have to go swimming. Theoretically, the filtration system would have removed a lot of the poop from the water without Henry around to constantly generate more, but still, there had to be *some* left. Henry's backwater had been so polluted, I guessed it would take far more than one night to fully sanitize it. The mere thought of going in there gave me the willies. At the very least, I'd need a mask and snorkel to see in that murky water, but since I lived two hundred miles from the ocean, I didn't own one—and the closest sporting goods store was thirty miles away.

So I wandered through Hippo River, observing the guards, trying to determine if there was any time in their rounds— perhaps during the shift change—when Henry's enclosure was left unobserved. But no luck. The guards relieved one another with military precision. I was almost ready to concede that I'd have to sneak into Hippo River at night when a commotion by the front gates grabbed my attention.

A crowd had gathered around someone. At first, I thought maybe a guest had collapsed from heatstroke, but no one in the crowd seemed worried. Instead, they were all giddy, clamoring for the attention of whoever was in their midst like hens trying to attract a rooster.

I scrambled up a tree to get a better look.

Two bodyguards loomed in the center of the crowd, the biggest men I'd ever seen, both wearing sunglasses and suits. They were so large, it was hard to see the person between them. I could only glimpse a lock of blond hair and flash of pink clothing—but that was all I needed to figure out who it was.

Summer McCracken had arrived.

Apparently, the rumors that she was home from boarding school were true. Summer always wore pink from head to toe; it was her trademark. And I knew she never went anywhere without bodyguards. Given his wealth, J.J. McCracken worried someone would kidnap his daughter, so he had her protected twenty-four hours a day. Despite the bodyguards' intimidating presence, the tourists still mobbed Summer. Full-grown men and women screamed her name and begged for autographs. She had a longer line of people waiting to take pictures with her than the Henry Hippo actors ever did.

I shook my head, not understanding this at all—until something occurred to me. There was one other option to investigating Henry's death by myself: Tell J.J. McCracken about it.

The police might consider investigating Henry's murder a joke, but J.J. certainly wouldn't. After all, Henry was *his* hippo. And he probably didn't even know about the murder theory. The only people who could have told him were Martin del Gato, Doc, and Pete Thwacker. But Martin had told Doc to bury the evidence—and Pete had barely even understood the murder theory in the first place.

The chances of a kid like me getting to J.J. McCracken were slimmer than slim. Summer was my only chance—but I had to act fast.

To look like another eager fan, I grabbed a piece of paper from a nearby trash bin. It was a discarded napkin with a smear of ketchup on it, but most of the autograph hounds were asking Summer to sign things that were equally unsanitary. As Summer passed, I plunged into the crowd around her.

It was a free-for-all inside. Unlike with the Henry Hippo actors, there was no official line set up for people to calmly stand in to meet Summer. Instead, everyone pushed and shoved, gouging each other with shoulders and elbows, jostling for position. I was jounced left and right, smashed forward, and then bounced back. An eight-year-old girl was nearly trampled beside me. It was already a hot day; surrounded by the crush of people, it was stifling.

I spotted a sliver of light between two incredibly fat women. I scrambled for it, but was only halfway through when the women slammed together, crushing me between them. For a moment, I thought I might suffocate in their flab. In desperation, I booted one in the ankle. She yelped and pulled away, allowing me to stumble free—and suddenly, I found myself in a small, open pocket of fresh air, face-to-face with Summer McCracken herself.

She was taller than I'd expected, a few inches more than me. Her blond hair hung to her shoulders and she wore a pink blouse, shorts, and sandals. But what really grabbed my attention were her eyes. They were an amazingly bright blue, like the wings of a morpho butterfly. The pictures of her never did them justice.

Summer looked at me, but didn't really appear to see me; she just dutifully reached for my napkin to sign it.

I started to say something—but then froze. For some reason, I was intimidated. Even at the time, I knew it was ridiculous; it wasn't like she was anyone important, like her father or the president. She was only a girl, only a year older than me. And yet, I simply stared at her like a dork. For a moment, all the noise seemed to drain from the world, and all I could think about were her eyes.

It took me a moment to realize she'd said something to me. "Wh-What?" I stammered.

"Do you want me to sign that?" Summer repeated, nodding to my napkin. I looked down and realized that instead of letting her have it, I'd kept it clutched in my hand.

The noise of the crowd suddenly came rushing back.

Mostly, it seemed to be people shouting at me to hurry up with Summer so they could have a turn. So I quickly blurted out what I had to say: "I need to talk to your father."

Summer looked at me curiously. "You and everyone else," she said.

"This is really important."

"Let me guess. You want a loan."

The crowd burst into laughter. My face grew warm as the blood rushed to it. I felt like an idiot and wanted to slip back into the crowd and disappear, but a sudden surge from the rear shoved me forward into Summer herself.

Instantly, the bodyguards were on me. They didn't think I was a threat; they were only giving Summer her space. Hands the size of baseball gloves grabbed my shoulders, steadying me and moving me back.

For a second, though, I was close enough to whisper to Summer. Before I even knew I was doing it, I told her, "Henry Hippo was murdered."

She stared at me a moment, surprised, her blue eyes boring into mine. And then, she shook her head in amusement. Suddenly, it occurred to me that Summer was probably approached by crazy people the time—and that I'd just been lumped in with the rest of the weirdos. Before I even had a chance to explain, the crowd swallowed me up again. Two seconds later, I was spit back out, left behind clutching my napkin while Summer and her groupies continued on.

I'd never felt so stupid in my whole life.

I'd behaved like a total freak in front of Summer McCracken. The only good thing about it was that she'd probably forgotten me the very next moment. At least, I hoped she would. It was preferable to her remembering me and avoiding me from then on.

Annoyed at myself, I resumed my watch over the guards at Hippo River. Large Marge had come on shift, so I selected a bench out of her line of sight and spied on her through the vines of a bougainvillea plant. She took her patrol very seriously, giving the stink-eye to any guest who so much as loitered in front of the barricades for too long.

It occurred to me that the need for so much security was suspicious. After all, what was the problem with letting guests see Henry's empty enclosure? It wasn't as if FunJungle was hiding the fact that the hippo had died. If anything, they were making it a huge deal. Numerous press issues had been released. Commemorative Henry T-shirts were already being sold. Pete Thwacker was even arranging for a public funeral.

The memorial was to take place in a few days. Martin had wanted it sooner, as Henry's corpse was still sitting on the Henry and Pals stage, slowly rotting. (There wasn't a freezer big enough to hold the body anywhere on the property.) But J.J. McCracken had decreed that his hippo be sent off with honor and dignity—as well as an event that would get a huge amount of free media coverage for FunJungle. This all took time to plan properly; guests had to be invited, the grave had to be dug, an extra-large coffin had to be built. In the meantime, hundreds of bags of ice had been packed around Henry's body to slow its decay, the theater's air conditioning had been turned up as high as it would go, and the building was sealed shut. (Even if the giant corpse hadn't been on their stage, the Henry and Pals Review would have been shuttered for a few days out of respect for the dead.. I'd heard rumors that Henry was being excised from the show altogether, and that it would soon be rechristened the FunJungle Friends Musical Spectacular.)

The point being, if it wasn't a secret that Henry was dead, why was his enclosure so tightly protected? I found myself wondering who'd even posted the guards in the first place. Martin? Pete? J.J. himself? What if the whole reason for them wasn't to discourage the random Henry fan from getting into the deceased hippo's enclosure—but to prevent someone like me from investigating? What if there was something inside there they wanted to hide? What if—

"Who killed him?" a voice asked, so close to my ear I jumped.

I spun around and once again found myself staring into the blue eyes of Summer McCracken.

She was tucked back in the landscaping, crouched behind the bench, almost as if she was hiding behind it. It had only been a few minutes since my embarrassing encounter with her, but somehow, she'd already changed clothes. She still had the trademark pink shorts on, but she now wore a FunJungle T-shirt over her blouse and had her hair tucked up into a baseball cap. The change was so startling, I would have assumed it wasn't even her except for her eyes. I couldn't collect my thoughts, spluttering, "I . . . uh . . . I don't know."

Summer frowned. "Then how do you know he was murdered?"

"I snuck into the autopsy."

Summer's eyes lit up, getting even brighter than they had before. But before she could respond, she noticed something behind me. I turned around to see her bodyguards hurrying in our direction, trying to act like they weren't worried, but obviously worried. Looking for her.

Summer ducked farther into the landscaping. "Meet me behind the Gorilla Grill in fifteen minutes," she said, then vanished with a rustle of leaves.

The bodyguards thundered past, not seeing her, and then I was alone on the bench again, feeling strangely excited.

It looked like I might have found someone willing to believe me after all.

6 · DIVING IN

It turned out, Summer McCracken *had* thought I was a freak. But that turned out to be a good thing. Right after I'd been sucked back into the crowd, Summer had asked her bodyguards, "Who was that nutball?" And they'd told her.

"They know who I am?" I asked, surprised.

Summer nodded. "It's their job. Daddy insists they know everyone at the park for my protection."

"But there must be at least two thousand employees here."

"Well, they don't know *everyone*, of course. But they try to. And you're not too hard to remember, 'cause you're the only kid. Plus, they say you've caused some trouble here."

I froze, worried. "Not really . . ."

"You didn't arm the chimpanzees with water balloons yesterday?"

"How'd they know that?"

"They get debriefed by park security," Summer said. "Apparently, you also taught the sea lions to make rude noises during their show . . ."

"The show needed some comedy. Even the trainers thought it was funny."

". . . and started a rumor that the hot dogs here are made of whatever animals died recently."

"That was an accident. I was joking and someone believed me."

"Whatever. Point is, my shadows told me to steer clear of you. Which is why I'm here."

We were seated on a small patch of grass behind the Gorilla Grill, not far from the restaurant's Dumpsters. It wasn't very scenic, but I had to admit it was a good place to avoid being seen. In all the months I'd been roaming around FunJungle—including dozens of meals at the Gorilla Grill—I'd never known this little spot of grass existed.

I'd arrived a couple minutes before Summer—long enough to start worrying that she'd played a joke on me, pegging me as an innocent rube and sending me to stand among a bunch of garbage Dumpsters just because she knew I'd do it. But then she'd wandered around the corner, smiling brightly, and asked if I was hungry.

I was—as a twelve-year-old boy, I was almost *always*

hungry—so Summer had slapped some cash in my hand and told me to go get us some burgers, fries, and Cokes. She couldn't do it, she said, because people would recognize her. I tried to protest—it didn't seem right to let a girl buy me lunch—but Summer had waved this off, laughing, and said, "Trust me, I can afford it."

So that's how we ended up having a picnic by the Dumpsters, Summer explaining to me how she'd ditched her bodyguards.

"I do it all the time," she said. "Daddy says they're for my safety, but honestly, how much more conspicuous could they be? Each is like the size of a house. The moment anyone sees them, they know I'm here, and then I have to spend my whole day signing autographs when all I really want to do is see the animals. Fortunately, they're not too hard for me to shake, 'cause they're *guys*. Dad's still living thirty years ago. He doesn't think women can protect me. So all I have to do is say I've gotta go to the bathroom."

"And then what, sneak out the window?"

"Please. Have you ever seen a public bathroom with a window? No, I just asked some girl if I could buy her hat and T-shirt off her. She was so thrilled, she practically let me have them for free. Then I put them on and walked right out the door. That's why I wear pink all the time; when I change clothes, my shadows never realize it's me right away. This time, they didn't even recognize me till I started running. And by then, they didn't stand a chance. Those guys might be big, but they're not fast. They're probably having a cow right now, thinking they're gonna be fired when Daddy finds out I got away again."

"D'you do this a lot?"

"I mix it up. If I do it too often, they'll put me under lockdown at home. So I play the good girl for a couple weeks, let them think I've reformed . . . and then, once they drop their guard, I bolt."

"Think they've called your dad?"

"Not today. Daddy's in India on business. It's the middle of the night there, and the last thing *anyone* wants to do is wake Daddy to tell him they screwed up. Besides, they know I'll come back. I always do. So, give me the scoop on the dead hippo."

I was caught off guard for a moment. Summer had been talking almost nonstop since we'd sat down to eat, barely letting me get a word in, telling me what she knew about me, rather than asking questions about me. At first, I'd assumed this was because she was conceited and liked to hear herself talk, but I was starting to think that maybe she didn't get to have normal conversations very often. Summer got interviewed by reporters a lot, but her bodyguards seemed to keep the rest of the world at arm's length.

And now, suddenly, she was looking at me expectantly, waiting for me to talk.

So I told her everything. About finding Henry dead, sneaking into the autopsy, Doc's murder theory, how I'd called the police to no avail, the heel print outside our trailer . . . Right up to how I'd been scoping out Hippo River. I was nervous at first, worried she'd think I was some loser with an overactive imagination, but she seemed really into what I had to say. Summer didn't simply listen the way Mom had, though. She interrupted me constantly. And yet, it wasn't annoying, the way it was when most people interrupted. It was kind of fun, because Summer had some good ideas and asked lots of smart questions. She turned out to not be self-absorbed at all. Instead, she was interested in all sorts of things. She was fascinated by my mother's work, forcing me to go off on a whole digression about her research, and then she'd been really excited by my life in the jungle, asking me about everything from whether I'd ever seen lions make a kill to how our pit toilet worked. By the time I finally finished my story, over an hour had slid by, and I had to keep reminding myself that this was *Summer McCracken* I was sitting there talking to. Because she didn't really seem much like the girl in the pictures of the supermarket checkout magazines. Instead, she seemed like, well . . . a friend. I hadn't had many friends my age; the kids in Atlanta had thought I was some weird jungle boy from Africa, and we lived too far from any other children in Texas. So making a new friend was a rare experience for me.

After my story was done, Summer nodded thoughtfully, taking it all in, and then said, "I know how to get into Hippo River."

For maybe the two hundredth time since meeting her, I was thrown. "You mean . . . You want to help me find what killed Henry?"

"Well, it's either that or go back home and watch TV. I don't know if you've noticed, but except for FunJungle, this area is awfully boring."

Summer smiled and I couldn't help but smile back. I couldn't believe what she was offering. Summer probably had hundreds of friends—and there must have been thousands of people who would have given anything to spend time with her—and yet, here she was, offering to help me investigate. Any concern I'd had about getting into Henry's pool quickly drained away. I wasn't alone in this anymore.

This was going to be fun.

Hidden in the lush landscaping around Hippo River was a door. It was how the zookeepers and maintenance workers accessed the hippo enclosures. I had known it was there—all the animal exhibits had an entry door tucked away somewhere—but I'd assumed it was impossible to get through. There was high security on all the exhibits at FunJungle, partly to keep the animals in—but more importantly, to keep humans out. Mom had told me plenty of stories about people breaking into zoo exhibits. When she'd worked at the Bronx Zoo, people routinely tried to steal animals, which were worth a lot of money on the exotic pet market. Three idiots had even tried to swipe an adult tiger once; two had ended up in the hospital—and one had ended up in the morgue. Unfortunately, most zoos couldn't afford very elaborate security, but FunJungle could. The doors were all double-bolted and alarmed.

In addition, the doors didn't have keys. Instead, each had a keypad. If you entered the right code, the door would open. The codes were changed every day and sent to authorized employees via encrypted e-mail, but there were still some ways around the system. For example, I wasn't authorized to have the code for Monkey Mountain, but Mom would just tell me the new one every morning. Then I could go see her whenever I wanted without making her come open the door for me. But for the most part, the security seemed to have worked very well.

To my surprise, Summer revealed there was a secret code: One that never changed—and that opened every door. Her father's personal code. J.J. McCracken wanted to go wherever he wanted, whenever he wanted, without having to learn a new code every time. So he'd had his own code built into the system. And he'd shared it with his daughter.

The door opened with a soft click, leading into a dark corridor that smelled like damp hay. Summer led the way in, not hesitating for a moment. She didn't seem to have any sense that what we were doing was wrong. Instead, she seemed to regard all of FunJungle as though she owned the place. Which, I realized, she kind of did.

Still, we'd taken care to do this when none of the keepers were around. It wasn't hard to arrange; with only one hippo left, there wasn't much need for keepers at Hippo River. All the keeper schedules were posted outside the administration building. We merely had to check the one for Hippo River before heading over. According to it, the hippo keeper wasn't due to check on Hildegard again until four thirty. As it was only two p.m., this gave us plenty of time to search Henry's enclosure.

My only concern was that the schedule wasn't rock solid. If any of Hildegard's keepers felt the need to check on her, for any reason, they could drop by Hippo River—and if they did, they'd certainly notice us swimming in Henry's pool. So I was still a bit nervous, though I did my best to hide it around Summer.

I followed her through the tunnel. The pumps that

filtered the river and powered the waterfall were so loud, we had to shout over them. The hydraulic system also appeared to be leaking; there were numerous slick spots and puddles on the floor. It was a much more dank and depressing access than Monkey Mountain, which had lots of windows into the exhibits and always smelled like oranges.

"Does anyone have the secret code except your father and you?" I asked.

Summer glanced at me over her shoulder, intrigued. "Henry's killer didn't need a code. You said he could have just thrown the weapons into Henry's mouth."

"Maybe. I was only wondering . . ."

"If *I* killed him?"

I blushed so hard, I could feel my ears turn red. "No. I didn't mean . . . Uh . . ."

I might have stammered for another five minutes if Summer hadn't burst into laughter. "Relax, Teddy. I'm just busting your chops. I don't know if anyone else has the code. I don't think my father would have shared it with anyone else, but he might have."

"Why'd he tell *you*?"

"'Cause this is *my* park. You've heard my father, right? It was all my idea."

"Do you sneak into the exhibits a lot?"

"Don't have to. I've been around FunJungle for *years*.

Daddy brought me all the time while it was being built. There's probably no place I haven't been in it."

"So this is the first time you've snuck in somewhere?"

"Of course not." Summer grinned mischievously, the way a young gorilla would when it had something it knew you wanted. Before I could ask her to elaborate, she ducked through a doorway. "Here were go," she said.

I followed her into the dankest room yet. It smelled like mold. There were several large bins inside. Summer was already digging into the first, pulling out what looked like a long, transparent hose.

"C'mon," she said. "Time to go swimming."

The bins held a variety of equipment to let keepers and maintenance men access the hippos' water. There were masks and swim fins, but instead of snorkels, there were the hoses, which had a mouthpiece to breathe through and then ran up to the surface. This allowed people to spend as much time as they wanted underwater without needing scuba gear, which J.J. McCracken considered dangerous and expensive. The hoses were heavy and unwieldy, but we eventually lugged all the equipment through the tunnels, up a flight of stairs, and out into Henry's enclosure.

It was weird being on the other side of the fence. I had spent countless hours looking *into* this enclosure, but I'd never had the chance to enter it before. As the viewing areas were all barricaded, no one could see us except for the tourists crowded at Umfundisi Scenic Viewpoint, and their view was so limited, it wasn't hard to stay out of their line of sight. To be safe, though, we piled the gear in a small, protected cove well-hidden from view.

I eyeballed the water cautiously, still concerned about hippo poop. But with Henry gone, the water looked significantly cleaner, more blue than brown. And it appeared that after Henry's body had been removed, someone had dispatched a crew to spruce up the place. Henry's favorite backwater, which had concerned me the most, didn't look like a sewage dump any more. The whole area smelled vaguely like bleach.

"It's been cleaned," I said.

"Thank God," Summer replied.

"But if the poop's gone, then the stuff that was in it might be gone too. . . ."

"Not necessarily. Hippo poop usually floats on the surface. If the things we're looking for were heavier, a lot of them might have dropped out."

I stared at Summer, impressed. She was right. I'd never met an American girl who knew about hippo poop before. Or *anything* about hippos, really.

Summer continued on, scoping out the river. "I think

it'd be best to look on the bottom of the deepest parts. It's probably only ten or twelve feet there." She selected a diving mask and then, to my astonishment, started to unbutton her shorts.

I must have done a poor job hiding my surprise, because Summer looked at me and said, "What?"

"We're not putting on bathing suits?"

"Did you bring one?"

"No, I . . . I thought they had them here or something."

Summer laughed. "For kids who want to break in?"

"I mean for the keepers. I thought we could use them."

"No such luck."

I could feel myself turning red again. Summer had a talent for embarrassing me, which she seemed to find amusing. "Don't have a heart attack," she said. "I'm keeping my undies on."

With that, she dropped her shorts and nonchalantly kicked them aside. It seemed wrong to stare, so I averted my eyes and looked at my feet instead.

"You can keep *your* shorts on if you want," Summer told me. "But it'll be a lot more comfortable if you don't."

I heard her footsteps race away, and then a slight splash as she dove into the pool.

When I looked back, she was already gone from sight; only her breathing hose was visible as it snaked out of the water.

I didn't really feel like taking my shorts off. But I suspected that if I kept them on, Summer would probably tease me about it, which seemed worse than just going swimming in my underwear. So, as quickly as I could, I peeled off my clothes down to my Jockey shorts, grabbed a mask, and slipped into the water.

As it was a broiling hot day, the water was wonderfully cool. It wasn't *completely* clean, though. Apparently, even Hippo River's high-tech filtration system couldn't remove every ounce of Henry's filth from the water. I could see my hands in front of my face and the glimmer of the glass viewing wall not too far in the distance, but that was it. The edges of the enclosure were obscured in a light haze of what I *hoped* was natural sediment and not leftover hippo poop. Summer had already vanished into the murk.

The air tasted stale, like water from a garden hose, but it was easy to breathe. I kicked for the bottom and found it closer than I'd expected. It was cement, flecked with the occasional piece of brown gunk. I wasn't sure what the brown gunk was, but opted not to examine any of it.

Something metal glinted nearby.

Excited, I swam over to inspect it, thinking it might be the murder weapon.

Instead, it turned out to be a metal groove fitted into the bottom of the tank. The edges were steel, with a gap of perhaps half an inch between them. I stuck my fingers into it and felt something metal that moved away when I touched it: something loose, snaking through the groove.

I'd never noticed the groove before—but for good reason. The metal was practically the color of the cement floor, standing out only in the direct sunlight. It was probably invisible from any of the above-water vantage points, and the glass warped the view too much to make the bottom visible from the underwater viewing areas.

I had no idea what the groove could be for. My first thought was filtration, but there was a standard filtration grate not far away. I moved my hands along the groove and found a few screws bolting the metal tightly to the floor. I followed the groove a bit, seeing that it passed under the wire mesh fence that marked the beginning of Hildegard's enclosure and kept on going as far as I could see. It seemed to be following the path of the river itself, as though it ran the entire length of the exhibit.

In the distance, the massive shape of Hildegard Hippo pranced with surprising grace along the aquarium floor.

My flesh went cold. You weren't supposed to swim with hippos. Even the gentlest ones were temperamental, prone to inexplicable attacks. Back in Africa, you didn't even want to be in a *boat* when hippos were around. I'd heard plenty of stories of hippos overturning canoes and fishing boats, then assaulting whoever had been in them. And I'd heard the occasional tale of them attacking swimmers as well. So my guard went up, even though the wire mesh was between Hildegard and me. FunJungle claimed the mesh had been designed to withstand the attack of a four-thousand-pound hippopotamus, but then, engineering had been known to fail.

I held as still as I could, watching Hildegard. It appeared she hadn't seen me. Instead, she jogged up to one of the underwater viewing windows. . . .

Suddenly something sharp jabbed me in the rear.

I yelped and whirled in the water.

Summer floated behind me, laughter echoing through her breathing hose. She held something out to me. It glinted in the diluted sunlight.

I gave her as nasty a glare as I could muster, which wasn't much. Then I held out my hand.

She dropped the object into it.

It was a small metal ball with six barbs sticking out of it: north, south, east, west, top, and bottom. Some of the barbs had been filed to sharp points; some were rather blunt. It had been done quickly, without much care for quality. One barb still had the remnants of an even smaller ball at the tip. Overall, it was maybe an inch across.

It was a jack. Or, it had been. Now it was most definitely a murder weapon.

I tried to ask, "Where'd you find it?" It didn't come out quite right, given the hose jammed in my mouth, but Summer got the idea.

She pointed toward the far side of the enclosure, where there was a small dip in the concrete floor. I wondered if there might be more filed jacks in there, enough to prove someone had made a concerted effort to feed them to Henry. I started to swim that way.

A shadow fell over me. Hildegard had noticed us. She now loomed on the other side of the wire mesh, her eyes narrowed in what looked like anger.

On second thought, one jack was enough. We kicked for the surface and scrambled out of the water.

There were showers in the keepers' locker room at Hippo River. Even though I was worried about getting caught, I was more worried about having hippo poop on me. I took the longest shower of my life, lathering up again and again in order to get every last ounce of anything that might have passed through Henry's digestive tract out of my hair. Summer teased me about it, but I noticed she spent even longer in the shower than I did.

After we finally felt clean, it was time to further investigate the murder weapon, so we headed to FunJungle Emporium. The largest store in the park, it sat directly across from Hippo River, right by the main gates.

There were dozens of other places to buy souvenirs at FunJungle, but most made an attempt to be thematically related to the area in which they were located. For example, Kangaroo Mercantile in the Land Down Under specialized in everything remotely Australian, from stuffed koalas to boomerangs to movies starring Australian actors. In addition, the stores were designed to look like local bazaars or quaint little shops, rather than western businesses. (The official FunJungle map went so far as to declare all of them "Attractions," as though they were actually fun to visit.) The Emporium, however, was practically a supermarket. It made no attempt to be picturesque or blend into its surroundings. Its purpose was obvious: To grab the attention of everyone entering or exiting the park and make them spend money. Half the store was FunJungle merchandise, aisle after aisle of virtually anything a logo could be slapped on: clothing, posters, toys, glassware, bumper stickers, children's books, postcards, beach towels, ashtrays, and cheap souvenirs that my dad always referred to as "future landfill." The other half of the Emporium was filled with things it surprised me anyone would buy at a theme park: jewelry, crystal, gourmet foods, greeting cards, baby pools, bicycles . . . virtually everything, it seemed, except what my family ever truly needed.

Summer and I wandered around the aisles, taking our time, as the Emporium had the best air conditioning of any building in the park: The doors were open at all times to lure in customers, so the cooling system was cranked down to fifty degrees to compensate. In some parts of the store—especially the frozen foods aisle—it was cold enough to make you shiver. Meanwhile, it was so hot outside that I'd already begun sweating on the short walk over. Without thinking twice about it, Summer opened a freezer, grabbed two Fudgsicles, and tossed one to me.

Eventually we found the aisle we were looking for. It was full of really cheap toys, stuff like rubber spiders and snakes, playing cards, fake jewelry, and action figures of all the FunJungle characters, even ones of Henry Hippo the store had forgotten to remove. Right in the middle of it all was a small cellophane packet of jacks.

Summer snatched it off its hook and tore it open, spilling the jacks into her hand. Then she plucked the one she'd found in Henry's pool out of her pocket and held it up to compare. "Looks like the same brand," she said.

I nodded in agreement. It wouldn't have taken someone with a metal file very long to shave the little balls off the jacks until the stems were pointy. Presto—instant murder weapons.

"Think the killer bought them here?" I asked.

Summer looked at me like I was incredibly naive—a look she seemed to give me often. "No, I think the killer stuck them in his pocket and walked out the door. He wouldn't leave a trail that way. And if he didn't have an issue with murdering Henry, he probably wouldn't have one with swiping a two-dollar packet of jacks."

I considered pointing out that we didn't know the killer was a *he*, but something told me Summer wouldn't appreciate that. She seemed to have made up her mind it was a man, so I let it slide.

Instead, I said, "So pretty much anyone could have done this."

"Pretty much," Summer agreed. "Steal them, sharpen them, then wad them in some food and toss it into Henry's mouth. Not too complicated. Although there *is* one thing we know about the killer. . . ."

Before she could finish the thought, a hand grabbed her shoulder. Summer and I spun around to find one of her bodyguards glaring down at her. "You have any idea what we've been through today?" he growled.

The second was suddenly behind me, gripping my arm as well. "'Course she does," he said. "She thinks we're playing a game here. Not trying to protect her life or anything." He swung me around and glowered at me. "What have you two been up to, Fitzroy?"

I gulped, worried. My arm felt like it was being pinched in a vise. But before I could answer, Summer piped up:

"*We* haven't been up to anything. I only ran into Teddy right now. There's no need to interrogate him."

"Maybe I'll be the judge of that," said the huge man holding me.

"Maybe my dad should know you're terrorizing his employees' children just because you're annoyed I gave you the slip again."

The bodyguard's angry gaze shifted to Summer, but he seemed to realize she was right. He lowered his sunglasses and gave me the full brunt of his menacing stare. "This doesn't mean you're off the hook," he warned. "I'm gonna keep my eye on you." Then he let me go, but did it so roughly I ended up sprawled on the floor.

"C'mon, Princess," the other bodyguard snarled. "Playtime's over. You've had enough fun today." With that, both men marched Summer toward the door.

She didn't even glance back at me, apparently not wanting to let the goons know I meant anything to her. But as she was led away, she opened her hand, letting the jack she'd found in Henry's pool drop. It bounced across the floor, stopping a few feet from me.

By the time I'd picked it up, Summer and her shadows were almost out the door. I could see both of them reprimanding her sternly as they went.

Up until that point, I had envied Summer, thinking she probably had the coolest life in the world. But as of then, I knew I wouldn't ever trade places with her. Not for a billion dollars.

Without Summer around, I quickly felt like I was in over my head again. I wondered what she'd been about to tell me before her bodyguards had shown up. I wondered what she thought our next step should be. Unfortunately, I had no idea how to contact her again; in all the time we'd spent together that day, I'd never thought to ask for her cell number or e-mail—or to give her mine. Without that information, I doubted she'd be any easier to get in touch with than J.J. McCracken himself.

So for now, it appeared I was on my own again.

Or was I?

I ran out of the Emporium and cut through a small alley marked by a sign warning visitors it was off-limits to anyone but park employees. It led to the administration building, and right beyond that was the veterinary hospital.

The hospital was state-of-the-art. Mom had told me it had better medical equipment than most hospitals for *humans*. It was only one story tall, with several large pens along the sides for sick animals to recuperate after surgery. It had an elaborate security system, though this was primarily to limit the number of people coming in and out, since people carried germs and there were sick animals inside. Still, I had been there enough times with my mother that the receptionists knew me. Any time a new animal came in for Monkey Mountain—or anywhere in

FunJungle—it had to be quarantined for up to three months to make sure it wasn't bringing any diseases into the zoo, and the quarantine was part of the hospital.

There was a call box and a security camera by the front doors. I fished through a nearby trash can until I found a lunch bag, then pushed the call button and faced the camera. I didn't have to fake being out of breath after running over.

"What is it, Teddy?" I recognized the voice as belonging to Roz, a sweet old lady who seemed to regard every animal in the hospital as her favorite.

"I need to talk to Doc," I told her. "Mom says one of the gorillas is sick."

The door immediately clicked open, allowing me into a small reception area where Roz sat behind a desk, a worried look on her face. "Which one?" she asked.

"Kwame," I replied, and Roz gasped with enough concern that I felt guilty and added, "He's not *super* sick. Mom just wants Doc to come take a look at him."

"Let me call him." Roz reached for her phone.

I held up the lunch bag. "Actually, Mom gave me a stool sample to give to him."

Roz recoiled, wrinkling her nose in disgust. "Oh. In that case, you know the way to his office, right?"

I nodded. Roz pressed a button on her desk and another set of doors clicked open.

I headed for them, hoping this would pay off. My dad had taught me a few things about stretching the truth. Over the years, he'd conned his way into lots of places to get the photographs he needed. But he always cautioned that lying was a trick best used as rarely as possible. You couldn't deceive someone many times before they stopped believing you. If Doc told Roz I'd suckered her, I'd have blown my trust with her and probably wouldn't ever be allowed into the hospital alone again.

There was a wide, shallow plastic tub by the doors with a thin layer of liquid disinfectant at the bottom. I dutifully stepped into it; most infectious agents that would be dangerous to sick animals traveled on the soles of people's shoes. Once mine were sterilized, I pushed through the doors and hurried inside.

The building was immaculate. It was supposed to be as clean as possible for the health of the animals, of course, but except for the quarantine area, it had barely been used. FunJungle hadn't been open long enough for many animals to need surgery yet.

I headed down a perfectly white and spotless hallway. Doc's office wasn't far along, but the door was open, so I could see that he wasn't there. I hurried on toward the operating rooms, passing other offices on the way. Most of these were empty as well. There were ultimately supposed to be a dozen vets on staff at FunJungle, but they weren't all hired yet—and those who *were* on staff spent most of their day out in the park, tending to sick animals on site. Few of these calls were emergencies; mostly, they were only preemptive checkups. If a keeper noticed anything unusual with one of their animals—a limp, listlessness, loss of appetite—they'd call the hospital and a junior vet would be dispatched to see what was wrong. Only Doc had the clout to do what few operations there were.

There were four operating rooms. Two were the size of a normal human operating room, for smaller animals, while two were much larger, big enough to perform surgery on a camel. (It wasn't a mistake that they weren't quite big enough for a hippo; the bigger an animal was, the more dangerous it was to move from place to place, so it was ultimately safer to do any surgery on it within its enclosure.) The first three operating rooms were open, no one inside. They were so clean, it appeared no one had been in them in weeks, if ever.

However, the door to the fourth, one of the larger operating rooms, was shut. I pressed my ear against it and heard voices inside. The thick steel door muffled them, but I could recognize one as Doc's. I knocked.

Doc opened the door a crack and peered out, looking flustered—but that changed to annoyance when he saw me.

"How the heck did *you* get back here?" he asked, sounding more irritated with me than usual.

"I need to show you something," I said.

"I'm busy," Doc snapped. He started to close the door, but before he could, I held up the modified jack.

"I found this in Henry's pool."

Doc stopped the door an inch from shutting it, surprised. For a moment, he wasn't quite sure what to do. A hundred different questions seemed to be tumbling around in his head. Finally, he turned to whoever was in the operating room, said, "I need a moment," then stepped into the hall with me and shut the door behind him.

"What were you doing in Henry's pool?" he demanded. He kept his voice low, so whoever was in the operating room wouldn't hear.

I tried to choose my words carefully. "I, uh . . . I heard you were looking for this."

Doc swiped the jack from my hand and looked it over cautiously.

There was a cold silence. I tried to fill it. "It's one of the murder weapons. . . ."

"I know what it is," Doc hissed. "The question is, how did *you*? You shouldn't have been looking for this."

Something told me it wouldn't be too smart to mention Summer's involvement. Or to answer Doc's question directly. "I thought you'd want to see it," I said.

"You're not supposed to be back here," Doc replied. "So scoot."

"But I thought—"

"Now." Doc shoved the jack in his pocket and turned back to the operating room.

I knew saying anything else was a bad idea, but I couldn't help myself. I couldn't let Doc take my evidence and leave me with nothing. "But this proves Henry *was* murdered! Don't you think we should do something?"

Doc turned back on me, his eyes narrowing. "*You* shouldn't be involved in this at all," he growled. "Next time you consider doing something stupid like going into the hippo pool, run it past your parents first. Now get out of here before I call security."

With that, he stormed back into the operating room and slammed the door behind him.

Right before the door closed, I caught a glimpse of what he'd been doing. A dead jaguar lay on an operating table, sliced open in mid-autopsy.

I stood in the hallway, stunned.

The dead jaguar was upsetting, but the conversation with Doc had really thrown me. So much about it was disturbing, I wasn't even really sure where to start.

I'd known Doc could be crusty, but I'd figured showing

him the jack would have produced a far different reaction. I'd hoped Doc would have been impressed by my detective work—or thrilled to see proof that his theory was right. Instead, he'd seemed angry. . . .

Well, not *just* angry. I realized there had been something else wrong with Doc.

He'd seemed worried as well.

Who was in that operating room with him? I wondered. I pressed my ear to the door, but the voices had faded, as though Doc and whoever else was in there had stepped away from the door. I listened to no avail for thirty seconds, then decided I'd tested Doc's patience enough and left, my mind full of questions.

What was I supposed to do now? If Doc wasn't interested in the jack, why had he taken it? Why was he worried? Was it because of the mystery person in the room? Or was it because another animal was dead?

I stopped outside the hospital, struck by another disturbing thought. Something had been bothering me about the jaguar since I'd seen it and now, I'd finally figured out what it was.

There *weren't* any jaguars at FunJungle.

There were *supposed* to be jaguars at FunJungle.
They should have been on display as of opening day, but their
display area—Carnivore Canyon—wasn't finished. It had
fallen several months behind schedule during construction.
This was because FunJungle's designers had mistakenly chosen to carve the canyon into the ground, rather than build a
fake canyon altogether—only to discover that the area they'd
picked to carve was solid rock. To get through it, they had to
use dynamite—but this couldn't be done as quickly as they'd
hoped, because the explosions spooked some animals and
could damage nearby exhibits. The first time the demolition
crew had blasted, the tremor had cracked a ten-thousand-
dollar glass wall at Shark Odyssey, threatening to release
ten million gallons of water—and six very hungry sharks—

on the guests. Shark Odyssey had been quickly closed for "Visitor Enhancement" and the demo crew had promised to be more cautious from then on.

There had been talk of delaying FunJungle's opening until Carnivore Canyon was done, because Carnivore Canyon had lions and tigers in it and zoo visitors are always disappointed if there aren't lions or tigers. In truth, those animals are usually boring—lions spend twenty hours a day sleeping and tigers are masters of hiding in the landscaping—but people still love them. Even so, J.J. McCracken had refused to put off the big day. Instead, he'd found a way to turn the construction delay into a money-maker.

J.J. had decided to make an event out of Carnivore Canyon's unveiling, turning it into a second grand opening for FunJungle. First, he had the new exhibit heavily advertised, making it sound so amazing that people who'd already come to the park were excited to come back. Then he'd organized a huge gala sneak peek at the exhibit the night before it opened for "special members." Special members were primarily people who'd paid a lot of money for the privilege— but a few invitations were being randomly awarded to park guests, which kept people coming. The party was two nights away, and it was going to be huge, with catered food and live music and fireworks; there were even rumors that a few movie stars and professional athletes might be there. I had hoped to go, as Carnivore Canyon had been off-limits to everyone during its construction and I was dying to see it, but Mom—who *was* invited—had sadly informed me the event was for adults only.

Until the Canyon opened, no cats were on view at FunJungle. The tigers and lions had been in quarantine for weeks, as had the raccoons, otters, and other carnivores that would be on display. (Since lions and tigers don't move much, the trick to a good carnivore exhibit is to feature many smaller, more active carnivores. Raccoons and otters might not have much marquee value, but they're fun to watch.) The delays had created all sorts of screw-ups for the delivery of many animals. Mom said the jaguars hadn't even arrived yet.

So how had a dead jaguar ended up in Doc's operating room?

I pondered this as I wandered through FunJungle. I wasn't sure where I was going or what I should be doing next. I thought about heading to Monkey Mountain to tell Mom all that had happened—that I'd met Summer McCracken and that we'd found the murder weapon together—but then she'd want to know *how* we'd found the murder weapon. I didn't want to tell her that not only had I decided to investigate Henry's death against her orders, but that I'd also broken into Hippo River to do it. She'd be livid.

Or maybe she wouldn't believe me at all; I didn't even have the murder weapon anymore. She certainly wouldn't buy that Doc had *stolen* it from me. Even though Doc was a crabby old jerk, Mom still respected him.

My cell phone buzzed in my pocket. I fished it out, thinking it was probably Mom, but found a text message instead.

It stopped me in my tracks.

Meet me at World of Reptiles. Black mamba exhibit. 7PM. Summer.

I was surprised that Summer knew my cell number—but only for a moment. Her father was rich and employed both my parents. It had only taken Summer a few minutes to learn about every prank I'd pulled at FunJungle; getting my phone number would have been easy for her.

I was even more surprised by how excited I felt. Suddenly, my heart was beating quickly and my skin tingled. I felt like I'd ridden the motion simulator for the first time. I wanted to believe this was because Summer had found a new lead in the case to share with me, but when I thought about it, I realized there was something more: I couldn't wait to see her again.

I texted back that I'd meet Summer at the black mamba exhibit, then found myself watching my phone, waiting for a reply. After five minutes, I realized this was stupid; why would she need to text me when she was going to see me soon?

I checked my watch. It was only five o'clock. Time instantly slowed to a crawl. Seven seemed an eon away. The seconds ticked by slowly as I bided my time, trying to find things to occupy my attention. I tried to focus on the case instead, but to no avail. I went on Life of a Bee twice but found even that couldn't distract me.

Eventually, the two hours passed.

Seven was when FunJungle closed for the night, although some exhibits shut down even earlier for the sake of the animals. All the guests weren't *gone* at seven, though; the stores by the front gates had resumed staying open after closing time in order to continue extracting cash from the guests. But there was nothing left to see and the guests were generally trickling toward the exit. World of Reptiles would be empty, which, I figured, was exactly why Summer wanted to wait until seven to meet me there.

World of Reptiles was probably the most conventional zoo building at FunJungle, since there's little way to make reptiles exciting. True, they can do some amazing things, but since they're cold-blooded, they often spend hours—if not days—resting. Usually under a rock.

Still, FunJungle's designers had done what they could to make the experience fun, which meant, for the most part, trying to distract the guests with things that weren't reptiles. The building itself was very cool, designed around a huge central glass dome so that it looked kind of like a gigantic turtle. Under the dome was an enormous tropical rain forest filled with waterfalls, streams, and towering trees (which were fake, but looked real enough) that had an airborne path of rope bridges strung between them. It was a like a giant arboreal jungle gym. There were lots of reptiles on display in the atrium, but the designers had included plenty of nonreptiles as well to provide some activity for guests to observe: parrots, scarlet ibises, small-clawed otters, and two families of capuchin monkeys.

An even more blatant distraction was the dinosaurs. They weren't real, obviously. They were robots. I had never been impressed with them. In the first place, they shouldn't have even *been* in a reptile house, seeing as dinosaurs weren't reptiles; science has proven a hundred times over that they were the warm-blooded ancestors of birds. Second, they didn't do much except act like they were eating and growl on occasion—although there was a velociraptor that sprang out of the bushes and occasionally scared little girls. The tourists loved them, though. World of Reptile's designers had shrewdly placed them right before the exit, which kept guests moving through the rest of the building in order to see them. To prevent pedestrian traffic jams, the designers didn't even let people *walk* through the dinosaurs. Instead, they'd installed moving sidewalks to hustle guests through them quickly.

The rest of the building had more traditional displays—generally, reptiles in glass cases—although I'd noticed most people tended to ignore them in their haste to get to the rain forest or the dinosaurs. This was a shame, as FunJungle's reptile collection was really impressive. There were Galapagos tortoises, a forty-foot anaconda, rare alligator relatives like caimans and gavials, snapping turtles, frilled dragons, basilisks, water monitors, and even a Komodo dragon, the world's biggest lizard. Most remarkable of all, however, was the extensive collection of poisonous snakes.

FunJungle had more poisonous snakes than any other zoo in the world: cobras, death adders, kraits, asps, coral snakes, cottonmouths, gaboon vipers, fer-de-lances, copperheads, taipans, bandy-bandys, bushmasters, sidewinders, two dozen kinds of rattlesnake, and a huge aquarium filled with sea snakes, which were fascinating to watch. The final snake on display was one the most deadly of all—the black mamba. Mambas aren't the most poisonous snakes (sea snakes are)—or even the most poisonous on land (that's the taipan)—but they're aggressive. Most poisonous snakes prefer to hide from humans, biting only as a last defense. If a mamba feels threatened, it'll come after you. And they're *fast*. Thus, they've killed more people than any other kind of snake.

It wasn't until I got to the mamba exhibit that I realized it was a strange meeting place for Summer to select. First of all, it was *inside* World of Reptiles, which was supposed to be locked at night. Luckily, the front door had been propped open with a brick, which I'd assumed meant Summer would already be waiting for me—but when I got to the mamba exhibit, I found myself alone.

Another strange thing about the meeting spot was that it wasn't very comfortable. There were plenty of exhibits in World of Reptiles with benches where we could have sat and talked; the central atrium alone had dozens. Meanwhile, the black mamba exhibit sat in the middle of a glorified hallway. Most people raced right past it to get to the dinosaurs. World of Reptile's designers had spruced it up a bit, filling the hall with planters full of tropical flowers, but still, it was kind of like inviting someone to your mansion and then asking them to meet you in the coat closet.

I did my best to distract myself while waiting for Summer to show up. I tried to focus on looking for the various poisonous snakes in their exhibits rather than at my watch every fifteen seconds. But I couldn't help myself. Where was Summer?

I checked my watch again, thinking it must be seven fifteen already, but found only three minutes had gone by. That wasn't unreasonable. Summer might have had trouble ditching her shadows again. Or misjudged how far World of Reptiles was from the front gates. Or been distracted by something in the atrium . . .

Why had she wanted to meet *here*? I wondered again. Was there something important about the mamba?

I turned my attention to the exhibit. Even among poisonous snakes, mambas aren't that interesting. They don't have the flared hood of a king cobra, the horns of a rhinoceros viper, the beautiful patterns of a coral snake. They're just black. Thin and black, which makes them very hard to find. I've always been good at spotting animals, but the mamba didn't seem to be anywhere in its case. . . .

As I leaned against the glass, it shifted slightly.

That seemed wrong. I took a step back and something crunched under my foot.

I looked down. The floor was covered with tiny glass shavings. They reminded me of the time in the Congo when Dad had to jury-rig a new windshield for the Land Rover and had cut the glass himself. . . .

Cut the glass.

I looked back up at the exhibit.

At the top, there was a two-inch gap where the glass had been removed. It was above my head, but there were several branches inside the exhibit from which the mamba could have easily accessed the gap and escaped.

Two heat lamps were on in the exhibit, but it was cool

out in the hall. The mamba, being cold-blooded, probably wouldn't have gone far after getting out.

The floor was black. The walls were black. The nearby planter was black. Exactly the same color as a mamba.

Now, I felt *my* blood go cold.

I looked around wildly, trying to locate the snake. To my dismay, the hall was kept quite dark in order to focus everyone's attention toward the exhibits. There were shadows everywhere. All I could see was blackness.

Something hissed behind me.

My ears prickled. In all my years in Africa, I'd never run into a poisonous snake, but Mom had given me explicit instructions about what to do if it happened. The trick was to make no sudden movements. Even an aggressive snake like the mamba wouldn't attack me unless it felt threatened. However, I couldn't stay frozen like a statue for hours, either. I had to figure out where the snake was. I twisted my head around as slowly as I could, struggling to keep my arms and legs still.

The hissing suddenly came from my right.

I leapt, startled, unable to control myself, and slammed into the glass of the mamba exhibit.

I whirled to my right, expecting the sting of fangs in my ankle at any second, and saw the source of the noise:

The irrigation system had kicked on for the tropical

plants, tiny sprinkler heads hissing as they sprayed water into the soil. I immediately felt foolish, but had no sense of relief. The mamba was still close, and now I'd made a sudden movement. Panic surged through me. I imagined the snake closing in from the shadows. I couldn't stay still any longer.

There was a groan behind me. The glass from the mamba exhibit had popped loose from its mooring in the wall. It toppled.

I ran.

An adrenaline rush is an incredible thing. I was already fifty yards away by the time the glass shattered on the floor, definitely a near-Olympic time for the distance, and I'd had to negotiate corners. I hurtled into the dinosaur exhibit, racing toward the exit, fearing the mamba's bite at every step, alert to every movement, every noise.

I rounded a stand of fake trees and something lunged at me.

I leapt away, screaming, and stumbled over my feet.

It was the dang velociraptor.

It didn't look anything like a mamba, of course, but I was too freaked out to control my reaction. I lost my balance, tumbled over the railing and thudded into the Triassic Period.

A tyrannosaurus suddenly loomed over me, roaring and gnashing its serrated teeth.

I wasn't concerned by it so much as the floor around me. There were fake plants everywhere, creating a thousand hiding places. Beneath all of them stretched dozens of electrical cables for the dinosaurs, each thin and black like a mamba.

To my right, only two feet away, one of them twitched.

I wasn't sure if it was a snake or a movement caused by the dinosaurs or just my mind playing tricks on me. I was well past the ability to keep my cool. I vaulted back over the railing, hit the ground running, and sprinted through the rest of the building.

I slammed through the exit door and didn't stop until I was a good hundred yards away from World of Reptiles.

The sun was setting, so it was still light outside. I could see the ground all around me. There were no black mambas out there.

I stood on a picnic table anyhow, just to play it safe.

The entire experience had taken a minute at most. It took me five times as long to get my breath back. And even then, my heart was still pounding in my chest like a jackhammer.

The truth now dawned on me: I'd been set up.

It was easy to fake a text message. Anyone could have sent it and signed it from Summer. I had no idea what her actual phone number was. I'd simply seen a message from her and assumed it was actually a message from her.

That had been foolish, I realized. But I hadn't been thinking right in my excitement to see her again. And frankly, up to that point, I had no reason to believe anyone would want to cause me trouble anyhow.

The thought flickered through my mind that maybe *Summer* had set me up, but I shoved that aside. She wouldn't do that. She was nice. She wasn't capable of sending me to meet my . . .

Death.

I froze at the thought of it. Had someone really tried to kill me? Or were they just trying to scare me off?

Either way, they'd sent me on a blind date with a black mamba. No matter what their intention, I *could* have ended up dead.

Certainly, one thing was clear: Whoever had killed Henry knew I was looking for them—and they were willing to do *anything* to keep me from investigating.

I was still jittery as I hurried home. I'd always found passing through the park at dusk relaxing, but now I was totally unnerved. Someone had made an attempt on my life; just because it had failed didn't mean they wouldn't make another. Were they watching me at that moment? I wondered. Did they have something else in store for me?

The park, as usual, was filled with animal noises, and that night, every one of them made me start in fear. I worried that any approaching employee could be plotting against me. I imagined assassins lurking behind every building. I know it was completely paranoid, but try having someone lead *you* into a trap with a black mamba and then see how normal *you* act afterward.

I ran home as fast as I could, but realized even that

wouldn't necessarily make me safe. If whoever had set me up could get my phone number, they could certainly find out where I lived. As I approached the trailer, I couldn't help but fear that someone might be waiting to ambush me there.

To my great relief, Mom was home. As I cut past the hot tub, I could see her through the window, making dinner. Even so, I came up the steps cautiously, making sure no one was lying in wait and forcing her to act normal in order to lure me inside.

No one was. Mom was her usual, chipper self. She was playing music instead of watching TV, humming along, dicing vegetables for stir-fry. Just being near her made me feel a hundred times safer (although I'd have felt even better if Dad had been there too, rather than halfway around the world in China).

Unfortunately, I had the opposite effect on Mom. The moment I came through the door, her cheerfulness faded. Mom always had an uncanny ability to sense when something was wrong. Not only with me. She could do it with almost anyone. I think that's another thing she picked up from watching gorillas for so long. Most of their communication was extremely subtle: a glance, a posture, a curl of the lip. Humans did a lot of the same things; most people just didn't notice.

Mom only needed one look at me. "What happened?" she asked.

So I told her. I knew she'd be upset to hear what I'd been up to, but she'd have been far more upset if I'd lied to her—and believe me, she'd have known if I lied.

Like the night before, she listened right through without interrupting. She kept cooking, her eyes usually focused on the stove, rather than on me. But this time, I could tell she was more on edge. She was angry when I told how I'd disobeyed her and continued the investigation, particularly the part about sneaking into Henry's pool. And then she got upset when I told her about the dead jaguar in Doc's lab . . . but when I got to the part about the mamba, she forgot about everything else and couldn't stay quiet any more.

She turned from the stove and I could see the fear in her eyes. "Teddy! Are you saying someone tried to hurt you?"

"I think so."

She knelt in front of me, clasped my arms in her hands and looked me right in the eye. "Listen to me," she said. "You need to stop this investigation right now. . . ."

"But that's exactly what whoever killed Henry *wants* me to do."

"You're a twelve-year-old boy. You're in over your head. . . ."

"*You* could help me. I mean, I was right that Henry was murdered, wasn't I? That's what all this is about. Someone killed him and now they're trying to cover it up. . . ."

"Maybe so, but it's not your job to find out who did this. And it's not mine, either."

"Then whose is it?"

Mom stared at me for a while without answering. I think she was considering telling me that it wasn't anyone's job, that Henry was dead and that was that and we should just leave well enough alone. Not because she didn't think it was wrong, but because she was so worried about what had happened to me.

Then she got to her feet and called Martin del Gato.

An hour later, I was back at World of Reptiles. This time, I wasn't alone. There was a whole crowd of people on account of me.

Mom was there. And Martin. So was Buck Grassley, the head of security at FunJungle, and three other security people: Large Marge and two guys I didn't know. There were also three men from maintenance and all the herpetologists. Everyone seemed annoyed at me for getting them out there at that hour of the night—except the herpetologists, who were far more concerned about their reptiles. They were dismayed by the disappearance of the mamba, but also worried that someone might have done something to one of their other animals.

The mamba had yet to be recovered, but the herpetologists had made several sweeps of the hall by its exhibit and assured us it wasn't there. Even so, the lights had been turned on brightly to put everyone at ease.

The maintenance guys and the security people all clustered about the mamba exhibit, taking measurements, verifying that I'd been telling the truth that someone had cut the glass and let the snake out. Every once in a while, I'd notice Large Marge nod in my direction, probably trying to convince everyone that *I* was the culprit.

Mom and Martin were having their own discussion. Mom was annoyed that Martin hadn't brought in the local police. Martin claimed they wouldn't come, as FunJungle was outside their jurisdiction. Technically, FunJungle was its own municipality. (It didn't just have its own security force; it also had its own fire department and power station.)

"This isn't merely a security issue," Mom said, trying to keep her anger in check. "My son's life is in danger."

"So he claims," Martin replied. "We'll find out."

For a moment, Mom looked ready to throttle Martin. "You think Teddy's making this up?"

"He's been known to cause trouble before."

"My son may have played a prank now and then, but he's not a liar or a vandal," Mom snapped, but Martin didn't appear convinced.

At that point, I was glad Mom hadn't told Martin *everything* I'd been up to that day. She'd only told him that I'd suspected Henry had been killed and had shared that with Summer McCracken when I bumped into her at the park, but left out the parts about my sneaking into the autopsy and Henry's pool. If Martin had known any of that, I'm sure he would have had security arrest me.

"How'd you even get the idea Henry was murdered?" Martin asked me suspiciously.

I shrugged. "One day he was healthy. The next he was dead. It seemed wrong."

Martin kept staring at me, not buying this.

"I thought it was just an overactive imagination myself," Mom said, then nodded toward the broken glass at the mamba exhibit. "But now that *this* happened, it's a different story."

Martin sighed, not committing either way, as though he still suspected that maybe I'd freed the mamba and pretended I'd been set up to cover my tracks. Before Mom could say anything else, Buck Grassley wandered over.

Buck was in his fifties. He'd grown up in the same town J.J. McCracken had; I'd heard they'd met in kindergarten and been friends ever since. Until J.J. had hired him to run security, Buck had been the county sheriff, though I don't think that had been too tough a job. There wasn't much crime in the area; the police mostly parked behind bushes and ambushed speeding drivers. A born-and-bred good old boy, Buck accented his park uniform with a cowboy hat and a bolo tie, carried a Bowie knife instead of a Taser, and talked so slowly, you'd think he'd been drinking molasses.

"Someone definitely let that snake out," he drawled. "Cut the glass, then hightailed it out of here."

"Any idea who?" Martin asked, looking pointedly at me.

Buck shrugged. "No fingerprints. And cutting glass ain't exactly brain surgery. Anyone with a $5.99 glass cutter from Ace Hardware coulda done the job. I got Matthews checking out the recordings."

"Recordings?" Mom asked.

"Yeah. We got surveillance cameras all over. On every entrance and exit to every building and most every hallway, too. Every exhibit in the park is wired. Just for instances like this. J.J. McCracken likes to protect his investments. These animals ain't cheap."

"This hall has a camera in it?" Mom asked.

Buck stuck a toothpick in his mouth and nodded toward the far end of the hall.

We all looked that way.

"I don't see anything," Mom said. I didn't either.

"No, I reckon you don't," said Buck. "But it's there all right. Embedded in the wall. Tiny little thing. Fiber-optics or some such. J.J. owns a company that makes 'em. Course, J.J. owns a company that makes pretty much everything."

"They all feed into a central computer," Martin explained. "Everything they see is digitally recorded."

"Matthews is reviewing it all right now," Buck added.

"So you can prove that Teddy didn't do this," Mom said.

"Or maybe, we'll prove that he *did*." Large Marge said. She butted into our group, giving me the evil eye as usual. It didn't bother me, though. I knew I hadn't done anything. Soon enough, Marge—and everyone else—would see who the real culprit was.

Buck's phone rang. He checked the caller ID and smiled. "It's Matthews," he told us, then answered. "What've you got?"

I couldn't hear what Matthews said, but Buck suddenly looked like he'd sat on a tack. "What?" he asked. "How did *that* happen?"

Whatever Matthews said next made him madder still. Buck noticed us all staring at him, then signaled us to stay where we were and stormed around the corner into the Triassic Period.

Martin started after him, desperate to know what was going on, but then Pete Thwacker came racing down the hall. "Martin!" he yelled. "What's going on? I've been trying to reach you for an hour!"

"Someone let the mamba out," Martin replied.

"Mamba? What's that? A dance?"

Almost everyone sighed with annoyance at once.

"It's a snake," Martin said, pointing to the sign. "The world's most dangerous snake. Someone let it out."

"In here?!" Pete scrambled onto a bench, terrified. "Shouldn't we evacuate?"

"Calm down, you idiot," Martin snapped. "You think we'd all be here if it wasn't safe? The herpetologists have cleared the hall."

Pete looked relieved, but also confused. He probably thought a herpetologist was someone who studied herpes. "Why did you bring them . . . ?"

"They're people who study reptiles," Mom explained. She pointed to a group of them. They waved back.

"Oh." Pete cautiously got down off the bench. "So if the snake's not here, where is it?"

The herpetologists all shrugged.

Martin said, "We're assuming it's still in the building. Which means we have to shut World of Reptiles down until we find it."

"So what do you want? A press release?"

"God, no! If we tell the media we're closing *another* exhibit, they'll start bad-mouthing the park. It's only the dang reptile house. We're gonna do this under the radar. Lock the doors and put a sign up saying the building's temporarily closed for some reason or another. . . ."

"Maintenance issues?"

"Whatever. Just don't mention the snake."

"Any idea how long it'll be closed?"

Martin turned to the herpetologists. "How long'll it take to find the snake?"

They all shrugged again. "Honestly?" one asked. "If it got into the atrium, there's a billion places for it to hide. We might never find it."

Martin gaped at them, aghast. "What?!"

"Miami Metrozoo lost a Burmese python once," the herpetologist replied. "It took them six months to find it— and that thing was thirty-five feet long. The mamba's small and black. It could be anywhere."

Martin rubbed his temples. He appeared to be in dire need of Pepto-Bismol. "That's unacceptable. Let's do everything we can. Get every available person in here tomorrow and sweep this place top to bottom. If we can't find the snake, then . . . I don't know. We'll cross that bridge when we come to it."

"You'd *think* about opening back up again?" Pete asked. "Do you realize what a PR disaster it'd be if a guest got bitten by a samba?"

"Mamba!" everyone corrected.

"You want to talk disasters?" Martin asked. "Think about what J.J. McCracken will do if we try to shut down a brand-new twenty-million-dollar building for a year."

While Pete considered that, Buck stormed back around the corner, mad as though *he'd* been bit by a snake. "We don't have the records," he announced.

This, on the tail of everything else that had gone wrong, made Martin look like he might explode. "What?! How on earth . . . ?"

"I don't know. I'm on my way over there to find out. Matthews says the entire security feed from World of Reptiles went down tonight for an hour starting at six thirty."

I quickly did the math in my head. World of Reptiles closed at six thirty, half an hour before the rest of the park. That would have given someone half an hour to enter the building, cut the glass and free the snake without being recorded. The missing hour of footage would also have covered the entire time I was in the building. So there was no proof of who had set the mamba free—and no proof I *hadn't*.

"It's the damn electrical contractor J.J. hired," Buck was saying. "Lazy cost-cutting nitwit. The best quality cameras in the world don't mean squat if the wiring's lousy. This isn't the first time this has happened, y'know. . . ."

My phone buzzed in my pocket. I answered it warily, fearing it might be whoever had tried to get me killed again.

Instead, it was Summer. "Dude," she said. "I heard someone tried to kill you!"

I was thrilled to hear her voice. "Yeah," I said. "Hold on." With all the conversations going on around me, it was way too loud to talk. I slipped around the corner into the dinosaur area, in such a hurry to get some privacy, it didn't even occur to me I was entering an area where the mamba might still be loose.

The dinosaurs had been shut down for the night. They were all frozen in mid-roar. I stopped by a dimetrodon to talk. "How'd you hear about me?"

"Daddy. Buck called him—and he called me because apparently whoever lured you in there used a fake text from me as bait. How sick is that?"

"Uh, pretty sick."

"Are you okay?"

"Yeah. Fine. I didn't ever really see the snake. . . ."

"Still. If it was me, I would have had a meltdown. I hate snakes. Can you meet up tomorrow?"

My heart nearly leapt out of my chest. I did my best to sound calm, though. "Uh, sure. Yeah. I think so."

"Cool. Cause you have to give me the skinny on everything that happened. I mean, whoever did this is obviously the same guy who knocked off Henry, right? We must discuss. Plus, I found another lead myself."

Something creaked softly behind me. I turned around in time to see Large Marge duck behind a stegosaurus. It was practically the only thing in the whole park big enough for her to actually hide behind. Still, it left her within easy eavesdropping range. I wondered how much of my call she'd already overheard.

"What is it?" I asked.

"Let's just say, Henry had more enemies than you'd think."

"Who?"

"I need to tell you in person. I don't trust the phones."

"Who'd want to tap your phones?"

"Who wouldn't? Meet me where we had lunch. Eleven sharp."

"Okay."

"Oh, and Teddy? I'm glad you're still alive."

"Me too."

Summer laughed, even though I hadn't meant it to be funny. "See you tomorrow," she said, then hung up.

I was upset the conversation had been so short, but excited to have an excuse to see her again. It almost made having someone try to kill me seem worth it.

10 · SUMMER'S LEAD

It turned out to be harder to make the appointment with Summer than I'd expected. For the first time in my life, Mom wanted me to stay by her side all day.

"I don't want you running around FunJungle all by yourself," she explained as we headed to Monkey Mountain. "It's too dangerous."

"Not during visiting hours, it's not," I replied. "No one's going to try to hurt me with a thousand tourists around." In truth, I wasn't completely sure this was true, but meeting up with Summer seemed worth the risk.

"It's not long-term. Just until security finds whoever tried to hurt you last night."

"That might take weeks! What am I supposed to do? Hang out in your office all day?"

"Maybe."

"Aw, c'mon, Mom. You let me be by myself all the time in Africa—and there were a ton of dangerous animals there."

Mom grabbed my hand and stopped walking, wanting me to pay complete attention to what she had to say. "This is different, Theodore. I knew you could handle yourself in Africa because animals aren't really that dangerous. They rarely try to harm people unless they've been provoked—and even on those occasions, they're not that hard to scare away. But humans are different. If a human really wants to hurt you, he won't give up that easily. He'll keep coming after you. He'll keep trying new tactics until he finds one that works. What you've gotten involved in here isn't a game. This is dangerous and you need to behave accordingly."

"Okay," I said.

I meant it too. Until that point I hadn't realized how worried Mom was about me—and her words got me more concerned about my safety as well. But from my point of view, meeting up with Summer to pursue our investigation *was* looking out for my safety. Mom might have believed we could trust FunJungle's security force to find out who'd been behind the mamba incident, but I didn't. First, they hadn't seemed too intent on investigating in the first place. Second, they weren't a real police force. Buck Grassley might have had some law enforcement experience, but most of his people didn't. Many didn't seem that much more competent than Large Marge, who couldn't have found a criminal if he was mugging her in broad daylight.

So it made sense that the best way to protect myself was to find the bad guy before he tried to hurt me again. If Summer had a lead, it ought to be investigated. And unfortunately, there didn't seem to be anyone willing—or capable—to follow up on it besides us.

Of course, I couldn't tell Mom any of this. I hadn't even told her that I planned to meet up with Summer again. She would have argued that our investigation stood a better chance of getting me into more trouble than getting me out of it. Moms are overprotective like that. Even mine.

So I pretended to be the perfect kid all morning. I went to work with Mom and stayed in her office, reading a book while she worked on her computer. Well, I *tried* to read a book. The truth was, I could barely concentrate. I was eager to see Summer again and find out what her big lead was— and I had to be constantly on the alert for a chance to sneak away. I'd never had time pass so slowly in my life.

Worse, Mom spent an unusual amount of time in her office that morning. Most days, she'd have been working with the gorillas in one way or another, taking care of them in their private quarters or maybe observing them out in their yard. But not that morning. She just sat at her computer. Didn't even take a bathroom break. As the minute hand slowly crept toward eleven, I was beginning to think I'd have to text Summer to say our meeting was off—when I got an idea.

One of Mom's innovations at Monkey Mountain was the camera grid. There were dozens of cameras in the exhibits which allowed her—or any other primatologist—to monitor the animals from their computers. There were thirty in the gorilla habitat alone; there wasn't a place the apes could go and not be recorded. This was exciting for Mom, as it was the first time she'd ever been able to watch her subjects without them *knowing* she was watching. As much as Mom could fade into the background in the wild, the gorillas never completely forgot she was there—and that would inevitably have some slight effect on their behavior. But the gorillas didn't know about the cameras. Obviously, being in a zoo affected their behavior too, but the exhibit at FunJungle was so well designed, Mom claimed it was as close to the wild as she could get without going back to Africa.

There were also security cameras in the building—and all those could be accessed from the researchers' computers as well. (I'd known about all of these before Buck Grassley had mentioned them the previous night, although I hadn't been aware that every building at FunJungle was as well-wired as Monkey Mountain—or that all the cameras fed into a central security bank.) Sometimes, when the gorillas were close to the glass of their exhibits, Mom used the security cameras to get better views of them.

Mom shared her office with another primatologist who was at the vet lab with a sick squirrel monkey that day. He'd left his computer on. I got on it and started surfing through the camera feeds. It didn't take long to find a park guest breaking the rules. In fact, I had several moronic rule-breakers to choose from: An obese man was blowing raspberries at the macaques, a skinny woman was trying to get a vegetarian colobus monkey to accept a hot dog, and a father was actually dangling his five year old daughter over a railing in a misguided attempt to let her pet a baboon. (Thankfully, the baboon was smarter than the father and kept its distance.) But the winners of the Most Annoying Visitors Award were a trio of teenagers.

They were banging on one of the gorilla exhibit's big plate glass windows, riling the apes. Of course, there were plenty of signs telling them not to do this for fear of upsetting the animals, but they obviously *wanted* to upset the animals. They laughed and howled as the gorillas reacted to their idiocy; Tembo, the silverback male, stood on his hind legs, making aggressive postures while the females and children leapt about, agitated. A lot of tourists had gathered to watch. Most seemed to realize the teens were doing something wrong, but no one had the nerve to tell those jerks to stop.

No one but my mother, that is.

"Hey, Mom," I said. "Look at this."

She glanced over and was instantly filled with rage. Mom never liked to see any animals being tormented, but she was extremely protective of her gorillas. As I'd suspected, she immediately snapped to her feet and stormed toward the door. "Stay here," she told me. "I'll be right back."

According to official FunJungle policy, Mom wasn't supposed to get involved in incidents like this any more than I was. She was supposed to call security, but she never did. I found it interesting that Mom didn't trust security to handle a couple rude teenagers but still thought they could find the criminal who'd come after me the night before.

I waited thirty seconds after she'd left, then whipped the apology I'd already written for her out of my book, set it on her desk, and slipped out the door.

As I scurried toward the exit, I heard Mom giving hell at the top of her lungs. At the risk of being caught, I doubled back and peered into the viewing room. The crowd of tourists had grown even larger, eagerly watching Mom berate the teenagers for their behavior. Though Mom wasn't a physically imposing woman, she could be *really* scary when she got angry. The teens cowered under her gaze, looking like they were facing an escaped lion, rather a ticked-off scientist. "You think it's funny, upsetting these animals?" Mom roared. "How'd you like it if *you* were trapped in a room and Tembo was banging on your windows? Because we could arrange that."

The teenagers whimpered apologies and accused one another of having started the trouble.

Mom had broken them quickly. It wouldn't be long before she was headed back to her office. I raced for the exit—and my meeting with Summer.

"It's about time," she said as I came around the Dumpsters. "I thought you were blowing me off."

"Sorry." I gasped, out of breath. I'd run all the way across the park to get there. "I had to wait until my Mom—"

"Relax. I'm just busting your chops." Summer grinned. She was wearing a T-shirt, a baseball cap, and sunglasses rather than one of her trademark pink outfits. She was so well-disguised that if she hadn't been waiting in our secret spot, I might not have recognized her.

"Did you have to ditch your bodyguards again?" I asked.

"Yeah, but not the way I did yesterday. They're still so peeved at me, there's no way they would've even brought me to the park today. . . ."

"Don't they work for you?"

"No, they work for my father. And if they want to keep me under lock and key all day all they have to do is claim there's a security risk. So I had to give them the slip early. I ducked out of the house before breakfast. My bodyguards sit in the hall outside my room, so I went out the window and down the trellis. One of our cooks gave me a ride here in return for some autographed stuff he can sell on eBay." Summer twirled in her outfit, mimicking a fashion model. "This is how I dress on the down-low. I've been here all morning. No one's recognized me yet. It's been awesome! I even had to pay for my own ticket to get in."

She was so excited, it sounded as though she were talking about having gone swimming with sharks rather than merely visiting a theme park. All I could figure was, for all the glitz and glamour her life appeared to have, Summer had so few normal experiences that she found them incredible. Going a whole morning without being recognized seemed to be the greatest thing she could imagine.

"How do you know they won't think you've been kid-napped?" I asked.

Summer shrugged nonchalantly. "I left a note."

"That makes two of us," I said.

"We ought to get going then. Pretty soon we'll have the National Guard looking for us."

We slipped out of the Dumpster area and headed quickly through the park—although not so quickly as to draw attention to ourselves.

"Where are we going?" I asked.

"To see Larry the Lizard," she replied.

"Uh . . . I hate to break this to you, but he's not real."

"Not the cartoon character, doofus. The guy who plays him. He's our lead."

"How?"

"Remember yesterday at the Emporium? I said we could tell something about who killed Henry from how they'd killed him?"

"Yeah. But you never got the chance to tell me what. . . ."

"You didn't figure it out? Dude, it's obvious."

"I've had a lot going on. Someone *did* try to kill me last night."

Summer grinned and I realized that, once again, she was teasing me. "Okay, I'll give you that. Here's the deal: Whoever did it had to know something about hippos."

"Not necessarily. The way they killed Henry was awfully simple. . . ."

"It wasn't. Think about it: If you went up to just about anyone and said, 'How would you kill a hippopotamus?' how many of them would say 'Give it peritonitis'? I'll bet most people don't even know what peritonitis is. A normal person would have shot Henry. Or poisoned him. Or stuck some live wires in his pool and electrocuted him. But to feed him a bunch of filed jacks to poke holes in his intestine? Would *you* have known that would kill a hippo?"

I felt embarrassed again—although this time, instead of making me seem naive, Summer had made me look stupid. How could I have not thought of that? "No," I admitted.

"And you're Tarzan Junior. You grew up with hippos in your swimming hole. Whoever killed Henry knew their hippos—and not many people do. So this was probably an inside job."

"You think one of the keepers did it?"

Summer shrugged. "There's a good chance, I guess."

"Then why are we talking to Larry the Lizard?"

"Background. We need to . . ." Summer trailed off in mid-sentence and suddenly veered to the side, yanking me behind a topiary bush shaped like Eleanor Elephant. She signaled me to stay still, then cautiously peered out from behind it.

"What's wrong?" I whispered, worried. "Is it the killer?"

"Worse," she replied. "Paparazzi."

I peeked out beneath the topiary elephant's armpit and saw a small cluster of heavyset men with multiple cameras strung around their necks stampede past. Luckily, they had another target in mind: A pitcher for the Houston Astros and his movie star girlfriend had just come through the front gate.

"Leeches," Summer growled. "They've probably been lying in wait all morning." She made sure the cameras were all pointing away from her, then dragged me off in the opposite direction. We were now going back the way we'd come, which meant we had to circle all the way around Hippo River to get to where we'd been going in the first place—wherever that was. Summer was too annoyed to tell me. Instead, she stormed along, grousing about photographers.

"People tip them off, you know. Random people. Someone at the park notices me, they call a magazine, the magazine gives them, like, a hundred bucks and sends the jackals down here. You try to do something normal, like go to dinner or a movie or even just get an ice cream—and next thing you know, there's a thousand lights flashing in your face and all these greasy guys are shoving up against you, calling you names to make you angry, and within thirty minutes there's the least flattering pictures of you possible all over the Internet and a million chat rooms are talking about whether or not you're fat. It's the worst thing ever."

"Yeah," I said. "Back when I was in the Congo, kids our age were dying of malaria and malnutrition and half their families had been killed in the war, but they'd always say, 'Thank God no one's taking pictures of us against our will.'"

Summer wheeled on me. For a moment, I thought I'd really screwed up and ruined our friendship before it even got started. But then Summer broke into a big smile, as though she appreciated my giving her crap. "Okay, you're right. I'm a pampered snob. But if you think the paparazzi's no big deal, let's see what you think when *you* have to deal with them."

"How's that supposed to happen?"

"Y'know the big shindig for Carnivore Canyon tomorrow night?"

"Uh, yeah. It's only, like, the biggest party there's ever been around here."

"Want to be my date?"

I didn't answer right away. I wanted to. The moment she asked, my immediate impulse was to scream "yes!" But it all seemed wrong somehow. Summer McCracken couldn't have been inviting *me*. It had to be a joke. She was teasing me again. . . .

Summer suddenly burst into laughter, and I realized I was blushing. "Whoa," she said. "It's not a *date* date, okay? My dad's coming back to town for it and I thought you'd want to meet him."

"Oh," I said, trying not to feel too deflated. "Of course. That'd be great."

"We'll try to get Daddy away from everyone and tell

him about Henry being murdered," Summer explained.

"You haven't told him yet?"

"He's halfway around the world and he's busy. Plus, I figure, if I tell him solo, he might think I've been drinking my cough syrup. But if you're there to back me up, maybe he'll buy it. So what do you say? Want to come?"

"Yeah. Of course," I said, though it seemed to me that someone as invested in his daughter's life as J.J. McCracken would give her the benefit of the doubt if she told him his mascot had been killed. I wondered if Summer was keeping our investigation a secret so she could play detective—but then got upset at myself for doubting her. After all, she *was* offering to tell her father the truth—and getting me into a swanky party to boot. Looking for ulterior motives to explain her behavior wasn't cool; I guess I was still having trouble believing someone like Summer really wanted to be friends with me.

"I'm not kidding about the paparazzi," she told me. "We'll try to avoid them, but they'll be everywhere. Like mosquitoes. You'll end up on the Internet."

I shrugged, trying to make it seem like I didn't think this was such a big deal, but down inside, I have to admit, I was a little excited by the prospect. "I can handle it."

"We'll see."

"Why are we going to talk to Larry the Lizard?" I asked.

Summer smacked her forehead. "Right! Totally forgot. Okay, the way I found him was, I was trying to get some info on all the hippo keepers. You know, to see if anyone had a grudge against Henry. I'd heard he'd attacked one of them, right? So my father's got this whole database on his computer with everyone at FunJungle's info. . . ."

"That's how you got my cell number?"

"Exactly."

"And your dad lets you use it?"

"Of course not. He has no idea I use it. But then, that's his fault for using my birthday as his access code. Anyhow, I found out there's four keepers who work with the hippos, but they all seem cool. Each has, like, fifteen years experience with hippos. The guy who got bit, he did hippo research for two years in Botswana. . . ."

"That doesn't mean he didn't kill Henry."

"I know. But they've all been doing this a long time. Sooner or later, a keeper's got to expect to get bitten by *something*, right? That's the name of the game. If you want a safe job, you become a secretary or something; you don't work with hippos. It doesn't make sense that one of them would have killed him for revenge."

"They could have had another reason. . . ."

"Possibly, but get this: While I was going through the database, I came across this other guy, Charlie Conner. Did you ever hear that Henry was in a circus before he came here?"

"Yeah."

"And that when he was there, he bit a clown?"

"I heard he bit three."

"Well, Charlie's one of them. So I figured maybe I should talk to him. The guy not only knows Henry's background, but he's got a motive."

"You think a clown would kill for revenge, but not a zookeeper?"

"Absolutely. Clowns are freaks. Plus, this guy didn't choose to work with animals. He just got attacked by one. That, my friend, is a recipe for revenge."

"So you just called him up?"

"Sure. He answered right away. Of course, the caller ID told him J.J. McCracken was calling, and everyone answers when my father calls."

"Was he disappointed when he found out it was you?"

"I didn't tell him it was me. I said I was from my father's office and we were looking into Henry's death. And the first thing he says to me is, 'I didn't do it. But I know who did.'"

I was so surprised, I almost tripped over my own feet. "He does? Who?!"

"I don't know. He wouldn't tell me on the phone. He was all paranoid, like maybe he's afraid the killer's gonna come after him next. That's why we're going to see him."

"How do you know it isn't another trap?"

Summer's step faltered, ever so slightly. She'd been so proud of herself for getting the lead, it apparently hadn't occurred to her that it might have been a setup. But then, she shrugged it off, as she seemed to do with so many things. "If it is, then I guess we'll know something important."

"What's that?"

"That Charlie's the *real* killer." She grinned, thinking this was funny.

I didn't. After all, no one had tried to kill *her* yet. But before I could point this out, she yanked me down a small alley between two exhibits. There, a tunnel plunged into the side of a building, the entrance to the mascot dressing rooms. There weren't any doors, because most of the costumes were too bulky to fit through them. Zelda Zebra was sauntering in ahead of us.

"Here goes nothing," Summer said, and slipped inside.

The mascot dressing room was an architectural afterthought. FunJungle's designers had originally envisioned an underground staging area connected to various points in the park via a network of tunnels—like Disney World had. Actors would have entered it near the employee parking lot and emerged at various points in the park as adorable animated characters. That way, they wouldn't have to walk all the way to their posts in the hot sun, a task that could take up to fifteen minutes in a big, bulky suit. However, that was all before J.J. McCracken got the estimate for what the tunnels would cost: Five million dollars. "Screw that," J.J. had said, and just paid for some extra dressing rooms.

If J.J. had ever entered one of those dressing rooms, however, he might have decided the tunnels weren't such a bad idea: They would have kept the frightening assortment of people who played the mascots where guests couldn't see them.

I'd heard that at theme parks in Florida and California, the people who played the mascots were usually young aspiring actors so desperate to break into show business that they considered dressing as a giant mouse to be a good career move. Central Texas had a dearth of such people. Our mascots had apparently been hired for two reasons: their body sizes roughly conformed to those of the animals they were playing—and they had to be inept enough at most jobs to take one that basically required them to stand still all day.

It was a group of people you'd expect to see in a police lineup, rather than a family theme park: a massive man with arms so tattooed they looked like the Sunday comics wore the bottom half of Eleanor Elephant while reading an old *Guns & Ammo* magazine; a lanky teenager who reeked of marijuana struggled to climb into her Gina Giraffe outfit; the scraggly man who played Uncle O-Rang had contorted wildly inside his costume so he could scratch his private parts. All of them probably should have been outside, amusing small children, but an impromptu cigarette break had been called. They all inhaled deeply, savoring their smokes, keeping an eye on the entrance in case a supervisor walked in.

Charlie Connor was smoking too. He held a huge cigar

in his little green hands. "I wasn't expecting a couple of kids," he grunted, looking us up and down with annoyance.

We looked him up and down as well. It didn't take too long, because he was a midget.

He was a few inches shorter than me, even though he was around forty. But his short stature wasn't what made him look strange. It was the fact that, save for the head, he was dressed as a lizard.

"You said you know who killed Henry?" Summer asked, ignoring the crack about us being kids.

Charlie fixed her with a hard stare—until recognition suddenly dawned on him. Then he broke into a wide smile. "Wait a minute!" he said. "You're that girl. The famous one. McCracken's daughter."

Before Summer could reply, everyone else turned toward her and gasped with excitement. Within seconds, they were all crowded around her, begging for autographs. Even the tattooed giant who played Eleanor seemed giddy.

"Hey!" Charlie snapped, trying to shove them all back. "She's here to talk to *me*. Not you yahoos."

He'd obviously been hired as Larry because of his size. Larry the Lizard was the shortest of Henry's pals. He was supposed to be some sort of chameleon, but the costume looked more like a frog with a tail. (In fact, a few people in PR had suggested removing the tail and simply calling him

Freddie the Frog.) Charlie seemed to have no great affection for his job; there were two obvious cigar burns on the costume, and the head, which lay by his feet on the floor, was slightly crushed, as though someone had sat on it.

Eventually, Summer signed everyone's autographs, answered a few questions, and then graciously asked if she might have a little time alone with Charlie. The other mascots reluctantly backed off, wondering what made the Lizard so special.

We sat down with him, trying to stay upwind of his cheap cigar, which smelled like burnt hair.

"Who killed Henry?" Summer asked again.

"Why are *you* asking questions about the hippo?" Charlie asked suspiciously. "You're what? Fourteen?"

"I want to know what happened to him," Summer replied.

"And who's this guy?" Charlie looked at me, but still spoke to Summer, even though I was only a few feet away.

"He's my friend. You can trust him."

Charlie looked us over again. While he was certainly excited to have an audience with Summer McCracken, it was obvious he wasn't keen on sharing any information with us. "First things first," he said eventually. "I didn't kill the hippo. This isn't me trying to avert the blame. I didn't like him, seeing as he nearly killed *me*—but I wasn't in this for revenge or anything."

"Of course not," Summer said diplomatically.

Charlie rolled up the leg of his lizard suit and pointed to a deep scar on his calf. "See that? That's what the jerk did to me. I'm minding my own business, working on a routine with some of the other clowns, and the fat jerk runs up and attacks me."

"For no reason?" It was the first thing I'd said in Charlie's presence, other than "Hello." I knew he was far more interested in talking to Summer than me, but I hadn't been able to keep that in.

Charlie turned to me, annoyed. "You think I was dumb enough to provoke that bag of pus? Everyone at the circus knew Henry was bad news. Truth be told, the owners didn't help the situation. They treated him like dirt. But then, they pretty much treated everyone like dirt, man and animal alike. Point is, I gave Henry a really wide berth, seeing as he didn't like little people."

"You're kidding." This time it was Summer who couldn't hold her words in.

Charlie pointed to his scar again. "Does this look like I'm kidding? First thing they told me when I joined the circus: 'Steer clear of the hippo. He don't like little people.' There was another little person in the clown troupe before I got there—Frankie. Henry had a go at him, too. This was his first week there. Frankie was only trying to be nice.

Brought Henry a carrot or something like that. They tell me the hippo acted real nice at first, even wagged his tail all friendly, like a two-ton cocker spaniel. . . . And then *boom!* Next thing anyone knows, he's got Frankie's head in his mouth. Nearly put the guy in the hospital."

"Was he okay?" I asked.

"Luckily, yes. Frankie came within an inch of losing an eye, though. And the hippo ate his toupee."

I had to bite my lower lip to keep from laughing. It was wrong, but I couldn't help it. The idea of a little person sticking out of Henry's mouth was funny. The fact that we were being told the story by a man dressed as a lizard didn't exactly help it sound serious.

I looked at Summer. She was biting her lip too. In fact, she was having so much trouble trying not to laugh, I had to ask the next question.

"So what happened when Henry attacked you?"

"He just got loose. I don't know what the handlers were doing with him. Moving him, feeding him, whatever you do with hippos. All I know is, one moment I'm minding my own business and the next, four thousand pounds of pissed-off hippopotamus is bearing down on me. Must've been thirty guys around, but he comes right after me, cause I'm a little person. Sank his teeth right into my leg. Thank God Bettina was around. . . ."

"Bettina?" I asked.

"The bearded lady. She took about a pound of testosterone pills a day to make her hair come in, so she was ripped. Strongest woman you ever met. She could bend a steel bar into a pretzel without breaking a sweat. Anyhow, when Henry had me in his teeth, she punched the jerk in the nose until he dropped me. Then the other clowns beat him back while Bettina got me to the medic."

"How badly did Henry hurt you?" Summer wanted to know.

"*Real* bad. That hippo totally messed up my leg. One of his teeth went straight through the muscle, one side to the other. Needed eighty-seven stitches and twelve shots. The doctor said God only knew what kind of bacteria could be in a hippo's mouth. They jabbed me for tetanus, typhoid, yellow fever, you name it. I was like a freakin' pin cushion. And I lost my job."

"Why?" Summer wanted to know.

"The circus life ain't exactly plush. There's no medical and dental. If you can't work, you're out. And I had to be on crutches for three weeks. No one wants to see a midget clown on crutches. That's not comedy. It's tragedy."

"So how'd you end up here?" I asked.

"Well, obviously, the circus wanted to get rid of Henry ASAP. So they offered him up cheap and FunJungle came sniffing around. I knew they were hiring—heck, everyone did—so I presented myself to them. I had good references, a degree from Clown College . . ."

Summer laughed. "Clown College. That's funny."

Charlie scowled at her. "It's not a joke. It's a prestigious institution serving those who seek the way of the clown. Not that this place gives a hoot. Here I am, a licensed practitioner of the harlequin arts—and they basically hired me 'cause I'm short. I thought they were looking for a real clown, not some yutz to stand around dressed as a lizard all day."

"You didn't know you were going to be in costume?" I asked.

"No, I did, but . . . I thought they'd let me *do* something. Acrobatics. Juggling. You know, let me *entertain*. But they don't. Apparently, the legal department's afraid us mascots might hurt a guest if we jump around too much. So we're just supposed to stand still and wave. I might as well be a shrubbery for all I get to do." Charlie angrily flicked the butt of his cigar toward the trash can. It bounced off the rim and landed on the floor, where it started to burn the carpet. Charlie made no attempt to pick it up.

"So who killed Henry?" I asked, unable to keep the question inside any longer.

Charlie stared at us for a while, enjoying keeping us in suspense. Then he said, "Pete Thwacker."

Summer and I looked at each other. I didn't know what to think. I didn't like Pete, but it was hard to imagine him killing Henry. Summer seemed a bit more excited by the revelation, though I wasn't sure if she even knew who Pete was. "How d'you know?" she asked. "Did you see him do it?"

"No. In fact, he didn't do the actual deed himself. He ordered someone else to do it. That's what I saw."

"How?"

"I was in costume. I was working over at Mbuko Hippo Overlook. That's usually reserved for the Henrys, but the one who was supposed to be there that day got food poisoning at lunch and had to go to the infirmary. While they were waiting to get another Henry, I got dispatched over there to fill in. It was a bad call. People don't want to see Larry the Lizard at Hippo River. They want to see Henry. In fact, most guests don't want to see Larry the Lizard at all. He's not a very interesting character. Plus, people think lizards are gross. Yet another reason this job bites."

"So what happened?" I prodded. Keeping Charlie on topic was like herding monkeys.

"I'm standing there, being ignored, and then to top it off, Henry has one of his incidents: He fires a load of crap at the tourists. A *huge* load. He must've been saving up for a week. He doesn't hit anyone, but he soils the glass at the overlook something awful, and it smells so bad, people are getting sick—so the park shuts down the Overlook till the cleaning crew can get there. Only, the rules state I'm not supposed to leave my post. Now, it's like nine hundred degrees outside, it smells like hippo crap, and I've got nothing to do. So I decide to heck with that and go find a shady spot to sit. I don't want the supervisor seeing me taking an unauthorized break, though, so I find a bench tucked back in the trees around Hippo River where there's not a lot of traffic. I'm there maybe a minute when I see Thwacker come along with some security guard. . . ."

"Which one?" Summer asked.

"I don't know. Some woman. A *big* woman. Built like a truck."

"Large Marge," I said.

Charlie looked at me, intrigued. "You know her?"

"Yeah. I know her."

"She's the one who *really* killed the hippo. I heard Pete tell her to."

My eyes widened in excitement. I could easily imagine Large Marge doing something as cruel as killing Henry.

"Right in front of you?" Summer asked.

"Damn straight. I think sometimes, people forget there's a human in this costume. But maybe they didn't see me. The costume's green; it blends into the landscaping. They were off tucked in the trees themselves."

"What'd Pete say?" I asked.

"He was royally pissed about Henry projectile crapping yet again. Going on and on about what a headache it was. The guests were all disgusted, as usual—and apparently this time, some old lady claimed she'd been hit. She said it had ruined her dress and she was gonna sue FunJungle for being unsanitary. Total crackpot, but still, it was a major headache for Thwacker. So he told this Marge he'd had it. He couldn't wait for Martin to find another hippo to replace Henry with. He couldn't deal with Henry one more day. The hippo was a disaster waiting to happen and Thwacker wanted him dead.

"So Marge gets all conspiratorial and says, 'Are you asking me to kill Henry?'

"And Thwacker says, 'Could you do it?'

"And Marge says, 'Not for what I'm getting paid right now.'

"So they negotiate. Marge doesn't seem too bothered by the idea of whacking the hippo. In fact, she seems excited about it. Like she's James Bond and she's been given orders to assassinate somebody. Thwacker's much more nervous, like he knows this is a bad idea, but at the same time, he can't take it anymore. The hippo's driving him nuts. They talk money for a bit, and then they reach an agreement."

"You heard Marge say she'd do it?" I asked.

Charlie hesitated. "Not exactly. The cleaning crew came

along, so Thwacker and Marge split. But it was pretty much a done deal. He wanted her to do it. She wanted to do it. A week later, the hippo turns up dead. What more do you need?"

I looked to Summer. She seemed happy with what she'd heard. I wasn't quite so satisfied, though. There were still a few things bothering me about the whole situation. But before I could ask anything else, the tattooed man shouted, "Supervisor's coming!"

Instantly, the room became chaos. The lazy actors were suddenly full of energy, stubbing out their cigarettes and squirming into their suits as fast as they could. Charlie snatched his lizard head off the floor and slammed it onto his shoulders.

"Gotta go," he said, then grabbed my arm and pulled me close. "In case anyone asks, you didn't hear *anything* from me. If I get in any trouble because of this, I'll come find you." Even though it was coming from a giant lizard, the tone of his voice still scared me.

Charlie turned to go, but in his haste, he slammed into an open locker, denting his nose. "Damn it," he muttered. "I've got to get a *real* job." Then he slipped into the tunnel and vanished from sight.

It was a good thing the Carnivore Canyon grand
opening party wasn't that night, because Mom was so angry
at me for running off that she probably wouldn't have let me
go. I'd never seen her so upset in my life. She'd been worried
sick—even though I'd left the note—and alerted security to
keep an eye out for me. (It spoke to how crummy FunJungle's
security was that I'd been running around the park for over
an hour and no one had spotted me.) After chewing me out,
Mom planted me in a chair in her office and didn't leave again
until it was time to go home for the night. Then she marched
me back to our trailer, made me dinner, and sent me right
to my room. She also confiscated my phone so I couldn't
communicate with Summer.

That was frustrating, because I knew Summer was probably in a heap of trouble as well. Once we left the dressing room, she'd checked her phone and found about a hundred messages from her mother and her bodyguards. "I gotta split," she'd told me, and raced out the front gates to grab a cab. I hadn't heard from her since and now wondered if she'd even be allowed to go to the gala event the next night, let alone bring a date.

I told Mom what I'd learned, of course. (I'd tried to leave Charlie out, but she'd dragged his name out of me.) I wanted her to know I'd disobeyed her for a good reason: my own safety. "If Pete and Marge really killed Henry, then they're also the ones who tried to kill me," I explained. "We should tell the police!"

"The police aren't going to believe that story for one second," Mom told me.

"Why not?"

"Because *I* don't even believe it. Pete Thwacker doesn't know a thing about hippos—and Marge is even dumber. You really think those two blockheads could put together that plan to kill Henry?"

"Maybe," I said. Although the truth was, this had already occurred to me. It was what had bothered me about Charlie's story. A couple weeks earlier, Pete had actually remarked at a press conference that hippopotamuses were basically whales with legs. I didn't doubt that he might have truly wanted

Henry dead—or that Marge would have been willing to do it for extra pay. But the two of them seemed more likely to go the poisoning or shooting route than doing something as subtle as killing Henry slowly via peritonitis. Still, that didn't mean they couldn't have done it.

"There's no 'maybe' here," Mom told me. "It's completely implausible."

"What if they got help from someone else? Like one of the hippo keepers? They'd know how to kill Henry without making it look like a crime."

Mom just shot me an angry look, as though the idea that one of the keepers would help kill their own animal was offensive to her. Then she got up, went into the adjoining office and made a phone call.

I didn't find out who she'd called until later that night. I was sitting in my room, reading, when Mom came in and said I had a visitor. I stepped out into our little kitchen and found Buck Grassley there.

"Evening, Teddy," he said. "Your mother tells me you've been looking into Henry's death on your own." Unlike a lot of the other adults at FunJungle, Buck always talked to me like I was a grown-up. He didn't seem upset that I'd been investigating. Instead, he seemed to be intrigued, like he was my grandpa asking how school had been that day.

"I guess," I replied.

Buck chuckled a bit. "It's a nice night," he said. "Why don't we all have a little chat outside?" It wasn't really a question. He held open the door for us.

I looked to Mom. She nodded that it was all right. So I went out.

We had a couple of cheap Target lawn chairs set up outside our door, facing the woods. Dad and Mom liked to sit there at night, stare up at the sky, and imagine they were back in Africa. Ever the gentleman, Buck waited for Mom and I to sit before he did.

It was still humid out, but the heat of the day had broken. The stars were bright and the woods were alive with the chirp of crickets.

"Your mother tells me you talked to Charlie Connor today," Buck said. "He told you Pete Thwacker and one of my own people might have had something to do with Henry's death?"

I thought it was interesting that he didn't call Large Marge by her name. Or call Henry's death a "murder." "That's right."

"I don't suppose Charlie told you what he did before he was in the circus?"

"No."

"He was in jail."

I swallowed hard, worried. Charlie had threatened me

not to mention his name and I had—and now he turned out to be a criminal. "For what?"

"Armed robbery."

"You mean like from banks?"

"No, nothing that big. He mugged people. Just a two-bit thug."

Mom stared at Buck, even more upset than me. "You hired an ex-con to work as a mascot?"

Buck shrugged. "He'd served his time. Got early parole for good behavior. The system considers him reformed."

"I'm all for giving people a second chance," Mom said, "But as a mascot here? Most of that job is working with children. You couldn't have given him a behind-the-scenes position instead?"

"I'm in security, not personnel. From what I understand, there's not a whole lot of people lining up to work as mascots. Those suits are hot and uncomfortable, and we've got to put people in them. I understand your concern, though. I have it too. So I've kept an eye on Charlie. . . ."

"Do you think he's dangerous?"

"To people? Not really. Charlie never actually used a weapon on anyone. He only used it to scare his victims. When he got busted, there weren't even bullets in the gun. But animals might be a different story. . . . I know he likes to hunt, so he's killed animals before. And he *did* have a grudge against Henry."

"So you think maybe *he* murdered Henry?" I asked. "And then accused Pete and Marge to distract attention from himself?"

Buck just gave another shrug. "First of all, we still don't have any proof Henry was murdered. . . ."

I almost interrupted him to say that wasn't true—that I'd even found evidence of the murder—but Mom signaled me to keep my mouth shut, so I did.

". . . but if someone *did* try to harm the hippo, I think Charlie would be as much as suspect as anyone else. Certainly more than one of my own people. I know Marge has a big beef with you, Teddy, but that doesn't mean she's a bad person, understood?"

I stifled a smile. "Understood."

Buck suddenly leaned forward, fixing me with a hard stare. "The thing is, these investigations can get dangerous. Someone's already made one attempt to scare you off and you could have been seriously hurt. Now there's a known felon in the mix. So from now on, let me and my people handle this, okay? This is a big park. I'm sure you and Miss McCracken can find something else to occupy your time here."

I reacted with surprise—which was exactly what Buck was expecting. Now that he had me on the hook, he let me wriggle a bit. He picked a chunk of cedar wood off the ground, took his Bowie knife from its holster and started to whittle, carefully shaving off the bark.

"Remember how we have all those cameras everywhere?" he asked. "Well, we've been reviewing all the tapes of Hippo River from the last few days. So we've got plenty of footage of you two and your little swim party."

"That was all my idea." I spoke so quickly, I wasn't even sure why I'd said it. Trying to protect Summer just seemed like the right thing to do.

"Was it now?" The tone of Buck's voice indicated he knew Summer well enough to guess whose idea it really was. He and Mom shared a smile, as though they thought my attempt at chivalry was cute. "What exactly were you doing in there?"

"Looking for the murder weapon."

"Did you find it?"

I hesitated before answering, then realized that this was as good as an answer. "Yes," I admitted.

"Where is it?"

"Doc has it."

Buck didn't seem quite sure how to respond to that. He fell silent for a bit, like he was mentally jotting down notes.

I realized I'd just dragged Doc into the investigation, which would probably make him even more annoyed at me than usual. But I still felt right in telling Buck about the weapon. I was glad *someone* in law enforcement was finally showing an interest in Henry's murder. I also felt some relief in letting Buck take over. After all, he was right. It *was* getting dangerous. The incident at World of Reptiles had been scary, but somehow, learning that Charlie Conner was a felon was even more unsettling. It seemed no one at FunJungle was exactly what they appeared to be. I wondered how many other people were hiding something.

"Why'd you give it to Doc?" Buck asked.

"I didn't, really. He took it."

"You mean he stole it from you?"

"No. I went to show it to him because I thought he'd want to see it. He'd suspected Henry was murdered during the autopsy, but couldn't find the weapon." I explained everything that had happened at the vet lab that day: How there'd been someone else in the operating room with Doc, how Doc had seemed on edge and taken the jack from me, how I'd caught a glimpse of the dead jaguar . . .

"Whoa there." Buck looked up from his whittling. "What dead jaguar?"

"It must have come for Carnivore Canyon, I guess. Doc was doing an autopsy on it."

"You mean to see if someone had killed it, too?"

"No," Mom said. "Nothing like that. It's just Doc's policy to autopsy any animal that dies at the park."

"So . . . he doesn't suspect there's a serial animal murderer here?"

"No. He thinks Henry is the only animal that's been killed." Mom suddenly seemed to doubt her statement and looked at me. "Is that right?"

"As far as I know," I agreed.

"But he still autopsies everything anyhow?" Buck asked.

"Yes," Mom said. "To determine the cause of death so that similar deaths can be prevented."

Buck had chewed his toothpick to pulp. He tossed it aside, then shaved off a new sliver of wood and stuck it in his mouth. "Teddy, you keep referring to this murder weapon as a jack. Can you describe it to me?"

I did. Then I explained how anyone could have picked up a package of jacks at FunJungle Emporium, turned them into murder weapons, and easily fed them to Henry. Buck listened intently, nodding thoughtfully, his mood darkening the whole time. I think he was starting to grasp that I was no longer just some bored kid crying wolf—although I'd have thought the murder attempt at World of Reptiles would have convinced him of that.

Mom grew more intrigued as she listened as well. "All these cameras you've got, Buck. Are any of them aimed at the tourist areas of Hippo River?"

"Plenty."

"So you could go through all the tapes from the days before Henry died and see if you can spot the killer throwing the jacks into Henry's mouth."

Buck frowned. "In theory, yes. But if it's as simple to feed Henry as Teddy says, then I doubt the tapes will do us any good. If the killer knows about the cameras—and I have good reason to suspect he does—then there are plenty of ways he could have avoided being filmed: going to the most crowded viewpoint and blending in with everyone else—or maybe wadding the jacks into some bread and giving them to a child to feed to Henry—or wearing a disguise. A baseball cap pulled down low over the eyes would be enough. Plus, we all know hundreds of people threw food to Henry every day. How could we tell which of them was the killer?"

"Good point." Mom looked defeated as she said it.

"Did you ever find out why all the cameras in Reptile World went down?" I asked.

"Power failure," Buck replied.

"Only for those cameras?" Mom asked.

"Yes. A fuse blew in the room where the recordings are kept."

"At the exact time that the mamba was being let out? That seems awfully suspicious."

"Yes," Buck admitted. "Yes, it does."

"Could the fuse be tripped manually?" Mom asked.

"It could."

"Where is it?"

"Inside the administration building."

"You need official access to get in there," Mom said. "Sounds like this was an inside job."

"Oh, I don't think there was ever any doubt of that." Buck stood and stretched. "Well, it's late and I've got a long drive home. I hope you've taken this little talk to heart, Teddy."

"I have, sir," I said.

"I have your word you're done investigating?"

"Sure."

"Good to hear." Buck tousled my hair and smiled.

"Am I in trouble for going into Henry's pool?"

Buck chuckled. "For what? Showing a little gumption? Nothing wrong with that. Reminds me of a kid I knew growing up around here. Little squirt named John James McCracken. He turned out all right." Buck sheathed his knife, then added, "Of course, J.J. always knew when to leave well enough alone. Hopefully, you do too."

Then he ambled off toward the employee parking lot.

I turned to Mom, expecting to be sent straight to bed, but to my surprise, she wasn't even looking at me. She was just staring after Buck, lost in thought.

I went inside and headed for my room.

"Where do you think you're going?" Mom asked.

I looked back through the screen door. "I thought I was grounded."

"Not anymore."

"I'm not?"

Mom shook her head. "I'm not saying I'm happy about what you did, but I see now that you didn't have much choice. You told me Henry had been murdered, but I didn't help you. No one did." Mom came inside and pointed to a seat at the table. I sat while she cut slices of cake for both of us.

"Do you think Buck can find the killer?" I asked.

Mom took her time before answering. "I'm not sure," she finally admitted. "Buck's a good man, but . . . I'm not so sure he's coming at this the right way."

"Why not?"

"Well, he seems far more concerned about Charlie than Pete and Marge. Now, yes, Charlie has a criminal past, but I find it hard to believe he'd kill Henry for revenge. If he really was angry at the hippo, wouldn't he have killed it back in the circus? Why wait until now?"

"I don't think Charlie knows that much about animals," I said. I was having a hard time imagining him doing something so clever as using the jacks to kill Henry. Or freeing the mamba. Plus, he wasn't tall enough to cut the glass on the mamba's exhibit without using a stepstool.

"Pete doesn't know anything about animals either," Mom admitted. "But then, maybe that's all an act. He was a very successful PR man at some of J.J.'s other companies before he was transferred here. He can't be as much of an idiot as he sometimes seems."

"Do you think he and Marge killed Henry?"

Mom sighed, then sat down with a glass of milk. "I don't know. I can see the motive. Henry's been a constant thorn in Pete's side. I can even see Pete getting so frustrated that he'd say he wanted Henry dead. I just can't see him actually going through with it."

"I can see Marge doing it," I said. "She's mean."

"Can you see Marge coming up with the plan with the jacks?"

"No. But I can imagine her feeding them to Henry if someone told her how to do it."

"How about setting the mamba free?"

I thought about that a bit. "Maybe if she thought it'd scare me. Not to kill me, though."

Mom took a long gulp of milk, then said, "I think Buck might be biased toward investigating an ex-con, rather than one of his own employees. Although there's plenty of other people who could have done this as well."

"Like who?"

"Pete wasn't the only person that Henry caused trouble.

For a hippopotamus, he had a lot of enemies. I know Martin hated him. Everyone in administration did. And the marketing department too. And if you're going to throw Charlie Conner in the mix, then you might as well count every other person he'd ever attacked or covered with crap."

"What about his keepers? I heard none of them liked him."

Mom immediately shook her head. "Maybe they didn't. But I've never met a keeper in my life who'd harm an animal. And anyone who works with hippos chose to do so. They'd know what the risks were. J.J. hired some of the best keepers from around the country to come here. Each of those people had years of experience with hippos. They wouldn't kill him."

"Even for money? What if they were really broke and someone offered them a whole lot of cash?"

"Like who?"

I thought a bit, but could only come up with one person who had a great deal of money. "J.J. McCracken? I'm sure he wanted to get rid of Henry too."

Mom considered that, then reluctantly admitted, "I guess it's possible. Whatever the case, that's an awfully long list of suspects, any one of whom could have killed Henry— and gone after *you*."

I got a queasy feeling in my stomach. Every minute Buck

spent going after the wrong suspect was a minute the real killer was still out there, free to come after me again.

Mom must have noticed I was getting worried, because she reached across the table and set her hand on mine. "It'll be okay," she said. "We'll get to the bottom of this. But for the time being, when I say 'Stay in my office with me,' stay there, all right?"

I nodded. "Does this mean I'm not in trouble anymore?"

"Yes. And I think it'd be okay if you came to the party tomorrow night."

"Really?"

"Sure. I'd like to meet this new friend of yours."

I blushed a bit, thinking of Summer. Mom laughed, then grabbed our plates and took them to the sink.

Despite the good front she was putting up, I knew the *real* reason Mom was letting me go to the party: She felt I'd be safer there with her than I would be at home alone.

Sadly, I felt the same way. Our trailer was a cheap prefab job with a cheesy lock on the door and walls you could practically poke your finger through. Plus, it sat in the middle of nowhere, thirty miles from the closest police station. True, we had neighbors, but they'd all be at the party the next night as well. You couldn't really come up with a less protected place to be.

That night, I went to bed with a chair jammed under the doorknob of my room, just to be on the safe side.

No one tried to kill me during the night and the next day passed uneventfully. I stayed with Mom at work, although this time it was a bit more fun. I think she still felt guilty about not taking my claim that Henry had been murdered more seriously, because she let me go into the gorilla exhibit with her, which violated about forty-three FunJungle rules and directives. I didn't go out where any of the tourists could see me, but it was still awfully cool. I hadn't been so close to gorillas since Africa. Kwame, the two-year-old, came right over to play with me.

Still, that was only about fifteen minutes out of what proved to be a very long day. I couldn't wait for the party, not only because it meant I'd get to see Summer again, but because I was going nuts cooped up in Monkey Mountain, waiting for Buck Grassley to do all the investigating. Every time the phone rang, I'd tense up in anticipation, hoping it was Buck calling to report that he'd solved the case. Maybe he'd gone through Charlie Conner's locker and found some jacks and a metal file—or he'd confronted Pete Thwacker and Pete had cracked like an egg and confessed to everything. The call never came, though. We didn't hear a thing from Buck all day.

Or from Summer, for that matter. I texted her a few times to see if she'd heard anything, but all I got back was a quick blurb: *Meet me at the check-in desk at 7.* And that was it. After a while, I decided not to reach out anymore or I'd start to look pathetic.

It was a slow day at the park as well, easily the slowest since the opening. Few people wanted to come pay full price to visit the park without Carnivore Canyon when the exhibit was going to be open the very next day. Plus, the park shut down an hour early to prep for the big party.

Mom and I headed home at six to shower and put on our best clothes, which wasn't saying much. Mom had never had a reason to own a fancy dress—or even a place to hang one. Besides, she'd always felt it was a travesty to spend hundreds of dollars on clothes she was only going to wear once or twice when the durable ones she wore every day cost a fraction of that. "With all the money people spend on fashion every year," she'd say, "we could cure every disease in Africa." She just put on clean slacks, a nice blouse, and a little perfume. All I had to wear was a collared polo shirt and my one pair of pants without a tear in the knees.

Not surprisingly, most of the other party guests had very different ideas about fashion. I'd never been to a big, fancy event before. (FunJungle's Grand Opening had been far more family-friendly and casual.) It had never occurred to me that women would ever wear diamonds to the zoo. Or ball gowns. Or even high-heeled shoes. But there they were.

The party attracted wealthy people from all over Texas. Even though Texas was a big state and it could be hours between cities, Texans still loved to drive. I'd heard of people driving from San Antonio to Houston just for dinner—and that was almost four hours each way. So it was no big deal for people to head in from every corner of the state for one of the biggest social events of the year. And then, to top that, there were people who'd flown in by private jet from other parts of the country.

All in all, over two thousand people were coming. There was already a long line to pass through the metal detectors into the party when Mom and I arrived. Everyone was grousing about the extra security—they'd already passed through the detectors at the front gates before being shuttled to Carnivore Canyon in golf carts—but I was pleased to see it. I felt safe for the first time in days.

Carnivore Canyon itself was too small to hold all those people, so the party took place on a wide lawn in front of the exhibit. J.J. McCracken had spared no expense. There were dozens of buffet tables piled with food, as well as several entire sides of beef roasting on spits. (Fans had been set up to blow the smell of meat away from Carnivore Canyon so it wouldn't drive the animals crazy with hunger.) There was a big dance floor, which was completely empty—and an outdoor bar, which was packed. There were strings of lights and disco balls and ice sculptures that had probably been lions and tigers at one point, but they had already melted beyond recognition in the heat. The press was out in force. I recognized several local reporters working the party. Camera flashes were popping everywhere. And that was merely the press J.J. McCracken had allowed in. I heard several people say the paparazzi were piled four deep outside the front gates.

Mom and I had little interest in the party itself. Instead, we made a beeline for Carnivore Canyon. All the hard work on the exhibit had paid off; it really looked like a natural canyon, carved by centuries of water running through rock, rather than something that had been built by men over a few months. An elevated walkway ran through most of it, letting you observe the animals from above, or see eye-to-eye with mountain lions as they perched on rock ledges or leopards nestled in the branches of trees. For the most part, there was no barrier between us and the animals; it felt like we were in their world, rather than the other way around. (Although there were a few points where a very fine wire mesh was strung, so thin you could barely see it.)

Surprisingly, there weren't many guests in the exhibit; most had come only for the party. Even the few who had ventured beyond the buffet tables paid little attention to the animals. Instead, they clustered on the walkways, sipping champagne and socializing.

While I found their disinterest annoying, it was also to my advantage. Mom and I had much of Carnivore Canyon to ourselves. There were no crowds to shove through, no pedestrian traffic jams. The guests might have been ignoring the animals, but that was better than throwing food to them. As it was close to sunset, the animals were at their most active, having spent the day sleeping. They eagerly explored their new habitats, bounding through the rocks and splashing in their pools. Three young mountain lions wrestled comically; otters slid down a slope into their pond, and a grizzly bear the size of a car paced on a ledge a few feet away from us. I was so captivated, I forgot about Summer. It wasn't until my phone rang at ten minutes after seven that I realized what time it was.

"Where are you?" Summer snapped when I answered.

"By the leopards," I told her. "Sorry. I'll come right out."

"No, stay there," Summer said. "Where you are is better."

I wasn't quite sure what she meant by that, but she hung up before I could ask. I got my answer soon enough, though. Summer got to the leopards quickly, bearing two skewers of chicken satay and a Diet Coke, her bodyguards in tow. She was wearing a pink dress and pink high heels. Her hair had been done; It looked like enough aerosol hairspray to rip a hole in the ozone layer had been deployed. I was now so used to seeing her dressed down, it took me a moment to recognize her.

We were a good way into the canyon, so only guests who truly cared about seeing the animals had ventured that far. There were only a few people about; they all recognized Summer as she passed, but had the good manners to not pester her for autographs. I noticed they all kept an eye on her, however, and then stared at Mom and me curiously once Summer began talking to us, wondering who we were and how on earth we rated highly enough to earn her attention.

"Yeah," Summer said. "It's *way* better back here. Did you see all the paparazzi out front?"

"Nope," I replied. "For some reason, they didn't seem that interested in us."

Summer laughed, then turned to Mom. "You must be Mrs. Fitzroy."

Mom smiled. "It's a pleasure to meet you, Summer. Theodore's told me a great deal about you."

I'm not sure why, but even that made me blush a bit. Summer and Mom talked a bit about Mom's research and life in the Congo before I finally got a chance to ask, "Where's your dad? I thought he was coming."

"He's right over there." Summer pointed with a chicken skewer. To my surprise, J.J. McCracken was already on the walkway, two exhibits farther down. He was talking to Doc.

"How'd he get past us?" Mom asked, a second before I could say the same thing. "We've been here all along. . . ."

"He came in the back way, through the keeper's entrance to the exhibit," Summer explained. "Daddy *hates* fancy events like this. He doesn't like crowds."

"But he always seems so happy at them," Mom said.

"He fakes it well. All part of the business, he says. If Daddy had it his way, the only way he'd socialize would be playing poker at the house. So he always slips in without anyone noticing, if he can. That's why I said to stay back here. He wanted to meet Teddy where no one would see him."

I coughed, surprised. "Your father wants to meet me?"

"Yeah. C'mon. He doesn't have much time." Summer quickly led us down the walkway. "The ribbon-cutting ceremony's soon."

The sun had set now and the stars were coming out above. Lights had come on in the exhibits to allow everyone to see the animals—but the walkway was getting dimmer by the second. J.J. McCracken was just a silhouette as we approached.

It wasn't surprising that we hadn't noticed him, despite being close by. Even though I'd seen thousands of pictures of him—maybe more—J.J. McCracken turned out to be an easy man to overlook. He was much smaller than I'd been led to believe, not much taller than his own daughter and surprisingly slight of build. He had very plain features that seemed mismatched on his face. J.J. made no secret of the fact that he wasn't attractive, often remarking that he was "about as handsome as a toad in a suit"—and claiming that Summer obviously got her good looks from her mother, who was a famous fashion model. (Summer's mother always said she'd been attracted to her husband's 'inner beauty' but most people figured his massive bank account had probably been pretty attractive too.) J.J. was wearing a tuxedo, but he looked uncomfortable in it, constantly tugging at his tie and shifting about like he had ants crawling over him.

As small as J.J. was, he had the personality of a man several times larger. I could sense it as we approached. He didn't notice us right away, as he was deep in conversation with Doc and staring down into the exhibit below.

I looked where he was looking. To my surprise, there were three jaguars down by a fake stream. I guess they'd arrived at FunJungle without anyone knowing.

"So what happened to it?" J.J. was asking.

"Toxoplasmosis," Doc said. "It's primarily a disease of house cats. Although wild cats can get it. And human infants, if they have pet cats."

"So it wouldn't have picked that up in the wild."

"No. It probably got sick en route here. Maybe even in the quarantine. Sometimes these idiots from customs don't take the right precautions and just lump all the cats together when they come into the country."

I realized they were talking about the dead jaguar. It must have come from outside the US if the customs service had quarantined it. Customs had a few big animal holding facilities on the borders that held every animal coming into America—be it a wild animal destined for a zoo, a farm animal destined for market, or even a family pet. Unfortunately, the facilities were underfunded and run-down and the animal care was known to be subpar at best. It wouldn't have been the first time a zoo lost an endangered animal while trying to bring it into the country.

"We have any proof of that?" J.J. asked, annoyed. "'Cause if we do, maybe we can get some kind of waiver, get customs to let us do all our own quarantining from now on."

"The government wouldn't let you do that. . . ."

"Oh, they might. I've got friends in high places, you know."

We were close enough now to see the frown on Doc's face. "It's not just customs at fault here. God knows why Martin insisted on bringing these animals all the way from the Amazon. There are a dozen facilities in this country where we could have got some. . . ."

"Six months from now. I'm the one who kicked Martin's ass on this, so if you've got a bone to pick, it's with me. Carnivore Canyon's opening tomorrow. We're supposed to have a jaguar exhibit with no jaguars?"

"No one would have even noticed. You've got lions and tigers. That's all the public cares about." Doc waved toward the tiger exhibit, which was not far down the walkway, then pointed back at the jaguars below. "These animals were bought from a shady breeding facility in Brazil and rushed up here. There's a good chance they could *all* have health problems."

"They look fine to me."

"That farm's breeding records were a mess. For all we know, these jaguars could be inbred worse than the royal family." Doc was about to go on, but J.J. had noticed us and held up a hand to silence him.

"We can talk more about this later," he said. "Go enjoy yourself. It's a party."

Doc turned and saw us. I think he was torn between frowning at me and smiling at my mother. Summer's presence put the smile over the top. "Evening, ladies," Doc said graciously. Then he left us alone. I noticed he didn't hurry out of the exhibit, though. He seemed as disdainful of the party as J.J. and only wandered a little farther down the walkway before stopping to watch some ocelots.

J.J. was far more friendly to us, instantly turning up the charm. "There's my princess!" he said, giving Summer a big hug that embarrassed her greatly. Then he turned to Mom and extended a hand. "Charlene, always a pleasure."

"Likewise, J.J." Mom took J.J.'s hand. "The exhibit looks wonderful."

"Doesn't it though? I think the designers have truly out-done themselves on this one." J.J. gallantly kissed Mom's hand, then set his sights on me. "And you must be the famous Theodore Roosevelt Fitzroy. These two ladies have a heap of good things to say about you."

Somehow, that single statement made both Summer and me blush. "It's very nice to meet you, sir," I said, extending my hand to shake.

J.J. pumped my arm with surprising strength, given his scrawny build. "No, the pleasure is all mine. I hear you and my daughter have been having quite a lot of adventures at this park."

"That makes two of us," Mom said.

"We heard you and Doc talking about the jaguars," Summer said. "Are they really inbred?"

J.J. studied his daughter for a moment, as though he didn't know whether to be pleased by her forwardness or annoyed by it. "I'd doubt it. I don't think these breeding facilities are nearly as poorly-run as Doc suspects."

"But what if they are? Will they have babies with three heads and stuff?"

"No. And it's a moot point, because if our genetic testing indicates they're inbred, then we won't let them breed, period. Of course, that's all small potatoes compared to the problems *you* believe this park has, Theodore." J.J. suddenly swung toward me. "Summer has recounted the tale of your investigation with great enthusiasm. Obviously, the idea that Henry was murdered greatly concerns me. I know he wasn't exactly Prince Charming, but for someone to kill him—at my very own zoo, no less—well, it makes me mad as a cut snake."

"Then perhaps you should use your influence to get the local police involved," Mom said.

"Oh, I don't think there's any need for that. Our security team is fully capable of getting to the bottom of this. . . ."

"As well as making sure the story doesn't leak to the press," Mom added.

J.J. gave her a friendly smile, but there seemed to be a little fire behind it. I don't think he was used to people standing up to him like that. "Well, yes. Maybe that seems ornery or blinkered to you, but imagine what a field day the press would have if they found out Henry was murdered. It'd be front-page news all over the world. Children would be devastated. And we'd look like we're running a secondhand outfit here—which might be exactly what the killer wants."

"Why?" I asked.

J.J. looked around cautiously, assessing how close the other guests were before answering. There was a small cluster of people nearby, so J.J. led us all down toward the tigers. A man-made waterfall thundered into the canyon there, loud enough to drown out most noise. Below us, four tigers slunk through the grass at the bottom of the exhibit, waiting for their dinner.

Carnivore Canyon was pioneering some new ground in keeping their animals mentally stimulated. In the past, zoos had simply thrown meat to their tigers, but after a generation or two of this, the cats would have no hunting instincts left. So zoos had begun to make the delivery of food less predictable, forcing the animals to work to find it by leaving it in different places every day and at different times. Now, FunJungle had gone a step further, creating a virtual hunt. Before food was delivered, the scents and sounds of various prey would be pumped into the exhibit via a series of tubes and speakers, leading the tigers on an ever-changing route through their exhibit before food was provided. It sounded a little corny to me, but it seemed to be working. The tigers below us were definitely exhibiting stalking behavior and seemed primed for attack.

They were so impressive, even J.J. McCracken was a bit distracted by them. He needed a gentle nudge from Summer to remember where he was. "Dad. The killers . . . ?"

"Oh yes," J.J. said. "When I first heard about the murder, I had a hunch who might be behind it. Now, I've had Buck and the security staff working on this case round the clock over the last two days, and what they've found has confirmed my fears. It's quite likely that Henry was murdered by saboteurs."

Mom, Summer, and I were all surprised by this. Mom was the first to speak. "Who?"

"There's two possibilities. One is the Animal Liberation Front."

Summer gasped sharply. "Why would animal-rights activists kill an animal?"

"To make us look bad. The ALF has been against this park since the moment it was announced. To them, we're just a prison for animals. They ignore all the work we've done to create state-of-the-art habitats, all the excitement we create in young people, all the money we generate for research and conservation projects. I even invited representatives from the ALF to tour FunJungle with me, to see everything we do to enhance the quality of life for our animals—but of course, they refused. These people don't want to listen to reason. They think they're right and we're wrong and they won't be happy until they've shut down every zoo, farm, and pet store in the USA. They're not sensible like the Sierra Club or the ASPCA. They're a dangerous group of radicals. In fact, technically, they're terrorists, since they've destroyed private property. They blew up a meat-packing plant last year in Nebraska."

I was surprised to hear this last fact. So was Summer. Mom appeared to have known about it. "But if the ALF was trying to make a statement against FunJungle, wouldn't it be more in line with their morals to attack a building, rather than an animal?" she asked.

"You'd think so, wouldn't you? But consider Henry. He's not just an animal. He's a symbol. Our mascot. The most famous animal in the world. Do you have any idea how much damage they've done by killing Henry right after the park's grand opening? Millions of dollars. Maybe more. We've had thousands of families cancel their visits. I've got warehouses full of Henry merchandise I can't sell now. And our stock price took a nosedive. Blowing up a building wouldn't have had an impact like that. Plus, it would have been an obvious terrorist act. The public would have instantly turned against them. Can you imagine anything more horrible than blowing up a zoo? No. But look at how Henry was killed. Subtly. Quietly. Most vets wouldn't have even noticed it was a murder. Only someone as meticulous as Doc. The death makes us look like we dropped the ball. Gives us a black eye. Here we are, claiming to be the greatest zoo in the world with the highest quality animal care—and we can't even keep our own mascot alive."

"So why can't you just say that Henry was killed?" Summer wanted to know. "That'd make whoever did it look bad, wouldn't it?"

"Maybe. If we knew who'd done it. But we don't . . . yet. So right now, all we could do is go public and say that someone killed Henry. We can't prove it was the ALF yet. Maybe it was just some lone jerk who hated hippos. It's still a black eye for us. We made Henry famous and then failed to protect him. Plus, the whole event goes from being a natural occurrence in nature—old hippos die—to a sordid tabloid story: 'Henry Hippo Murdered!'"

"But you said Buck had found some evidence that it *was* the ALF," I reminded him.

"No, he found evidence that it was sabotage. We don't know who's behind it yet. Buck's leaning toward the ALF . . . but there's also the chance this is corporate warfare."

"You mean, another corporation killed Henry?" Mom asked.

"Exactly. Do you know what a dent FunJungle has put in the business of other theme parks in this country? We've sucked away thousands of guests from them. Millions of dollars in profits. They're not happy about that."

"Still," Mom said incredulously, "you don't honestly think a corporation would murder your mascot?"

J.J. shrugged. "Why not? Technically, it's not even murder. Henry's an animal. Legally, it's only destruction of property—and I know that's fair game in the corporate world. Again, look at the economic damage they've done. They couldn't have hit us any harder. The buildings might cost a lot, but they're insured. But Henry . . . Say what you will about the bucket of lard, but he *was* FunJungle to most people. The damage to our image—to our brand—has been irrevocable. It's as though I went down to Disneyland and assassinated Mickey Mouse."

I was taken aback by all this. It all sounded crazy to me—which was compounded by the fact that J.J., lit by the floodlights from the tiger exhibits below, looked a little maniacal as he spoke. But even more shocking was the fact that it kind of made sense. After all, humans had a history of behaving badly in order to make a buck. If a man would kill a rhinoceros for the thousand dollars its horn would bring him, what would stop a corporation from killing a hippopotamus when billions were at stake?

Somewhere close to us, I heard the clank of metal banging on metal. The walkway trembled slightly and then the tigers began to growl. It sounded as though the hunt was picking up.

"What was the evidence Buck found?" I asked.

J.J. smiled at me, as though pleased. "I thought you might ask that. Unfortunately, I can't tell you for fear of jeopardizing the investigation."

I frowned and Summer started to complain, but J.J. cut her off and spoke to me. "I know it's not cool. After all, there wouldn't even *be* an investigation if not for you, Theodore. And for that, I am greatly indebted. That's why I wanted this time with you, so I could talk to you man-to-man and express my gratitude in person. You're a good kid. You're smart and you've got guts. I know you're not gonna like leaving this case to someone else, but I also know you'll understand why it has to be that way. Buck has this under control. He'll find whoever killed Henry. He just needs some time to do it. So all I ask of you in the meantime is patience. Sit back and trust Buck to do his job. Can you do that for me?"

I had to admit, J.J. understood me awfully well. He grasped exactly what I was going through. I wasn't happy to step aside, but I appreciated J.J. taking the time to explain everything to me like I was a grown-up. I could see why he was such a good deal-maker. It was hard not to like him. "Yes," I said. "I can do that."

"Like I said, smart." J.J. patted me on the shoulder happily. "Now, don't think you're totally out of the loop, son. If you have any more thoughts on this case, you let me know. Call my office and I'll be on with you as fast as I can. But as far as the investigation's concerned, I need you on the sidelines. It's beginning to look like there's some really dirty people involved here. It could get dangerous."

There was a soft thump on the walkway, not far behind me.

"It just *did*," Mom said.

She was looking past us, fear in her eyes. Beside her, Summer had the exact same look.

There was a low, guttural growl from behind me.

I spun around. A pair of bright orange eyes leered at us from down the walkway.

One of the tigers was out. And it was still on the hunt.

The tiger was on the walkway between us and the main entrance to Carnivore Canyon. It was locked in a crouch, legs cocked, ready to pounce, its tail flicking from side to side.

I began to tremble with fear. So did Summer and J.J. Only Mom seemed composed. She took my hand in hers and squeezed it reassuringly. "Stay calm," she said quietly. "That's a defensive posture. The tiger's more afraid than we are."

I had a hard time believing that. In all my years in Africa, I'd never come face-to-face with a hungry predator. It was terrifying.

J.J. took a step back, away from the tiger.

The tiger snorted angrily.

J.J. froze.

"No sudden movements," Mom told us. "No loud noises. Anything sudden might trigger the attack instinct."

"Daddy, I'm scared," Summer whimpered. It was the first time I'd ever heard her actually sound like a thirteen-year-old.

Behind the tiger, I could see something metal propped against the outer railing of the walkway. The top end of a ladder. The rest of the ladder descended into the exhibit, which explained how the tiger had got out.

It also meant the other three tigers in the exhibit could get out too.

The tiger's escape had been amazingly quiet. Even now, its growl was so low, it was almost below the range of our hearing, easily covered by the distant cocktail party chatter. In fact, there was a cluster of guests on the walkway not far beyond the tiger who hadn't even noticed it yet. They were gabbing away, oblivious to the fact that their lives were in danger.

"Was that tiger caught in the wild or bred in captivity?" Mom asked.

"Captivity," J.J. replied. "The Columbus Zoo, I think."

"So it's used to humans. It probably doesn't even think of us as prey."

"Why's it ready to attack, then?"

"To defend itself. It's scared. It's in a new place. There's a loud party going on. Bright lights are shining into its exhibit. It thinks we're a threat."

"So what do we do?" Summer asked.

"Don't agitate it. Let it relax. I'm speed-dialing security." Mom had her phone open and slowly pressed the buttons with her thumb.

"It could be five minutes before they get here," J.J. said. "We could be dinner by then."

"Not if the tiger decides we're not a threat."

A shriek pierced the air. One of the party guests behind the tiger had finally noticed it. She dropped her champagne glass and ran.

The rest of her friends did too. They scurried as fast as they could in their high-heeled shoes, which wasn't very fast at all.

The tiger whipped around, startled. It saw the humans running, which triggered its attack response. It was a second from taking off after them. . . .

When J.J. McCracken bolted in the other direction. Summer disappeared from my side as he yanked her along.

Later, J.J. would claim he was sure the tiger was already heading in the opposite direction and that he was taking advantage of the distraction to get a message to security. But I knew what he was really doing. He was panicking. If he'd waited another second or two, the tiger would surely have headed after the other guests—but as it was, J.J.'s sudden movement brought the tiger's attention back toward us.

It swung around, poised to attack, and saw the McCrackens fleeing. But Mom and I were now left as the closest targets.

The tiger roared loud enough to make the walkway vibrate. Then it sprang.

Before I could run, Mom tackled me. She pinned me to the walkway, shielding me from the tiger with her own body.

The giant cat quickly closed the distance between us, covering fifteen feet with each pounce. Within seconds, it was only ten feet away. . . .

Someone suddenly darted past us from behind, heading toward the tiger. I couldn't see who it was in the darkness. Only that he was armed with a broom.

The tiger ignored him, still focused on us. It sprang, teeth bared, claws extending from its paws. . . .

The man swung the broom like a baseball bat, catching the tiger full in the face.

The tiger tumbled to the walkway, shook its head, and sneezed.

"Down!" the man ordered.

To my astonishment, the tiger cowered like a scared kitten. It even whined a bit.

The man cocked the broom over his shoulder again. "Back," he ordered.

The tiger turned around and slunk toward the ladder with its tail between its legs.

The man chanced a look our way, and the light from the exhibit illuminated his face.

It was my father.

"You all right?" he asked.

I'd never been so happy to see anyone in my life. I leapt to my feet and hugged him as hard as I could.

"We are now," said Mom. I could hear the emotion in her voice. She was as thrilled by Dad's arrival as I was.

Dad gave me a comforting squeeze, then looked back at the tiger, which had returned to the ladder. It placed a paw on the rail, considering the climb back down into its enclosure.

Then it gave Dad a mischievous glance and bounded down the walkway toward the party.

"Oops," Dad said.

In retrospect, it seems crazy that I ran after a tiger that had just tried to attack me, but that's how safe I felt with Dad around. He went after the tiger and before I knew it, Mom and I were following. Maybe it was that, within a second, Dad had established his dominance and reduced the tiger from a wild animal to an overgrown housecat. Much of an animal's behavior involves its position in the dominance hierarchy. An animal that doesn't know its place will be confused and agitated. However, one that knows its place—even if it's on the bottom—will be far more relaxed.

The tiger, Kashmir, was only two years old. Although fully grown, he was still a kitten at heart. Now that he'd calmed down, he wanted to play. Only, no one at the party knew that. The moment Kashmir gamboled out of the exhibit, chaos erupted.

The screams of terror echoed back into the canyon as we ran down the walkway. Mom paused, holding me back, though not out of fear; she'd already fully recovered from our scare. She was looking at the ladder that extended from the tiger exhibit. It was about thirty feet tall, fully extended, and it leaned against the walkway rail at a gentle angle that would have been easy for the tiger to scale. Thankfully, there were no other tigers on their way up, though one was prodding it curiously with a paw, as if considering the climb.

"Help me get this out," Mom said. "The last thing we need are *two* tigers crashing the party."

I helped her heave the ladder up over the railing. It was only aluminum, so it didn't weigh too much. There was an inch-thick piece of rope tied to one of the top rungs. It was only a foot long, having been cut clean through. I looked across the exhibit and saw the other end of the rope dangling on the far side, where it was tied to a rock at the top of the cliff.

I realized how whoever had rigged the ladder to free the tigers had done it, but before I could say anything, we heard a roar from Kashmir, followed by a renewed round of screams from the party guests.

"Wait here," Mom said. She dropped the ladder to the walkway, then ran toward the party.

Despite her warning, I followed her. Whoever had rigged the ladder might have still been around. I felt safer near my parents, even with a tiger loose.

By the time we exited Carnivore Canyon, any semblance of the genteel gala event had evaporated. Guests were shrieking at the top of their lungs, stampeding in every direction, shoving and clawing at one another to get away. There was no sense of dignity or chivalry; I saw a security guard flatten three old ladies in his dash for safety. (No one else from security was anywhere to be seen; every one of them had fled their posts.) Many people had run straight out of their shoes; the lawn was strewn with high heels, as well as thousands of champagne glasses, plates of food, and purses everyone had quickly cast aside. There were also quite a few guests strewn on the lawn as well; whether they'd been shoved over or had simply tripped and face-planted into the grass was unclear.

Rather than chase any of them, Kashmir had settled on far tastier and easier prey: a massive roast in the midst of an abandoned buffet table. The tiger happily bounded onto the buffet, which promptly collapsed under its weight, catapulting a tray full of sushi into the bobcat exhibit.

Doc came running up the walkway from Carnivore Canyon. He took one look at the pandemonium and burst into laughter. "Now *that's* what I call a party," he said.

Two of the carnivore keepers rushed over. Both seemed less worried about Kashmir than they did about their jobs. "Oh, boy," the first said. "McCracken's gonna have our heads for this."

"It's not your fault," Mom said. "Not unless one of you left a ladder in the tiger pit."

The keepers looked at her, incredulous. "Why would there be a ladder in the tiger pit?" the second asked.

"To help the tigers escape," Dad explained.

"Why would anyone want to do that?" said both keepers at once.

Mom and Dad both turned to me, the same thing occurring to them at once. "To make FunJungle look bad," Mom said. It was a lie, an attempt to hide the truth from me, but it didn't fool me for a second. I was thinking the same thing Mom and Dad were: Once again, the escape of a deadly animal had been engineered when I was close by.

Dad took my hand and squeezed it tightly.

"I thought you were in China," I said.

"Your mother called me and said you were in trouble. So I jumped on the first plane back."

I knew that wasn't as easy as he made it sound. Flying halfway around the world on the spur of the moment was never simple, especially when you were starting from rural China. Later, I found out Dad had spent the last thirty-six hours traveling, most of it uncomfortably, in the backs of trucks and on cargo planes, just to get back to help me. He'd also forfeited a high-profile assignment *and* the chance to see giant pandas in the wild. But Dad acted like it was no big deal; he didn't want me to think I'd caused him any trouble, even though I had.

Mom gave both of us a huge hug. She was crying a little, though I wasn't sure if that was because she was happy to see Dad, worried about me, or relieved to be alive. Everyone who was left was now staring at us. Most times, I might have found Mom's public affection embarrassing . . . but I didn't that night. Even if we were on live television, I could have hugged both my parents for an hour straight.

There was a whine from Kashmir. The tiger had licked an ice sculpture and got its tongue stuck to it.

Dad reluctantly pulled away from Mom and me; there were other things to take care of. "Can you get this guy back home?" he asked the keepers.

"Yeah," they sighed. One took the broom from Dad and they both approached the tiger so nonchalantly, it might as well have been a baby duck.

"Bad Kashmir," one said. "Bad tiger. Time to go home."

Mom was still clutching Dad's hand. "Thank God you got here in time," she said. "How'd you know what to do?"

"I shot some publicity stills of the tigers a few weeks ago. I had to go in the pit with the keepers, so they showed me all their training techniques. They use the broom a lot. It sends the right message, but it doesn't hurt the tiger."

"Where'd you get the broom?" I asked.

Dad looked at me blankly. "I don't know," he admitted. "It all happened so fast. When I got here, someone told me you were in the Canyon, so I came around through the exit, thinking I'd catching you coming out. Then I heard the tiger and I saw you, so I ran to help and . . . I guess the broom was just there."

"On the walkway?" Mom asked suspiciously.

"Yes. Maybe someone from the cleaning crew left it there."

"Or, more likely, someone who knew the tiger was going to be out. Did you see anyone else on the walkway as you came in?"

Dad shrugged. "A few people. But I didn't pay any attention to them. The only people I recognized were J.J.

and his daughter. They were running like hell."

"Hey," Doc said. "What *did* happen to Moneybags?"

"Guess he's still hiding somewhere," Mom said.

At that moment, my phone buzzed. I pulled it out and found a text from Summer. *R U OK?*

I wrote back, *Yes, where R U?*

Meanwhile, Kashmir had managed to pull his tongue free from the ice sculpture. Now he'd returned his attention to the roast, which he tore to shreds, ignoring his keepers as they shouted at him and prodded him with the broom.

"Is it okay to come down now?" Pete Thwacker's voice startled all of us, as it was coming from directly above. We looked up and found him eight feet up a light post. He was clinging to it so hard his fingers had turned white.

"I'd stay up there another half hour, just to be sure," Dad said.

As usual, it took Pete a few seconds too long to realize someone was joking. "Ha-ha," he sneered, then shimmied down. "I suppose this is all one big joke to you, but people's lives were endangered tonight."

"Is that so?" Mom asked sarcastically.

"I was nearly killed!" Pete insisted.

Dad studied the distance from Pete to the tiger. It was a good fifty yards. "Yeah. Looks like that was a real close call there."

"Tell me about it. If it weren't for my lightning reflexes, I'd be tiger chow." Pete surveyed the lawn mournfully. "This is terrible. The mother of all PR disasters."

The guests who'd been sprawled on the grass were slowly getting to their feet. While many seemed relieved to be alive, an equal number seemed distressed by the damage done to their clothes. One woman screamed in such horror, I thought perhaps a second tiger had attacked, but it turned out she was only reacting to a grass stain on her dress. "My Vera Wang!" she cried. "It's ruined!"

My phone buzzed with a new text from Summer. *Long story. Will call soon. Promise.*

"I'm cursed," Pete said. His voice trembled, as though he was on the edge of a nervous breakdown. "I knew I shouldn't have taken this job. I should have stayed in the soap division. There's no PR emergencies with soap. Soap never tries to kill anyone. The problem with animals is, they don't know how to behave themselves. They escape. They die. They try to make baby animals in front of church groups. Every day, another crisis. It's driving me crazy. I'm losing my hair! Look!" He ran his fingers through his hair, then displayed a few follicles that had come out in the process.

The keepers had resorted to gently swatting Kashmir with the broom to get him off the buffet. The tiger picked the entire roast up in his mouth and dragged it down the walkway toward his home.

"How on earth did someone get a ladder into the tiger pit?" Doc asked. "It had to be twenty feet tall to reach the walkway. We'd have seen someone carrying it in, wouldn't we?"

"It was set up before the party," I said.

Everyone looked at me curiously.

"It was tied to the far side of the exhibit with a rope," I continued. "All they had to do was cut the rope and the ladder dropped to the walkway."

"How'd you figure that?" Dad asked.

"The rope's still tied to the ladder." I thought back to the metal clank I'd heard right before the tiger got out. "They cut it while we were talking to J.J."

Mom, Dad, and Doc all frowned.

"Must've been someone who works in Carnivore Canyon," said Mom. "The broom, the access to the exhibit . . ."

"Not necessarily," Doc said. "I've been in and out of the Canyon all afternoon. Until right before the party, I hadn't seen a security guard all day. I *did* see that ladder, though. It was lying on the walkway. I figured some construction guys had left it behind. Practically anyone could have rigged it. . . ."

"Oh great," Pete sighed. "Another murder attempt with a thousand suspects. That's all I need."

Normally, I might have been annoyed at Pete. The murder attempt had been made on *me*—and yet there he was, acting like *he* was the one with problems. But I realized his behavior was significant: He looked so frazzled, so at his wits' end, it was impossible to imagine him as the criminal mastermind of everything that had happened. He didn't have the stomach for it. And no matter how much he might have hated Henry when he was alive, it was now evident that Henry's sudden death had been a tremendous amount of work for him.

"I've spent three days planning a funeral for a damn hippopotamus," he whined, "And all the news is going to care about is that we've got some screwball setting the tigers loose." His cell phone rang. He stared at it balefully, then reluctantly wandered off to answer it.

"No," I heard him say. "No one was injured. The tiger has been contained without incident."

I took in the aftermath of the party. Most of the guests were long gone, having hightailed it for the exit, though a few were trickling back, probably to collect things or family members they'd left behind. The woman with the big grass stain on her dress was now having a conniption over a broken strand of pearls. Other people who'd fallen were dusting themselves off and assessing the damage. The janitorial staff sat on the periphery, unsure whether they were supposed to start cleaning up or not.

A helicopter zoomed overhead, a spotlight scanning the grounds.

"It's the news," Doc grumbled. "Someone already tipped them off."

"Go away, you vultures!" Pete screamed.

Three golf carts emblazoned with the official seal of the FunJungle Security department pulled up. Buck Grassley and five security guards leapt out, sedation rifles at the ready. Each of Buck's men had run in terror when Kashmir had showed up, but now that their boss was here and they had guns, they made a big show of looking tough.

"Right on time," Doc said sarcastically.

"Where's the tiger?" Buck asked.

"Back in its exhibit," Mom said.

Buck appeared annoyed to have missed his hero moment; the rest of his men pretended to be equally upset. "You were at the scene of the crime?" Buck asked Mom.

"That's where I called you from. *Fifteen minutes ago.*"

Buck either didn't recognize Mom's anger at how long it had taken for him to show up—or he ignored it. "I'm gonna need statements from all of you."

"The tiger got out because someone propped a ladder in its exhibit," Dad said. "That's it. We're going home."

He took Mom and me by the hand and led us toward our trailer.

"You can't leave!" Buck shouted. "This is a crime scene!"

"I just flew halfway around the world to see my family," Dad replied. "If I'd been one minute later, they'd have been mauled thanks to your security failures. So I'm taking them home now. Feel free to investigate, and if you have any questions, you can ask us in the morning."

Buck simmered angrily, but there wasn't much else he could say. He stared after us as we walked away, then turned on his deputies and barked, "Someone get that damn news copter out of here!"

Mom was beaming at Dad. It looked like she'd fallen in love with him all over again. "Thanks for coming home."

Dad beamed back at her, then at me. "I think you better tell me *everything*," he said.

So I did. Mom helped. It took the whole walk home, plus the time Mom spent cooking us dinner. (We'd planned to eat at the party, but the tiger had put an end to that.) Dad took everything in, then sat thoughtfully while we ate. We'd almost made it to dessert before he finally spoke up. "Obviously, there's a lot of questions that still need answers, but two things really bother me in your story. The first is the dead jaguar. . . ."

"Why?" I asked. "We know why it died. Doc said it was toxoplasmosis. . . ."

"It's not *why* it died so much as that the death seems to have been covered up. Did you know the jaguars were even here yet?" Dad turned to Mom, who shook her head.

"Most zoos keep a detailed log of which animals have arrived and which have died," Mom explained. "It should be accessible to all the employees. In the Bronx, before e-mail, they'd just tack the lists up in the keepers' building every week. With computers, it's gotten even easier to keep everyone informed."

"But I've never seen any such list here," Dad said. "Which makes me wonder how many other animals have died."

"We should find out," Mom said.

"Absolutely," said Dad.

"What's the second thing that bothers you?" I asked.

"The metal track at the bottom of Hippo River."

"Really?" It seemed odd to me that, out of everything that I'd told him, my father had focused on that. But Mom always said Dad had a gift for seeing the big picture. "What do you think it's for?"

"I have no idea," Dad admitted. "But tomorrow, we're going to find out."

Pete Thwacker was right. The next morning, the news was all about the escaped tiger. And not just the local news. Even though it seemed to me there were far more important things going on in the world, Kashmir was the lead story on every channel. You might have thought Iran had strapped nuclear weapons to the tiger's back for all the coverage. Every show had plenty of footage of Kashmir wreaking havoc: Several park employees had used their phones to film him, then uploaded their videos to YouTube. I even caught a glimpse of myself and Mom in one shot, standing to the side and watching, although there was no mention of us by name—or that fact that we'd been in direct danger.

My family wasn't really surprised we'd been left out of the

story. What *did* surprise us was the revelation that FunJungle knew who had let the tiger out. At some point in the night, they'd even issued a press release to that effect: The event had been an act of sabotage perpetrated by the Animal Liberation Front.

Pete himself appeared on all the major morning news shows via satellite. He was surprisingly well-kempt and confident, given the state of mind he'd been in the night before. "The ALF has a history of sending threatening letters to FunJungle and other zoos, despite our commitments to conservation and quality animal care," Pete stated. "Now they have attacked. Setting Kashmir free was a blatant terrorist attack designed to both make FunJungle look bad and hurt our bottom line without any consideration for the safety of our guests last night. Thankfully, our keepers handled the situation professionally and no one was hurt. The sad thing is, that while the ALF claims to be looking out for the animals' best interest, it is they, in fact, who are doing harm to the animals in their desperate bid to discredit us."

"How's that?" the news anchor asked.

"Our internal investigation has uncovered evidence that the ALF was also behind the death of our beloved Henry the Hippo."

Mom, Dad, and I all turned to the television, stunned by Pete's announcement.

His interviewer was visibly startled. "Are you saying Henry was murdered?"

"No. But he definitely died—whether premeditated or not—because of actions perpetrated by the ALF."

"What is your evidence?"

"I'm not at liberty to reveal that at this time for fear of jeopardizing the ongoing investigation. But I can say that full details will be released as soon as possible, most likely after the funeral services for Henry this afternoon."

Even I had to admit, while Pete was a moron when it came to animals, he was awfully smart when it came to PR. In just a few sentences, he had turned the scandal over the escaped tiger around to focus the blame on the ALF—and even got in a plug for Henry's funeral as well. After his interview, the news program's staff had forgotten entirely about Kashmir; all they could talk about was Henry.

Pete—or his minions in the PR department—worked the same magic on the other morning shows as well.

"I thought FunJungle didn't want anyone to know Henry was murdered," I said.

"I suppose they'd rather have people talking about that than the escaped tiger," Mom replied.

Pete's words were bittersweet for me, though. While I felt redeemed to have finally got the word out that Henry had been murdered, it was annoying to get no thanks for all my hard work—and to be so shut out of the investigation that I had to hear the recent developments on the news like every other person in America. Plus, something about the quick reveal that the Animal Liberation Front was responsible rubbed me the wrong way. Despite all the claims that evidence had been uncovered showing their link to Henry's death, I hadn't found anything along those lines, and I'd been the first one to investigate.

I told Mom and Dad this. To my surprise, they were as uncomfortable with Pete's accusations as I was.

"I know plenty of people who've been involved with the ALF over the years," Dad said. "They're radical and even destructive, but I have a hard time imagining them doing something like this."

"Then why is FunJungle saying they did?"

"To deflect attention from whoever *did* do it," Mom said.

"Then . . . do they know who did it?"

"Not necessarily," Dad replied. "But finding the real criminal isn't the point of PR. It's making everyone think no one at FunJungle is to blame."

"So then, FunJungle might not really be trying to find the bad guy at all? They might only be trying to find someone to take the fall?"

"Possibly."

"But then the real bad guy gets away."

"Not if we can help it," Dad said.

So we set off to learn answers to the questions Dad had posed: How many animals had died at FunJungle, and what was the metal groove in Hippo River?

I was thrilled to have Dad home and helping the investigation. Even though Summer had lent a hand, things were different with my father. Despite the attempts on my life, with him at my side, the investigation felt less dangerous and more like one of our adventures.

Plus, Dad's presence made investigating easier. First, he was highly respected around FunJungle. And simply put, he was an adult.

When you're a kid, everyone's naturally suspicious of you. I know I didn't have the best reputation around FunJungle, but still, if an adult acts like they belong somewhere, more often than not, no one gives them a second glance. As a kid, you stick out. There are plenty of places you're not supposed to go. There are plenty of questions you can't get away with asking. It's very hard to be taken seriously when everyone's wondering where your mother is.

Dad didn't even have to make up a story to be allowed into the veterinary hospital. He simply pushed the buzzer, waved at the security camera and said, "Hey, Roz, it's me."

Roz quickly buzzed both of us in, then greeted us with a warm smile. "Welcome back!" she cooed to Dad. "How was China?"

"Wonderful," Dad said, and then regaled her with a few amazing tales of giant pandas to get her in a good mood. Dad had a way with women—particularly older women like Roz. They'd just stare at him dreamily as he told his stories. (Mom always said they were imaging themselves thirty years younger.) If Roz had any idea we'd nearly been munched at the party the night before, she didn't show it; she just hung on every word.

Once Dad had her really hooked, he smoothly segued to the task at hand. "I could talk to you all day about this, but we both have work to do. I was told you had a list of all the animals that have died at FunJungle."

Roz reacted, more curious than suspicious. "What do you need that for?"

"McCracken wants photographic documentation of every animal that's come to FunJungle. His office gave me a list of every animal that's been shipped here, but they said it's not completely accurate because it doesn't take into account the animals that have died. I don't want to go running around all day looking for an animal that no longer exists, so they sent me here for the list."

"I see. Only, I don't have any list like that."

"You don't?"

"No. No one ever told me to keep one."

"Could you remember all the animals that died?" I asked.

Roz grimaced, finding the thought of doing this distasteful. "I suppose . . ."

"It'd be a great help," Dad said, flashing his best smile.

That put Roz over the edge. "Well, let's see. Sadly, there have been quite a few. First, there was Carl the Capybara. Such a shame. He was a real sweetheart. So adorable. I think he had some sort of gastric disorder."

Roz's true love for animals was definitely showing through. A capybara is the world's biggest rodent. It looks more like a compacted Airedale than a giant rat, but I'd still never heard anyone refer to one as a "sweetheart" before.

"And then there was Sidney the Sloth. I never got to know her. She got some sort of infection in transit and died en route. I'm sure she was lovely, though. All sloths are."

"She died before she got here, but they still named her?" Dad asked.

"Oh no, darling. *I* named her. I name all the animals, no matter what. Sidney's so much nicer than calling her Sloth Number 6, don't you think?"

"I suppose," Dad said, though I could tell he didn't mean it.

"Then there was Alistair . . ."

"Let me guess," I said. "An alligator?"

"No. An anaconda. I'm not partial to snakes myself, but he was darling. Unfortunately, some foolish cargo employee let his tail get crushed during delivery. It got infected, and by the time he got here, it was too late to save him."

Dad was growing concerned now. Not because of the deaths, but something about them. "I don't need to know the details behind how they all died," he said. "I only need to know their, uh . . . names."

"Let's see. There was Harriet the Howler Monkey, Oswald the Ocelot, Agnes the Agouti, Wally the Wildebeest, Andrea the Anteater, and Jerry the Jaguar. Plus, there were quite a lot of little creatures that died en route, frogs and fish and such, but I'm afraid I don't have names for them all. Doc didn't autopsy the small ones. He just had them buried, I think."

I doubted this last part was true; it was probably something Doc had told her to protect her delicate sensibilities. As much as Doc liked animals, he couldn't take the time to bury every one that died. He got rid of the small ones the way most people did—by flushing them down the toilet.

"That's quite all right," Dad told Roz. "You've been extremely helpful. Thanks for your time."

"Feel free to come by anytime," Roz cooed.

The moment we were out the door, Dad asked me, "Did you notice what all those animals had in common?"

I nodded. "Except for the wildebeest, they're all from the Amazon rain forest."

Dad smiled, proud of me. "Exactly."

"That's suspicious, right?"

"Extremely. First, that's a very long list of large animals to die in such a short time. But even if the deaths *were* natural, the probability is that you'd have dead animals from random places all over the world. Instead, we have a pattern. Almost every large animal that died is from the exact same region. And that suggests something's wrong here."

"What about the wildebeest?"

"He's probably not significant. I'm betting he truly died from natural causes."

"But all the others were murdered?"

"I didn't say that. But I'd bet good money they didn't die for the reasons Roz says they did."

"You think *Roz* is in on this . . . ?"

"No. I think she's been lied to."

"But the only person who does the autopsies is Doc. . . ."

"I know."

I frowned. "I can't imagine Doc killing all those animals. Sometimes, I can imagine him killing *people*. . . . But never animals."

"Same with me. And I'm not saying he did. But I'll guarantee he knows something about all this."

"He's probably in the hospital right now. Why don't we go back and talk to him?"

"All in good time," Dad said. "There'll be plenty of opportunities to talk to Doc. Right now, we have to find out about that metal groove in Hippo River, and we only have a limited time to do it."

16 · BAD PLANS

What Dad meant was, to learn about the groove, he wanted to look at the blueprints for Hippo River. Unfortunately, the blueprints were in the administration building, which had the tightest security of any building at FunJungle. They didn't use security guards like Large Marge there; they used tough ex-military guys who wore crew cuts and constant frowns. The men were armed only with Tasers—guns were deemed inappropriate at a theme park, even one in Texas—but every one of them looked like he was itching for the chance to use his. I'd always assumed the extra security was because J.J. McCracken had his office in that building, but now I began to wonder if there was something inside that J.J. wanted protected.

Given their reputations, Mom and Dad could talk their

way into pretty much any zoo building, but the administration building was different. It was staffed with people who really didn't care about animals or the people who studied them; they cared about things like daily operations and profit margins. They were people like Martin del Gato, Pete Thwacker and his PR department, designers, architects, and a staggering number of lawyers. Most of the zookeepers had never been inside it. Neither had I—or Mom or Dad. The people who worked in administration might have been suspicious of our presence in the building, particularly in the rooms we had to enter, so Mom and Dad had decided we should only visit when there would be almost no one inside: during Henry's funeral.

It wasn't as though all the employees *wanted* to go to Henry's funeral; there were probably plenty of folks in administration who'd never even bothered to go see Henry when he was alive. But J.J. McCracken wanted the funeral to be an event. He and Pete envisioned a huge crowd of grieving employees and guests that would make for great television—and thus reinforce the image of FunJungle as a place that truly cared about its animals. "It ought to look like Princess Diana's funeral," J.J. had reportedly said. "But bigger, if possible."

Lots of employees had grumbled that this was ridiculous, but most agreed to go anyhow for two reasons: It was paid time that they wouldn't have to work—and there was going to be an open bar at the reception.

Even though the administration building would be virtually empty, though, we still had to get in. And to do that, we needed the help of the one person the security staff would easily turn a blind eye to: Summer McCracken.

With Mom and Dad's permission, I'd sent a huge e-mail to Summer the night before, detailing where we were with the case and what we needed her help for. She'd sent back only two words in response: *I'm in.*

The funeral was to take place just outside of FunJungle. J.J. had decided he didn't want the actual grave within the park itself; he felt it would be morbid—and give the impression he wasn't taking good care of his animals. Finding the perfect spot had been a challenge; a team of PR men, geologists, engineers, landscape architects, and funeral planners had spent much of the last few days prowling the entire property for it. Finally, they had settled upon a small grove of trees to the side of the Albert Aardvark parking lot. It wasn't that beautiful a spot, but J.J. had promised to spruce it up postfuneral with a small shrine to Henry where his fans could visit even after park hours. More importantly, the proximity to the parking lot allowed easy access for funeral guests, any news channel that wanted to film the proceedings—and the industrial crane that was needed to lower Henry and his coffin into the grave.

J.J. had been disappointed about the crane, believing

pallbearers would have been far more dignified. When Martin had pointed out that the coffin alone weighed a ton, J.J. had suggested using elephants. Martin had finally convinced him that even elephants couldn't hoist the huge coffin—only a crane could—so J.J., determined to bring some nobility back to the proceedings, had cajoled the Archbishop of Houston to preside over them. (I'd heard that the Archbishop had balked at first, considering it undignified—until J.J. had hinted that he might recruit a prominent rabbi instead. Apparently, lack of dignity was less important to the Archbishop than letting the world think Henry was Jewish.)

The funeral was planned for noon, so we'd arranged to meet Summer outside the administration building at eleven thirty. It was going to have to be a quick encounter. J.J. and the PR department had insisted on Summer's presence by her father's side for the ceremony. Otherwise, every magazine in the country would be running articles asking where she was.

The eleven thirty target quickly fell by the wayside, however. The funeral wasn't going to start anywhere near on time. The park staff had prepared for every eventuality except one: that the funeral might be *too* popular. Thousands more people had showed up than expected. It hadn't been necessary for J.J. to badger his employees into attending the funeral after all; evidently, there were legions of Henry fans who needed closure. The crowd filled the Albert Aardvark, Betty Baboon, and Carla Camel parking lots—and still, there was a half-mile line of cars backed up down the entrance road. A few devoted mourners had actually camped out the night before, staking out prime locations close to the gravesite. Now everyone jostled for space in the steaming parking lot while the special events team scrambled about, trying to get more speakers so the entire crowd could hear the ceremony—and more Port-a-Potties so everyone could pee; as it was, hundreds of guests were already slipping off into the woods around the parking lot to relieve themselves. Meanwhile, even J.J. McCracken's family got stuck in the traffic jam.

Mom, Dad, and I could do little but lurk around the administration building while doing our best to look like we *weren't* lurking. Mom told me to stop checking my phone because it looked suspicious, but I couldn't help it. I kept expecting Summer to text us an ETA, but she never did.

Although I was pleased Summer had agreed to help us, I was beginning to find her lack of communication annoying. Despite her promise to tell me the "long story" of what had happened after she and her father had fled the tiger the night before, she hadn't. And short of one brief text—*R U OK*—she hadn't made much of an effort to check up on me. If *she'd* been the one who'd nearly been eaten by a tiger, I'd have beaten down her door to make sure she was all right. Mom suggested that perhaps Summer hadn't been able to get away from her bodyguards long enough to text or call, but I didn't believe that: Summer had been able to elude her bodyguards for an entire day when she wanted to. That she hadn't been able to find a few minutes to reach out to me made me think she didn't value our friendship as highly as I did.

So by the time Summer finally arrived, I was feeling pretty angry. It was nearly noon, and she was flushed from the heat. Her usual pink had been deemed inappropriate for such a solemn day; instead, she wore a stylish black dress—although it was accented with a pink scarf. "Sorry," she gasped. "I had to ditch a horde of fans. We gotta make this quick. Dad thinks I just went to get a Coke."

With that, she led us past the main entrance of the administration building and around the side to a loading dock where supplies went in and trash came out. There was a security keypad there. Summer quickly typed in her special code and the door clicked open.

As we slipped into the building, I couldn't keep my thoughts to myself any longer. "So, are you ever gonna tell us what happened last night?"

If Summer realized I was upset, she didn't show it. "Oh, man, I'm sorry about that." She led us into a staircase and practically sprinted up it. "Daddy didn't mean to leave you guys. He thought you were with us, and by the time he realized you weren't . . . Well, it looked like your father had things under control."

I found her glibness aggravating. This wasn't exactly the long story she'd promised—and there was something strange about the way she said it, as though she didn't believe what she was saying herself. I glanced at my parents and saw they weren't buying it either.

"And you just left the party after that?" I asked.

"Well, there really *wasn't* any party after that, was there?" Summer burst through a door onto the third floor and quickly led us down the hall. "We didn't leave the park, though. We snuck back out through the keeper's route, notified security, and then came back here. Daddy spent the whole night on the phone trying to take care of the mess."

Our plan to come to the administration building during the funeral had worked perfectly. There didn't appear to be another person inside. It was so deserted, I half expected to see tumbleweeds blowing through the halls.

"Do you know anything about the investigation into the tiger's escape?" Mom asked.

Summer stopped outside a nondescript door. It was marked only with a room number—333—and another security keypad. "Not much. Daddy and Buck are playing this pretty close to the chest. . . . Although I do know Buck thinks the ALF has an inside man at the park."

"Why's that?" I asked.

"How else could they get the ladder into the tiger pit *before* the party?" Summer checked her watch, then made a worried gasp. "I've really gotta motor," she said, then typed her security code on the keypad. The door clicked open. "Let me know what you find," she told us, then bolted down the hall before we could ask another question.

Once again, the brevity of our encounter made me feel as though Summer was hiding something. Before, when I'd spent time with Summer, I'd always enjoyed every minute. But now I felt irritated.

I wasn't doing a good job of hiding my feelings, because Mom put a hand on my shoulder and asked, "Is something wrong?"

I couldn't bring myself to admit the truth; the feelings I had embarrassed me. So instead, I said, "I just wish we had some more time with her. I wanted to ask her what evidence Buck has against the ALF."

"Why?" Dad asked. "It wouldn't matter."

"What do you mean?" I asked.

"I'm sure Summer only knows what Buck and J.J. want her to know," Dad said. "And that might not necessarily be the truth."

We entered room 333. It was a long room with a bank of windows looking out over the entrance to the park. Beyond the front gates, we could see the sea of mourners who had gathered for Henry's funeral.

"You don't think *anything* we've been told about the ALF is true?" I asked.

"Frankly, I don't trust J.J. McCracken one bit," Dad replied.

I thought about asking him if he trusted Summer, but for some reason, I didn't. Maybe I was afraid of hearing his answer.

At both ends of the room, the walls were filled with banks of very thin drawers, each only about three inches tall, but four feet wide. In the middle of the room was an extremely long conference table. Past the far end of the table was a huge glass box atop a large pedestal. Inside the box was a model of something.

We all headed over to it. On the way, I glanced out the window. I could see Summer three stories below, sprinting back toward the funeral, moving surprisingly fast for a girl in dress shoes.

The model in the box was FunJungle.

Well, it was sort of FunJungle. FunJungle with changes. They were so dramatic, I instantly forgot all about Summer.

The most obvious difference between the model and the

real FunJungle was the tower. It was the tallest structure in the park by far, jutting several inches higher than anything else. And, in case people might not notice a giant tower in the middle of the Texas plains, it had been painted a glaring maraschino cherry red. It was obviously a lookout tower, an uglier version of the Eiffel Tower, with a big flat disc jammed on the top like a crashed flying saucer.

"What do you think that is?" I asked.

"Probably a rotating restaurant," Mom answered flatly, as though she didn't approve. "Ever hear anyone mention a big tower that's supposed to be built in the park?"

Dad shook his head. "What's in this spot now? A picnic area, right?"

"There's picnic tables, yes," Mom replied. "They still call it a viewpoint, although it's maybe ten feet higher than any other spot in the park. It's got one of those idiotic African names the PR department made up. Mooboodooboo Mountain or something."

"So they still might be planning on building this, then," Dad said. "That's right in the middle of the park. If they were going to put an animal exhibit there, they would have done it already."

I noticed something on the far side of the model. "Mom. Dad. Look at this."

I was looking at SafariLand. Right alongside the monorail, a new track had been added. Only, this track was twisted, with loops and plunges in it.

"Oh, no . . ." Mom gasped.

It was a roller coaster. One of the new steel kinds that had only a few giant posts to support the winding track. It went right through the safari area. Some thoughtful designer had even put a herd of toy gazelles grazing under the corkscrew loop.

We quickly scanned the model, looking for other discrepancies between it and the real FunJungle. There was a river rafting ride near Carnivore Canyon, a smaller coaster in the children's zoo, a log flume by the Swamp—and boats in Hippo River.

I couldn't believe what I was seeing—and when I looked at Mom and Dad, they seemed to be feeling the same sense of shock.

"This is disgusting," Dad said.

"It's worse than disgusting," Mom replied. "It's *evil*. How could they . . . ?"

"Maybe they're not really going to build them," I said hopefully. "Maybe they've changed their minds about all this."

"The fact that they've even *thought* about it is bad enough," Mom snorted.

Dad headed toward the closest wall of thin drawers. "Let's see how serious they are," he said.

Mom and I joined him. We all yanked open drawers.

Inside, laid out flat, were blueprints. Mine, at the bottom right corner of the wall, were for the zebra paddock.

Dad was at the other side of the wall. "I've got the aardvark pen," he said. "What do you have, Teddy?"

"Zebras."

"Must be organized alphabetically," Mom said. She went to where she guessed the H's would be. It only took her two tries to find what she wanted. "Here we go. Hippo River."

There were a lot of blueprints, as though the exhibit had been redesigned several times. Mom pulled them all out and spread them on the conference table.

Some showed Hippo River as I knew it, detailing the design of the enclosures, the thickness of the glass walls, or the specifications for the pumps that controlled the water filtration. On one, some of the problems had been noted in red ink. Several circles were drawn around the backwater where Henry had so often chosen to relieve himself, above which someone had written "How do we get rid of this???"

Other plans had a very different representation of the river. The overall structure was the same, but what was going on around it had changed dramatically. It was all summed up by a cheerful artist's rendition of what the Hippo River Water Safari should look like. Several gaily-colored tour boats motored through the paddocks, filled with joyful tourist families who gasped in amazement as friendly hippos swam around them. In the background was the boarding station, where a throng of tourists seemed only too happy to stand in line for this incredible adventure.

The picture was ridiculously unrealistic. In the first place, the crowd didn't look like any group of tourists I'd ever seen in FunJungle. No one in line was shoving or sweating. All of the children were behaving like angels. None of the boat passengers appeared the slightest bit worried by the two-ton creatures surfacing right next to them. Everyone seemed to have stepped right out of a Norman Rockwell painting. An accurate representation of FunJungle guests would have shown one of the children trying to feed cotton candy to the hippo—and several adults tossing garbage in the river.

Far more inaccurate were the hippos themselves, peeking from the water, mouths wide open, almost smiling, like it was wonderful fun to watch boats churn by all day long. In Africa, the only time a hippo emerged from the water with its mouth open was when it was attacking. Usually they lurked right beneath the surface, their beady little eyes poking out above the water, watching the world in an unsettling way. There was no way any self-respecting hippo would allow a constant parade of boats to motor through its home. I couldn't imagine what the ride's designers *thought* the hippos would do, but hippos in Africa were well known for attacking boats, often flipping them or knocking holes in the bottom. And now, J.J. McCracken was hoping to take tourists by the thousands right through their territory.

"They can't really be thinking of doing this," Mom said, although she sounded like she was trying to convince herself. "These have to be old plans. Surely, *someone* had to have the sense to point out what a disaster this would be."

"I don't think so," Dad said sadly. "They must still think this is possible. That's what the metal groove is for."

He placed another set of blueprints on the table. These showed how the boat system would work. The boats didn't have motors. They were pulled along a track. A thick wire led from the bow of each to a chain tucked in the metal groove—the chain I'd felt when I'd been looking for the murder weapon. As it moved through the groove, it tugged the boats along.

"They want to run machinery through an exhibit with live animals?" Mom gasped. "How long do you think it'll be before a hippo ends up caught in the wires? A day? This has to be the worst idea in theme park history."

"Not quite." Dad slapped another set of plans on the table. "This is worse."

These were for the rafting ride, which was to be set inside the Asia Plains. The artist's representation showed another group of irrepressibly happy people strapped into eight seats on a huge circular raft—sort of an inner tube designed for public transportation—which careened down an artificial river. Although the water was stained Ty-D-Bowl blue, several dozen antelope contentedly drank from it, ignoring the constant parade of tourists. A small herd of elephants joyfully sprayed the boats with their trunks, unfazed by the deadly crocodiles sunning themselves nearby.

"Maybe they're fake," I said hopefully. "Like robots."

"There's no robots in the blueprints," Mom said. "I can't believe this. They expect the animals to *drink* this water? Do you know how many chemicals they use on a ride like this?"

"It won't work, will it?" I asked.

"Not the way they expect it to, no. But after a few animals die, they'll probably find a way. They'll put in fake animals and try to convince everyone they're real. Or hell, maybe they'll drug the real ones so they don't attack the boats."

"But even *building* it's going to be bad for the animals, right?" I asked. "Won't having a rafting ride or a roller coaster in the middle of their homes affect them?"

"In the worst possible way." Mom angrily stared out the window at FunJungle. "J.J. lied to us. He told us that this park was all about the animals. About the research. He crows about conservation and providing the highest quality care . . . but it's all just lip service."

I noticed another set of blueprints. They were for an array of fireworks cannons to be used for a "FunJungle Fireworks Fantasy." While not as insidious as building a roller coaster in the breeding grounds, the idea of doing a nightly fireworks display was still dangerous. Twenty minutes of loud explosions every evening would probably stress every animal in the park into having a heart attack.

"J.J. has advisors, right?" I asked. "*Someone* must have told him this would be bad for the animals."

"I'm sure someone has," Dad replied. "That doesn't mean he has to listen to them."

"But why would J.J. plan this? I thought he wanted to build the world's best zoo."

"No," Dad said. "He wants to build the world's *most profitable* zoo. My guess is, he's testing the waters now. Seeing if the animals bring enough guests through the gates to make him rich. And if they don't, he'll build something that will."

"He said he was different," Mom spat. "But he's not. These plans are proof: J.J. McCracken cares more about his money than his animals."

A funeral dirge suddenly blared through the speakers outside. The ceremony for Henry had finally begun. Startled by the sudden burst of sound, I dropped a roll of blueprints. It rolled under the conference table and I got down on my knees to grab it.

"We need to tell someone about this," Mom said. "We need to stop them from going through with it."

"Who are we supposed to tell?" Dad asked. "McCracken owns the park. He can do anything he wants. These plans might be cruel and idiotic, but they're not illegal."

"Unlike breaking and entering," someone said.

I peered through the legs of the conference table. Several men had entered the room. Most wore the sensible shoes of building security—although one wore cowboy boots. Those went with the southern drawl I'd heard: Buck Grassley.

"Arrest them," he said.

17 · THE FUNERAL

The security guards rushed my parents. No one noticed I was under the table.

"We're not breaking the law!" Dad protested. "We're allowed to be here! We're park employees."

"You're covert members of the Animal Liberation Front," Buck shot back. "Caught red-handed plotting another attack."

"That's a lie and you know it!" Mom shouted.

"I can prove it, should I need to." I could imagine Buck smiling as he said it.

Mom and Dad were unarmed and outnumbered. From under the table, I watched in horror as they were quickly subdued. I could hear the metal clicks of handcuffs being snapped on their wrists. More than anything in the world, I wanted to protect my parents, to attack the legs I saw before me, bite and kick if I had to, but I knew it'd be futile. I'd end up getting arrested too. Unfortunately, I had no idea what else to do.

Mom and Dad dug their feet into the carpet, struggling to keep from being dragged away. Mom pleaded with the security guards, urging them to think for themselves and let her go. Dad was shouting at Buck: "You're making a big mistake here! McCracken's going to have your ass when he finds out about this!"

"McCracken?" Buck laughed. "Who do you think sent me here?"

Dad made a last attempt to wriggle free. He almost did it, but the guards overpowered him. They all flailed about for a moment, and then one fell to the floor.

He landed on his hands and knees. . . . And found himself staring right at me. "There's a kid!" he gasped.

"Run!" Dad yelled.

I was already on my way. I burst from under the table, gunning for the door.

Buck Grassley's satisfied grin quickly gave way to shock as I appeared. He lunged for me, but fell short. His fingers brushed the back of my neck as I sprinted into the hall.

"Go, Teddy!" Mom called out. "Don't worry about us!"

I wanted to turn back to her, to see her and Dad, but

there was no time. Buck and his security men were right on my tail.

So I ran. Through the hall, down the stairs, and out the loading dock doors. I put everything I had into it. I had no idea where I was going. I only knew that if I wanted to help my parents, I couldn't get caught.

The security men stayed right behind me. They were all in great shape, as fast as I was. Even Buck proved to have surprising stamina for an old man.

FunJungle was almost empty. Nearly every guest had decided the funeral was too important to miss. Normally, there would have been ample crowds to lose my pursuers in, but that day, it appeared there were *only* security guards in the park. Two more emerged from behind Hippo River and tried to cut me off.

So I ran toward the only cover I could think of. The funeral.

The Archbishop was beginning his eulogy as I exited the park. "Ladies and gentlemen, friends and families, we are gathered here today to honor the memory of a wonderful hippopotamus. . . ."

The sea of mourners stretched past the front gates. I plunged in.

It was a strange crowd, to say the least. Some people stood reverently and wept. Others had merely set up folding chairs and brought a picnic lunch. Some people wore somber black. Others were dressed from head-to-toe in Henry paraphernalia. In the distance, at the front of it all, was a stage where the most distinguished guests sat. I could barely make out J.J. and Summer, along with Summer's mother, Martin del Gato, the governor of Texas, and both state senators. The Archbishop stood before them all at a podium while behind him, the crane slowly winched Henry's giant coffin off a flatbed truck and maneuvered it toward the grave.

"It is with great sadness that we mark Henry's passing, and beseech you, O Lord, to welcome him into Hippo Heaven. . . ."

I did my best to slip lightly through the crowd. The security men weren't nearly as reverent. They elbowed mourners aside and stomped on people's picnics. "Stop that kid!" Buck ordered. "He's wanted in connection with Henry's murder!"

Thankfully, only the people within close range heard him. The speakers were cranked so loud, his order was mostly drowned out by the thundering eulogy.

Still, I was in trouble. Many people were too stunned to act, but a few were spurred to action. One burly guy almost got me, but I gave him the slip by ducking through a small cluster of orthodox Jews reciting the kaddish.

"Henry was no mere hippo. He was a friend to millions of people he never met. A beacon of hope to the world. An ambassador of love and honor from the animal kingdom to our own . . ."

Another mourner made a grab for me. I now realized that coming into the crowd was a mistake. I had to get back out again, but that wouldn't be easy. I couldn't see very far ahead: Almost everyone was standing and I only came up to their chests. For all I knew, the sea of mourners went on another mile in every direction except the one I'd come from—and going back was out of the question because Buck's men were right behind me.

The only thing I could see was the crane. I knew no one was gathered around that. Pete had made sure there was a wide empty swath underneath the path the coffin would travel, just in case something went wrong.

So I went that way. Buck kept shouting at people to stop me. Occasionally, someone turned from the ceremony long enough to try. Hands lashed out at me, but I kept ducking and jiving. One hefty woman in a commemorative Henry T-shirt managed to snag my arm, but I wrenched her pinkie back and she released me with a howl.

"As many of you know, Henry didn't always have an easy life. FunJungle rescued him from a run-down circus where he was treated poorly. But luckily, his years of struggle and torment were rewarded with a wonderful life here, in a state-of-the-art facility more suited to a hippopotamus of his caliber. . . ."

Toward the front of the crowd, I encountered the die-hard mourners: the Henry devotees who'd camped out to get the best spots. These people all stood in respect. Many were openly weeping. Each had been completely fooled by FunJungle's PR machine into believing Henry was a wonderful creature. "Why did *he* have to die?" I overheard someone sob. "Why Henry, when so many terrible animals are allowed to live?"

Everyone was so tightly packed together, it became much harder for me to slip through them. They had invested so much time and energy to get their good viewing positions, they didn't want to let anyone get in front of them and reacted with indignation as I shoved past. As tough as the going was for me, though, it was much harder for the security agents. I heard several get gut-checked by annoyed mourners who thought they were jockeying for a better spot. It was stifling in the crowd, but I could see daylight ahead. I forced my way between two bawling women and found myself in the open, right at the base of the crane.

The stage wasn't far away. Almost everyone's eyes were locked on the Archbishop, although I could see Summer bent over with her face in her hands. At first it looked like she was crying, but then I realized the truth: She was trying not to laugh at the overblown eulogy.

Two more security guards charged at me from behind the podium. Buck had called for backup.

I could hear Buck himself not far back in the crowd, informing everyone that I was connected to Henry's death. A few mourners came at me with white-hot hatred in their eyes.

I was surrounded. There was only one way to go. I grabbed the crane's tread and scrambled up.

The Archbishop's voice suddenly caught in the midst of his eulogy. I was now out in the open enough to be noticed. On the stage, everyone turned toward me. Martin was livid. Summer was shocked. I couldn't quite make out what J.J. was thinking.

A security guard's hand brushed my ankle. He was coming up after me, a beefy guy with tiny, mean eyes. "Give yourself up or we'll do this the hard way!" he threatened. Then he snatched his Taser from his holster and flipped it on.

Electricity crackled between its contact points.

I kept climbing, though I was running out of room. I quickly reached the cab where the operator worked the controls. The crane stretched ten stories higher, but that was a dead end and there was no way I was going up it.

The cab's door suddenly swung open, nearly clocking me in the head. The crane operator lunged out, trying to grab me himself. "Get off, kid! You're not supposed to—"

I leapt aside, barely dodging his grasp, just as the guard behind me made a jab with his Taser. He missed me—and hit the crane operator in the arm. The operator gagged as 3,000 volts of electricity shot through him, then collapsed backwards into the cab, landing on the controls. A lever with a bright red handle shifted beneath his weight.

There was a loud twang as the main support cable was unlocked, then a whoosh as it quickly snaked up the crane.

Thousands of mourners looked up in horror at once. Then they all screamed as Henry's coffin dropped.

"Jesus Christ!" the Archbishop gasped, and then dove for cover.

I scrambled into the safety of the crane's cab.

The coffin smashed into the ground and burst open—as did its contents.

Despite Martin's best efforts to keep Henry cold, the hippo's corpse had been slowly rotting for days. And it had spent the last few hours slowly roasting in the Texas sun. It was probably bloated from the heat and ready to rupture anyhow, but the sudden impact with the ground made it explode. A wave of putrid flesh and bodily fluids rained upon the crowd. The mourners who'd been so devoted as to get the best seats possible were now in prime position to get the most disgusting souvenirs of Henry's death imaginable: a piece of the actual hippo himself.

Something that looked like a gall bladder splattered on the window of the crane's cab.

The cab had protected me from the worst of it, unlike everyone else within a hundred-foot radius. The security guard who'd tried to Taser me had been hit head-on. Covered with rotten innards, he instantly forgot about me, screaming as he ran for the showers.

The crowd below was now a sea of shrieking, disgusted people. Some desperately wiped themselves off; some stood rigid in shock; quite a lot were vomiting.

While everyone was distracted, I made my break. I leapt from the cab onto the treads of the crane, nearly losing my balance as they were now slick with Henry's guts. The smell from them was overpowering, far worse than it had been a few days before. I fought the urge to blow chunks, dropped to the ground, and fled into the open countryside beyond the stage.

I only had a second to glance at Summer. The stage had taken a direct hit. It—and most of the dignitaries—were coated in flesh. However, Summer and her family were surprisingly unsullied. Their bodyguards had thrown themselves atop them as protection right before the hippo blew.

Summer locked eyes with me as I ran past. She didn't look happy to see me—and in that moment, my worst fears were confirmed:

She'd turned me in.

I didn't want to believe it, but it made sense. Buck said

J.J. McCracken had sent him to arrest my family, but the only way J.J. could have known we were in the blueprint room was from Summer. If a guard had spotted my family on the security cameras, he would have notified Buck directly, not J.J. Summer's father was at the root of all that was wrong at FunJungle. He was planning to turn the animal exhibits into theme rides. He controlled the security force. He was the one who'd proposed that the ALF was behind the attacks—but who also had the ability and the money to fake any evidence he needed to prove it. Maybe Summer had known J.J. was behind everything all along—or maybe she'd only found out recently. But given the choice between bringing down her family or mine . . . she'd chosen mine.

I hightailed it toward the scrubby forest that surrounded FunJungle. The splatter of Henry's remains ended abruptly beyond the stage, with only the occasional fleck of red gunk strewn on the ground. I left it all behind, disappearing into the trees.

I had no idea where I was going. I just ran.

My parents had been arrested on trumped-up charges. J.J. probably intended to pin the murder of Henry and everything else that had happened on them. Even though *our* lives were the ones that had been in danger.

And Summer had betrayed me.

I couldn't think of another person I could trust. I couldn't even come up with anyone else I considered a friend. But now I had to find *someone*. I was only a kid in way over my head. I needed to solve the crime and present the evidence to someone who could help my parents, but I couldn't do that alone. I'd been on the case for days now and I still had no idea who had killed Henry—or freed the mamba—or helped the tiger escape. Maybe J.J. had—or maybe he was just looking for someone to frame for it. Did his plans to build the theme park rides tie in to Henry's death somehow—or were they two separate works of evil? And if J.J. wasn't the killer, who was? Everyone I'd met seemed to have a motive. Anyone could have done it.

I suddenly realized I was alone. I'd left the crowd far behind, so far that it was almost quiet. If anyone was still chasing me, I'd have heard them coming.

I was too exhausted to run anymore. I bent over, clutching my stomach, having no idea where I was or how far I'd come. I was lost and on my own. I'd never felt so helpless in my life.

The world spun around me. For a few seconds, I thought I might pass out. . . .

I looked for something to focus on and steady myself. To my surprise, there was a rabbit sitting a few feet away. It had frozen in fright at the sight of me, not daring to twitch a muscle. It occurred to me that I'd done exactly the same thing the night before, facing down the tiger—and a few nights before that while watching the autopsy.

The autopsy . . .

I was struck by a flash of insight.

There was one more lead. And maybe, if I was right, there *was* someone I could trust.

I wasn't quite sure, but it didn't seem I had any other choice. And the more I looked at the pieces, the more everything seemed to make sense.

I was still scared and worried, but now, at least, I felt a tiny glimmer of hope.

I scrambled up a tree. I'd run much farther than I'd realized. FunJungle was about a mile away. I could see the crane jutting into the air. I could barely hear the distant screams of panic and horror from the funeral. And I could smell Henry.

I dropped to the ground and headed back toward the park. I couldn't spare the time to be cautious. My parents were in trouble, and if I wanted to help them, I didn't have long to solve the case.

I found Doc out at the farthest end of SafariLand, where he'd just overseen the birth of a wildebeest. He was sitting in the shade of a cedar tree, watching the baby struggle to its feet for the first time. Despite such a joyous event, he appeared quite sad, his eyes rimmed with red, as though he was close to crying.

He'd skipped the funeral, of course. Doc knew the whole thing was a sham and would have had no tolerance for it.

It hadn't been too hard to find him, even though I couldn't show my face inside the park. I'd simply called the vet hospital looking for him. Roz was at the funeral, which was probably lucky for me; I was afraid she might recognize my voice and alert Buck. Instead, there was a temp who happily informed me where Doc had gone.

SafariLand was the easiest part of FunJungle to sneak into. Given its massive size, it was difficult for security to patrol. I circled through the woods to the back fence and found a place where I could scramble up a tree and drop over. Then I just snuck around until I spotted Doc's truck. Much of the time I was right out in the open, but I was so far from the viewing areas no one could tell I was only a kid. Instead, everyone probably assumed I was one of the keepers who occasionally wandered through.

To my surprise, Doc showed none of the gruffness he usually greeted me with. Instead he appeared strangely relieved to see me. "How'd you get here? Buck's turning this whole county over looking for you."

"How'd you know?"

"It's all over the park's radio channel. His men are combing the woods, the trailer park, everything."

"They got Mom and Dad."

Doc nodded sadly. "I heard that, too."

"J.J.'s saying they're members of the ALF, but they're not."

"I know. I . . . I'm sorry. I had no idea this would happen. Otherwise I'd never have . . ." He trailed off, at a loss for words.

Suddenly I understood. "You knew I was in the auditorium during the autopsy, didn't you?"

Doc nodded. "I saw you up in the lighting grid after you made that noise. I knew Martin would prevent me from doing anything with the information that Henry was killed, so I let you know. But I never thought *you'd* investigate. I figured you'd tell the police. . . ."

"I tried. They didn't care."

"Or your parents. I hoped there was a way to get someone to look into Henry's death, to wonder *why* somebody would murder a hippopotamus. I just didn't realize how far up it all went. . . ."

"You mean to J.J.?"

Doc scratched his chin thoughtfully, watching the baby wildebeest as it took its first stumbling steps. "I don't know. He's not the cleanest businessman in the world, I'll tell you that. He's never up to exactly what he says he is."

"He's planning to build thrill rides in the park."

Doc turned back to me, stunned. "Where?"

"Through the exhibits." I quickly explained how I'd found out and what had happened to my parents as a result.

Doc shook his head. "I should have known. I *knew* this place was too good to be true." He spat in the dirt. "So your parents told you to come to me?"

"No. But I figured you might know what was going on."

"How so?"

"You do all the autopsies around here."

Doc stared at me a long moment, then broke into a smile. "Your mother always said you were smart."

"Why are all the animals that died from South America?"

"Because that's where the emeralds are from."

That revelation caught me off guard. It took me a moment to collect my thoughts. "Emeralds? What emeralds?"

"Sorry. I should start at the beginning." Doc rubbed his eyes. He looked tired and worn-out, like a man who hadn't slept in a week. Something seemed to be weighing on him. "I think Martin del Gato killed Henry."

Even though I'd considered Martin as a suspect before, I was still surprised to hear his name. "Why?"

"Because he killed all the other animals."

"All the ones from the Amazon?"

Doc held up a hand, signaling me to be quiet. "I'll explain it all. Just sit and listen."

I did as I was told, finding a spot of shade under the tree.

Nearby, the baby wildebeest staggered to its mother and took its first drink of milk from her teats.

"Before FunJungle, Martin ran a dozen other companies for J.J. and they all made money," Doc said. "However, this place was the brass ring. If Martin made it a success, he'd become J.J.'s right-hand man. . . . But if he failed, J.J. would want a fall guy. Now, Martin's a very good businessman.

That's why J.J. picked him. Unfortunately, the zoo business doesn't work like any other business, because at a zoo, your main attractions are alive. Martin didn't get that. He didn't know squat about animals and he didn't bother to learn. He figured they were like cars or soup or detergent. He thought he could make them do whatever he wanted, but of course, he couldn't, and so he made mistakes. . . ."

"Like choosing a hippo for the mascot."

"Right. Every keeper knew that was idiocy, but when they tried to protest, he didn't listen. All those mistakes started to pile up. He made dozens over the years—and each cost money. Exhibits had to be designed over and over again. Construction fell behind schedule. Animals died. The park started to hemorrhage money. Martin cooked the books to hide that from J.J., but he knew he couldn't get away with it for long. So he started looking for a way to line his pockets before he got canned. That's where the emeralds come in."

My phone buzzed. I checked it and saw it was Summer calling. It was the tenth time she'd tried to reach me. I ignored the call and stuffed the phone back in my pocket.

"J.J. owns a jewel-importing business," Doc said. "Martin ran it for a while, so he had contacts at an emerald mine in Venezuela. He arranged for them to smuggle stones to him—and figured out how to get them across the border without anyone noticing."

"The animals," I said.

"Exactly. Customs agents don't pay much attention to animals. Animals can be dangerous. The agents know enough to check their cages for contraband. . . . But they never think to look *inside* the animals. Heck, they'd need an X-ray machine to do it."

"Martin got the emeralds inside the animals? How?"

"The mine set up a shady animal distributor and Martin arranged contracts with FunJungle. Whenever he needed a new shipment of emeralds, he'd send a request for a big animal, like an anaconda or a jaguar. They'd go out and catch one in the wild—which is totally illegal—then do a little surgery, sewing a pouch of jewels inside the animal. Customs never noticed. Of course, the animals usually got sick because the surgery wasn't done right, but that didn't bother Martin. In fact, it made his job easier, because when they died, he had a legitimate reason for having me cut them open to get his emeralds out, rather than having to make one up."

"But why'd you help him?"

Doc wavered a moment, as though he didn't want to admit the next part. "My daughter. She's an actual member of the Animal Liberation Front. She means well, but . . . sometimes, she doesn't think things through. She was involved in that attack on the meat-packing plant last year. She managed to keep anyone from finding out she was involved—except Martin. The jerk listened in on my phone calls and overheard her. Then he blackmailed me. If I didn't do his dirty work, he'd turn Susie in to the FBI."

"That's why you couldn't go public with the news that Henry had been killed if Martin didn't want you to?"

Doc nodded. "I've hated every minute of this. Watching animals die for no good reason and not being able to do a damn thing about it. It goes against everything I believe in. There's been a hundred times when I wanted to call the police, but . . . I love my daughter."

"Was Martin the person in the operating room the day I came there?"

"Yes. I'm sorry for the way I treated you. I was surprised you were there—and with the jack, no less. I probably shouldn't have taken it from you . . . but I panicked. I was afraid Martin would come through the door any moment and see you. That's why I told you to talk to your parents before you did anything else."

I nodded, realizing I'd completely misjudged Doc all along. He hadn't really been angry at me all those times. He'd only wanted me to keep my distance for my own safety. "Did you keep any evidence against Martin?" I asked.

"Tons." Doc pulled out his keychain and unclipped a portable flash drive. "It's all on here. Detailed accounts. Photos. Everything. We need to get it to J.J."

"But I thought you said he was corrupt."

"That doesn't mean he likes people killing his animals. Once you show him that Martin's the real culprit here, he'll make sure justice is served."

"But your daughter . . ."

Doc shook his head. "I can't protect her anymore. Your parents are in trouble now because of all this. *You're* in trouble. I can't sit by and watch anymore. My daughter made her mistakes; now she'll have to pay for them."

He got to his feet, looking like it was a struggle, as though he was burdened by what he was about to do to his daughter.

I almost felt bad about what I had to say next. "The thing is, Doc, none of this proves Martin killed Henry."

Doc paused, thinking. "No, I suppose it doesn't. But I do have proof that Martin's been responsible for many other animal deaths here—and I know he hated Henry. He always called that hippo the greatest mistake he'd ever made. He couldn't wait for him to die. He even fantasized about killing him. I recorded him in my lab one day. The audio clip's on the flash drive too."

I had to admit, it seemed like a pretty good case, although something still bothered me about it all. Before I could say anything, the sound of engines cut through the silence. The newborn wildebeest and its mother looked up, startled, while a herd of impala stampeded away in fear.

Two Land Rovers crested a rise in the distance, coming fast. I instantly knew they meant trouble. No one was supposed to drive quickly inside SafariLand for fear of harming the animals.

"Security," Doc said. "They must know you're here." He hustled me into his truck. By the time I'd buckled my seat belt, he already had it in gear. We rocketed away in a cloud of dust.

Behind us, the Security Land Rovers gunned their engines and took up the chase.

The dirt roads in SafariLand hadn't been built to drive quickly on. They were mostly used by the safari vehicles, which always had a dozen tourists in them and therefore moved at a top speed of three miles an hour. In fact, FunJungle's designers had demanded that the roads *not* be cared for, as it would help the guests feel like they were really in Africa. Thus, the roads were muddy, pocked with potholes, strewn with rocks and often had animals that weighed half a ton sitting in them. In short, it was extremely dangerous to speed on them—but that's exactly what Doc and I were doing.

We flew over the top of a hill so fast we left the ground, only to find a herd of elands blocking our path. Doc swerved wildly to avoid them as they scattered in panic.

I gripped the dashboard so tightly my fingernails scratched the paint. "How are we supposed to get to J.J.?" I asked.

Doc risked turning away from the road ahead for a split second to give me a worried look. "I thought *you* knew how to do that. Aren't you tight with his daughter?"

"I thought I was. But I don't think I can trust her."

"Why not?"

Behind us, the Land Rovers roared over the top of the hill.

"She was the only one who knew we were in the room with the blueprints. And then security just happened to show up there?"

"That doesn't prove she told them."

"Buck said J.J. sent them. How'd J.J. know we were there unless Summer said so?"

"There are other ways. J.J. has this park wired tighter than Fort Knox. How do you think security found you in SafariLand now? Summer didn't tell them that."

I gritted my teeth, unsure of what to believe.

"It couldn't hurt to call her," Doc said. "I don't see that we have many other options. . . . Oh, boy."

We rounded a clump of trees to find a mother rhino with a month-old calf blocking the road. Doc slammed on the brakes, skidding to a stop only a few feet from them. The mother snorted angrily and lowered her head, aiming her horn at us. Rhinos are fiercely protective of their young and have extremely bad eyesight; their eyes are so far to the sides of their head, they can barely see anything in front of them. The mother rhino probably couldn't tell if we were a rival rhino or a hungry lion. All she knew was, we were a threat.

"Hold on," Doc said. "This could get hairy."

He threw the truck into reverse and punched the gas.

The rhino charged.

Despite the fact that it's as aerodynamic as a cinderblock, a rhino can run up to thirty-five miles an hour. The speed of our truck in reverse on that crummy road was less than that. We jounced along backward, Doc trying to steer over his shoulder, while the rhino churned toward us, ready to do damage.

I could hear security's Land Rovers on the other side of the trees.

Doc suddenly cut to the right. His truck slewed wildly through a patch of mud, nearly pitching me out the door.

The Land Rovers rounded the trees.

The rhino thundered past us. Maybe it didn't see us turn—or maybe it perceived the incoming cars as a bigger threat.

The lead Land Rover braked and swerved. The rhino broadsided it. The security guards yelped in surprise as their car upended and toppled onto its side.

The second Land Rover spun out in the mud, nearly slamming into us.

Doc gunned the engine. Our tires spun wildly for a moment before finally catching. We sped off, showering the second Rover—and everyone inside it—with mud.

The rhino wasn't hurt by its crash; it might as well have been bitten by a mosquito. Instead, it got angrier. While the security men hid behind the upended Rover, the rhino jabbed the car with its horn, smashing the exposed engine to bits.

The second Rover resumed the chase, though we'd gained some ground.

I dialed Summer. She answered on the first ring. "Dude! Where've you been?"

"Trying to not get arrested," I said. "How'd Buck know we were in the blueprint room?"

"I screwed up. Apparently, Dad has something built into the system that alerts him whenever I use his security code."

"But you used it before at Hippo River. . . ."

"And he knew. He's known every time I've ever used it. . . . He just never busted me for it."

"So why'd he send Buck after you *this* time?"

"'Cause this time he didn't know it was me. I told him I was getting a Coke—and suddenly someone's breaking into his top-secret blueprint room. He assumed his code had been compromised. He'd already dispatched Buck by the time I got back."

"And you didn't alert us?"

"I didn't know he'd done it! He didn't tell me. The funeral was about to begin."

A family of warthogs darted across the road in front of us. Doc nearly flipped the Rover trying to avoid flattening them.

My stomach did a backflip. "Why'd your dad tell Buck my folks were in the ALF?" I asked.

"What?" Summer gasped. "I don't know anything about that."

"You didn't know he had my parents arrested?"

"No! He . . . I don't think he'd do that."

"Well, he did. Buck arrested them and said your dad had ordered it."

"I don't . . . I can't believe that. That's not right." Summer's confusion sounded genuine. Either she really didn't know what had happened, or she was an incredible actress.

"Where's her father now?" Doc asked, and I repeated the question.

"He's here," Summer replied. "In his office, freaking out. That stunt you pulled at the funeral royally screwed up his day. He's had to offer free lifetime passes to everyone who got splattered by hippo guts."

"See if she can get you to him," Doc said. "As fast as possible."

"Me?" I asked. "You're not coming?"

"I don't think I can get through *that.*" Doc pointed ahead of us.

The entire herd of water buffalo was stretched across the road. There were fifty in all, ranging in size from week-old calves to thousand pound bulls. They completely blocked our exit route and they weren't about to move.

We could hear the second Land Rover coming, just around the bend behind us.

Doc snapped the flash drive off his keychain and slapped it in my hand. "Get out before they see you! I'll divert them!"

I didn't have a moment to protest. He practically shoved me out the door.

I tumbled down a small slope into a patch of tall grass. My foot planted right into a water buffalo poop. Despite this, I lay perfectly still, not daring to move a muscle.

Doc floored the accelerator and turned off the road, speeding across the fake savanna.

The Rover rounded the bend. No one saw me hidden in the grass. They shot past me, following Doc.

I waited for them to leave me behind, then carefully made my way toward the exit.

Water buffalo are dangerous, but they're not as skittish as rhinos. They didn't perceive me as a threat. Still, they all kept a close eye on me as I wandered past. I fought every instinct I had to run; that would have only put them on edge.

Summer was still on the phone, saying, "Teddy? Are you there?"

"I'm here," I whispered. "But I need your help. I have to get to your father right away. I know who killed Henry."

"Oh my God! Who?" Summer said it so loudly, the water buffalo went on alert.

"Keep it down!" I hissed. "I'll tell you when get there. Can you meet me at the service entrance of the building?"

"No can do. My shadows have me on lockdown. I've given them the slip one too many times."

"Well, then, how . . . ?"

Summer told me the secret code; it was the date of FunJungle's grand opening. "Daddy's gonna kill me for sharing that. His office is on the top floor. Let me know when you're on your way up."

"I will . . . if I make it."

"Oh, and Teddy . . ." There was a long pause, as though Summer was having trouble getting out what came next. "I'm sorry we abandoned you with the tiger last night. . . ."

Before I knew it, I was saying, "That wasn't your fault. Your dad's the one who ran—"

"Like a coward. I know I've been AWOL since then. I kept meaning to call you, but . . . I was too embarrassed by what we'd done. We nearly got you killed! Can you ever forgive me?"

Despite everything that had happened that day—and

despite being surrounded by dangerous animals at the moment—I felt relief wash over me. Doc had been right; I'd completely misjudged Summer. "Of course," I told her.

"Thank you, Teddy. For understanding . . ."

The sound of an engine cut the silence behind me. The second Land Rover was racing back my way. The guards must have caught up to Doc and realized I'd jumped out. Now I could see them yelling and pointing toward me. The driver honked at the water buffalo to get out of the way.

The buffalo stiffened in response.

I wasn't through the herd yet. Heads with giant horns perked up all around me.

"I gotta go," I told Summer, and hung up.

Seeing that the buffalo weren't about to move, the guards leapt from the Rover and started toward the herd and me.

I knelt down and found a rock the size of a potato. The buffalo were all watching the guards, slowly forming a defensive wedge with the biggest bull in front.

I heaved the rock, nailing him in his rear haunch.

The buffalo bellowed in surprise and ran.

The others took his lead. Within seconds, their delicate state of alertness became panic. They stampeded the way they were facing: toward the guards.

The guards' eyes all went wide with terror. They fled back to their Rover.

My path to the exit cleared like the Red Sea before Moses as all the buffalo charged the car. They piled around it, gouging the metal with their horns. The guards screamed for help.

I ran the other direction. There was a steel door at the edge of SafariLand, but it was designed to keep people out, not in. I pushed through it and hauled ass down the service road, looping around the edge of the park. I didn't see another person until I got to the administration building.

There was a guard posted outside . . . but it was Large Marge. Instead of keeping an eye out for me, she was playing a game on her phone. I slipped past her with ease. I couldn't believe it. For once, I was having some luck. . . .

And then Charlie Connor exited the mascot changing room. His shift must have been over, because he was in his street clothes, lighting a new cheap cigar. He went ballistic at the sight of me. "You!" he shouted. "You're dead! You sicced security on me!"

Marge snapped to attention and saw me. Her hand immediately dropped to her holstered Taser. "Freeze, Fitzroy!" she ordered.

I ran instead.

Marge thundered after me. She snapped out her radio and informed everyone, "This is O'Malley! I've spotted Teddy Fitzroy outside the administration building!"

Meanwhile, Charlie Connor came at me from the other direction. "I told you not to tell anyone you talked to me! But you went right to Buck and gave him my name!" He lunged at me, but I sidestepped him.

Large Marge wasn't quite so nimble. She slammed into Charlie and fell, flattening him to the pavement. I chanced a look back. All I could see of Charlie were his feet, sticking out from under Marge like the Wicked Witch of the East's after Dorothy's house landed on her.

I reached the loading dock, entered Summer's code on the security keypad, and yanked on the door.

It didn't open.

INVALID CODE, the keypad read.

My heart sank. I couldn't believe it. Summer had betrayed me again.

Marge staggered to her feet, leaving Charlie Connor laid out like a pancake, and charged at me. Like a rhinoceros, she could move surprisingly fast for her size.

I was about to run, but took one last chance on Summer. Maybe she hadn't tricked me. Maybe I'd simply entered the code wrong in my haste.

I tried again.

The door clicked open.

I ducked through it. Marge was almost on top of me. She jammed her foot in the crack as I tried to slam the door shut, then threw her bulk against it and knocked it open.

I ran down the hall and into the stairwell.

"He's in the administration building!" Marge screamed into her radio. "The fox is in the henhouse!"

I charged up the stairs, dialing Summer as I ran. "I'm coming!" I gasped.

Now that we were climbing, Marge quickly fell behind, but I didn't slow down. I knew every member of Buck's force would be converging on the stairwell soon.

"There're two guards on this floor," Summer told me. "They're waiting for you outside the stairs—but they'll expect you to stop when you see them. Don't. Keep going straight for my father's office. It's at the end of the hall. I'll do what I can."

I faltered, uneasy with this. But there didn't seem to be any other option. I heard the stairwell doors bang open down on the first floor and the shouts of more security men as they entered. And I could hear Marge gasping for breath as she thudded up.

So I charged on. I reached the top floor and hit the stairwell door with everything I had.

The security men were right there, two massive guys, but like Summer had said, they were expecting me to stop. It took them a second to recognize I wasn't going to, and by that time, I was upon them. They swiped at me, but I darted between them, then sprinted for the imposing doors of J.J. McCracken's office.

The guards spun around and came after me. They were much bigger than me and I was exhausted. I could feel their hands reaching for my shoulders. . . .

Summer threw the office doors open as I approached. "Teddy! C'mon!" I could see her startled bodyguards grabbing for her just beyond.

The security men tackled me as I reached the door. We slammed into Summer's bodyguards and went down in a pile on the floor. I was buried under a mountain of men.

"What in the world is going on here?" J.J. McCracken leapt up from behind his gigantic desk and then gasped as he laid eyes on me. "You! How did you . . . ?"

"It's urgent!" Summer protested. "Teddy knows who killed Henry!"

In that moment, I hated myself for any doubts I'd ever had about Summer. She'd been a good friend all along. I was the one who'd failed *her* by questioning her loyalty.

The security men and the bodyguards all seized me at once, yanking me to my feet, glaring at me like they were ready to pummel me.

"Let him go!" J.J. snapped.

The guards all looked at him, surprised.

"The boy's gone through a heck of a lot of trouble to

get here," J.J. told them. "He's not getting out again. So let's hear what he has to say." J.J. fixed me with a hard stare. "Who killed my hippo?"

"Martin del Gato," I said.

"I told you he'd say that," said a reedy voice.

Then Martin del Gato stepped out from behind the door and took his place by J.J.'s side.

Martin didn't look the slightest bit unsettled by my accusation. Instead, he sneered at me haughtily, like a poker player who had the ace of spades up his sleeve. "This little brat needs to accuse *someone* to get his parents off the hook and he's always had it in for me."

Behind me, Buck Grassley and a few more guards raced through the door. Large Marge staggered in behind them, gasping for breath after hauling herself up five flights of stairs.

"It's about time you got here," Martin snarled at them. "Arrest this kid. I'm sure he's complicit in all this with his parents. At the very least, he cost this park a ton of money today."

Buck snapped at his men. They wrenched my arms

behind my back to handcuff me, but I squirmed away and raced around the office.

"My parents are innocent!" I shouted. I pulled out the flash drive and waved it at J.J. as the guards pursued me. "The proof's on here! It's from Doc. Martin's been using your animals to smuggle emeralds from Venezuela!"

Martin's sneer faded. J.J. shot him a suspicious glance, then looked at me. Finally, he shifted his gaze to Summer, as though seeking her idea on what to do.

"I'd check it out," she said.

The guards cornered me by J.J.'s desk and closed in.

"Keep your hands off him!" J.J. ordered.

The guards froze, inches away from me.

"This is ridiculous!" Martin snapped. "The kid's bluffing!"

"Then you don't have anything to worry about, right?" J.J. took the flash drive from me and plugged it into his computer. It only took him a few seconds to find the first incriminating documents. He turned to Martin, stunned. "What's going on here?"

Martin stepped back, wild-eyed, all his confidence blown, and desperately tried to lie his way out. "Okay, I admit, I smuggled emeralds. . . . But I did it for the park! I was only trying to cover the cost overruns. Trying to keep this place solvent . . ."

"By stealing from me?" J.J. growled. "By killing my mascot?"

"I'm not the one who killed Henry." Martin spun and pointed at Buck. "*He* did!"

Buck stared bullets back at him. "Now you're just talking crazy."

"I'm not! Buck found out I was smuggling and tried to blackmail me into giving him a cut. He confronted me one night at Hippo River after I'd brought in a big shipment. . . ."

Buck grabbed Martin and started to arrest him. "Enough of your lies . . ."

"Leave him alone," J.J. ordered. "I want to hear this."

Buck looked at J.J., surprised.

Martin pulled away. His haughty demeanor had vanished. Now, he was begging for mercy. "I had over two pounds of emeralds in a plastic bag . . . and Buck wanted them. I needed to hide them fast, so I threw them into Henry's pool. I figured they'd just sink to the bottom . . . but that lousy hippo ate them!"

"So you killed him?" J.J. asked, aghast.

"Not me! Buck did it! He saw the whole thing. I wanted to wait for Henry to crap the emeralds back out again, but I guess the bag got jammed in his stomach. After a few days, Buck got impatient and fed Henry the jacks. It never occurred to him that Doc would want to do an autopsy. I kept Doc from going through all Henry's stomach contents, though. Buck and I returned to the auditorium later and got the emeralds."

J.J. gaped at Martin and Buck, at a loss for words for once in his life.

"Tell me you don't really believe this?" Buck asked. "You've got proof the guy's a criminal—and now he's just trying to bring down everyone else. I'll bet he's the one who killed Henry! He always hated that hippo." Without waiting for an answer, he snapped a pair of cuffs off his belt.

As he did, I noticed the Bowie knife he kept sheathed there.

Suddenly everything fell into place.

"Martin's telling the truth," I said. "Buck killed Henry. And he freed the mamba and let the tiger out."

Every pair of eyes in the room shifted to me.

"Aw, now don't tell me we're gonna have to listen to this little troublemaker," Buck snarled. "He's done more damage to this park than anyone. . . ."

"Shut your piehole," J.J. snapped. "Let him talk."

Then he turned to me expectantly.

My mouth went dry. For a moment, I doubted everything I'd come up with. But when I went over it in my mind again, it all made sense.

"Buck was waiting outside the theater the night of the

autopsy," I said. "It must have surprised him to see me, because he followed me home. I found his bootprint in the dirt outside our trailer." I pointed to Buck's cowboy boots. Their heels were half-circles, the kind I'd assumed had been from dress shoes.

"That doesn't mean squat," Buck protested. "Half this county wears cowboy boots. . . ."

"Let the kid speak or so help me, I'll duct-tape your mouth shut," J.J. snapped.

Buck backed down like a whipped dog and glared at me hatefully.

"The walls on our trailer are really thin," I continued. "Buck heard me tell the police Henry had been murdered, so he tried to scare me off with the mamba the next day. He runs the security system, so he knew how to shut off the cameras in Reptile World to hide the fact that he was there."

"And when that didn't scare you off, he set the tiger on you," Summer put in.

"No," I said. "That's what I'd been thinking too, but the tiger wasn't meant for me. It was meant for someone else who was on the walkway that night: Doc."

"What?" J.J. asked. "All of a sudden, he wanted to kill Doc, too?"

"I didn't want to kill anyone!" Buck shouted.

"Shut up!" J.J. roared at him.

"At first, Buck thought I was the only problem," I explained. "But the night before the party, I told him that Doc was the one who'd learned how Henry had been murdered— and who'd autopsied all the other animals. Then Buck realized Doc was the real threat. He knew about Henry's murder, the smuggling, everything. If Buck got rid of Doc, he got rid of all the evidence. So he rigged the ladder to set the tiger free. The rope was cut clean through and it was an inch thick; only a knife like Buck's could do that."

"So?" Buck asked. "Lots of men have knives like mine."

"But you're the only one who could get one past security. Every party guest had to pass through two metal detectors that night. But not you. Plus, it explains why you took fifteen minutes to respond to our emergency call. You were hiding in Carnivore Canyon and couldn't leave until after we did. Then you had to go out through the back exit and loop all the way around."

"Sounds open-and-shut to me," said Summer.

"No!" Buck snapped, a little too quickly. "It's all speculation! You don't have proof."

"I'll bet we could find some," I said. "You couldn't have erased *every* security tape. There's thousands of hours of them. There's bound to be one of you getting the jacks at FunJungle Emporium, or sneaking into the theater after the autopsy, or following me home that night, or rigging the ladder into Carnivore Canyon. . . ."

"This is insanity." Buck spoke directly to J.J. now. "The kid's making everything up. He's just trying to protect his parents. There's evidence against them. . . ."

"All of which *you* provided," J.J. replied. He pointed to two security officers. "Go to the security room and lock down every tape we've got from the past two weeks."

"J.J., please." Buck now looked desperate and wounded. "We've been friends a long time. You're gonna tell me you don't trust me?"

"Trust? Let's talk about trust." J.J. began to tick things off on his fingers. "First, my own manager of operations killed my animals to smuggle emeralds into the country. Now, he's accused my head of security of killing my mascot, then plotting to kill a twelve-year-old boy and my vet. My head of security claims it was the boy's parents who killed the hippo, but the only person who appears to have been doing any actual investigating around here at all is the boy—who managed to turn a lovely funeral into a national travesty on live television today. That doesn't include my PR director who's botched everything he's laid his hands on, a security staff that's so incompetent they couldn't find their own rear ends with a mirror, bodyguards who can't control a thirteen-year-old girl—and my own daughter, who's been slinking around behind my back every chance she's got and thinking I wouldn't notice." As J.J. spoke, he was getting angrier and angrier, as though he'd been struggling to hold his rage in for some time but was now ready to explode. "Frankly, it doesn't seem that I should trust *anyone* here at all. Because every single person I've trusted has been up to something and I'm sick of it!"

The entire room fell silent, ashamed.

"It's not like *you're* completely honest either," I said.

J.J. wheeled on me, stunned I'd dared accuse him. "What did you say?"

"My parents and I saw your plans. You're going to build thrill rides in the animal exhibits."

"Daddy?" Now it was Summer's turn to look betrayed. "How could you?"

I'd heard J.J. McCracken could outtalk any businessman in the world, but apparently this didn't hold true for his daughter. He crumbled under her gaze, stammering, "Those weren't . . . Those are just prototypes. They're not . . ."

Buck Grassley suddenly bolted for the door. He was surprisingly fast for an old man—and everyone was too distracted by J.J. to respond quickly. Buck slipped past his security men and Summer's bodyguards and dashed for the hall. . . .

. . . When Large Marge stepped into his path and

punched him in the nose. There was a loud crack, a small spurt of blood, and then Buck dropped flat on his back, unconscious.

Marge cracked her knuckles and looked J.J. McCracken square in the eyes. "Who're you calling incompetent?" she asked.

I raced across FunJungle as fast as my legs would carry me. It was tough going, though. The concourses were so packed with tourists, there was barely room to move.

There had been plenty of concern that the string of publicity disasters would hurt FunJungle's business, but if anything, the opposite had occurred. The park was busier now, a month after all the trouble, than it had been before. The scandal about Henry's murder had been headline news all over the world; if you believed that there was no such thing as bad publicity, J.J. McCracken couldn't have bought more of it. The footage of the escaped tiger and the plummeting hippo coffin had been viewed millions of times on YouTube; now people wanted to see the places the events had taken place themselves.

Which wasn't to say people weren't coming to see the animals at all. They were—although the more cautious guests tended to avoid Carnivore Canyon, no matter how much time Pete Thwacker spent insisting that no more tigers would escape. As I ran past SafariLand, I noted that the wait for the tram was an hour long. In addition, a line of people snaked out the door of the Polar Pavilion—although they might have been less interested in seeing the penguins than getting out of the 100-degree heat.

Doc, ever the pessimist, groused that it was all too good to last. Given the financial straits Martin del Gato had left the park in, he figured it was only a matter of time until FunJungle had to start selling the wildebeests to hot dog factories to make ends meet. (Dad insisted Doc was joking, but I wasn't so sure.) Mom pointed out that, of everyone, Doc should be optimistic. After all, he could have been in jail.

I rounded Amazon Adventure and Hippo River came into view.

J.J. McCracken had decided not to press charges against Doc. Either J.J. believed Doc wasn't really guilty because Martin had blackmailed him into helping with his scheme— or he simply didn't want to lose his best vet for five to ten years. He'd also kept Doc's daughter's connection to the ALF a secret—as had everyone else involved. But J.J. had gone after everyone else who'd betrayed him with a vengeance. He'd used his political clout to ensure that Martin and Buck were arrested without bail and put his top attorneys on the case to make sure they both went to prison for a long time. Of course, J.J. also made sure Pete Thwacker informed the press of all this to convince the public he was the good guy in this scandal.

I reached the Hippo River Restaurant and found it closed. This was surprising; the restaurant was usually open all day and there was always an hour wait. Now, there was only a cluster of disgruntled tourists who kept checking their guide maps to see if they'd read the hours wrong.

I checked my phone, thinking I'd made a mistake as well. But there was the text from Mom: *Come to HR restaurant ASAP!!!*

I called Mom. She didn't answer. Instead, fifteen seconds later, she opened the door and furtively waved me inside, as though worried she'd be caught in the act.

"What's going on?" I asked.

Mom put a finger to her lips and signaled me to follow her.

The restaurant looked a lot bigger when it was almost empty. Most of the lamps were off, so it was dark and cave-like, the only light coming from the massive windows that looked into the hippo enclosures.

On the other side of one window, Henry's replacement, Horton Hippo, slept at the bottom of the river. The fact that Horton was actually outside was surprising to me. Personality-wise, Horton was the anti-Henry. He was extremely timid and unaggressive for a hippo, preferring to spend most of his time in his holding pen where the guests couldn't see him. While this aggravated Pete, even he admitted that a hippo who hid from the tourists was infinitely better than one who fired poop at them.

None of the people in the restaurant was watching Horton, though. Instead, they were all clustered at the window into Hildegard's enclosure: Dad, Doc, all four of the hippos' keepers, Pete, two of his underlings from the PR department, Large Marge—and Tracey Boyd, an officious woman who'd replaced Martin as director of operations. (She'd started only two days before, so I hadn't met her yet.) There were also several Klieg lights, reflectors, and cameras—still and video—mounted on tripods: Dad's handiwork. Hildegard herself loomed on the other side of the glass.

As Mom led me over, Dad and the keepers waved, looking happy as kids on Christmas morning.

Tracey gave me a sideways glance. "What's *he* doing here?" she asked.

"Teddy's like a bad penny," Marge muttered. "He turns up everywhere."

Marge had been promoted after Buck's arrest; J.J. had been impressed with her performance in his office. Summer and I had protested, revealing that Marge had actually plotted to kill Henry herself, but this turned out to be a misunderstanding. When Pete had told Marge he wished Henry was dead, Marge hadn't realized it was only a figure of speech and tried to run her own private sting operation. To me, this was further proof of Marge's incompetence, but J.J. had viewed it as initiative. Marge was now head of park security, which meant she had even more freedom to tail me suspiciously each day.

"This is my son," Mom told Tracey. "I figure after all he did bringing Henry's murderer to justice, he deserves to be here for this."

Tracey looked to Doc for confirmation. Doc nodded that it was okay, though it seemed to pain him to do it.

"What's going on?" I asked for the second time.

"Hildegard's in labor," Dad said.

It took me a moment to process that. "But I thought she and Henry never, uh. . . ."

"Apparently they did," Mom said. "While no one was looking."

A huge grin spread across my face. "And no one ever noticed?"

"A pregnant two-ton hippo doesn't look that different from a nonpregnant two-ton hippo," Doc told me. "Although I suspected something was up. . . ."

"And you never told anyone?"

"No. I told people. People who needed to know. I just didn't tell *you.*"

Even Doc's crustiness couldn't wipe the smile from my face. I knew most of it was for show. Mom had told me Doc really felt indebted to me for helping bring Martin down, though he'd never said a word of thanks to me.

I looked through the window at Hildegard. Unlike humans, animals are usually very calm during labor. Hildegard just sat by the glass, occasionally rearing up to poke her nostrils out of the water.

The restaurant door banged open and J.J. and Summer McCracken entered, flanked by bodyguards. Even J.J. couldn't hide his excitement. Summer rushed across the room toward us. "Tell me it hasn't happened yet."

"It hasn't," I said happily. What was already an incredible day had just got even better. I hadn't expected to see Summer again for months; she was heading back to private school that day. Sadly, we hadn't had much opportunity to see each other since the incident in her father's office. The press had been hounding Summer like crazy—half the magazines in the country still seemed more interested in her reaction to Henry's murder than in the story behind it—and J.J. had warned her bodyguards that if she gave them the slip again, they'd be fired. We'd had lunch at the zoo twice and I'd been invited out to the ranch once, but that hadn't been nearly enough time for me. I would have been happy to spend every day with Summer—though I wondered if she felt the same way about me. Now that there was no murder to solve, my life had become routine again, while hers had remained busy. I hadn't even had a chance to see her in the past few days; we'd had to say good-bye by phone. Or so I'd thought.

"Aren't you supposed to be on a plane?" I said.

"It's *our* plane," she replied. "It leaves whenever we want it to. And we couldn't miss *this*. . . ."

"Of course not," J.J. agreed. He might have been a tough businessman to everyone else in the world, but he was a total pushover for his daughter. When she told him she'd never speak to him again if he built thrill rides inside the animal exhibits, he had immediately promised not to. Or at least, he'd promised for now. . . .

"Hey!" Dad said. "It's happening!"

We all turned to the window. Hildegard stood on her hind legs and grunted loud enough that it echoed through the restaurant.

"Don't be alarmed by that," Doc told us. He was never crotchety in front of J.J. "That's a good sign."

"Isn't this amazing?" Watching the hippo, Summer grabbed my hand. I'm not sure if she even knew she was doing it. She was riveted to Hildegard, her eyes filled with excitement.

I'd seen animals give birth plenty of times before. More than I could count. But I'd never held a girl's hand before. For the first time, I got the idea that Summer might want to be more than just friends. "Yes," I said. "It's amazing, all right."

Thankfully, it was so dark in the restaurant no one could see my face had turned red as a baboon's bottom.

Hildegard gave a push and, within seconds, the baby was out. Everyone cheered. Even Doc cracked a smile for once.

The baby hippo already weighed fifty pounds and knew how to swim. Hildegard nudged it toward the surface for its first breath.

Up at Nugudugu Overlook, the guests shouted with joy as the baby emerged. I caught J.J. and Pete share an excited look. Both seemed to be seeing dollar signs.

Summer squeezed my hand, thrilled by what we'd just witnessed.

The baby hippo swam back down to Hildegard's side and began to nurse.

I couldn't stop smiling.

Dad had been shooting pictures constantly, making sure he got the entire birth on film. Mom stood by his side. "I'll be darned," she said. "It's a boy."

"Henry Hippo Junior," J.J. McCracken proclaimed. "I believe we can market that."

TAKE A SNEAK PEAK AT TEDDY FITZROY'S NEXT FUNJUNGLE ADVENTURE IN *POACHED*

Available February 2014 wherever books are sold.

I would never have been accused of stealing the koala if Vance Jessup hadn't made me drop a human arm in the shark tank at FunJungle.

It wasn't a *real* human arm. It was a plastic one Vance had stolen from a department-store mannequin. But it *looked* real enough through the glass of the tank, which was how all the trouble started.

Vance was the toughest, meanest kid at my middle school. He was in the eighth grade, but he'd been held back. Twice. Which made him a fifteen-year-old eighth grader. Plus, he was big for his age, nearly six feet tall with biceps as thick as Burmese pythons. Every other kid looked like a dwarf next to him.

There was a very long list of things I didn't like about

Lyndon B. Johnson Middle School, but Vance was at the top of it. He'd been bullying me since my first day of seventh grade—and it was now mid-December. I didn't know what he had against me. Maybe it was because I was new at the school and thus fresh meat. Or maybe it was that, having spent most of my childhood in the Congo, I was different from all the other kids. Whatever the case, Vance homed in on me like he was a cheetah and I was the weakest wildebeest in the herd.

Vance stole my lunch. He gave me wedgies. He flushed my homework down the toilet. I reported these incidents to my parents, who angrily informed the school principal, Mr. Dillnut. Unfortunately, Mr. Dillnut was afraid of Vance himself. So he merely threatened Vance with detention— and then ratted me out as the kid who'd squealed. If anything, this made Vance even *more* determined to harass me. Only now he warned me that if I ever got him sent to the principal again, he'd hurt me.

So I fought back the only way I knew how: I played pranks on him. Covertly, of course. I filled his locker with aerosol cheese. I submerged a dead roach in his chocolate pudding. I caught a king snake and hid it in his gym bag. That one worked out the best. Vance was changing in the boys' locker room when the snake popped out and scared him silly. Vance shrieked like a girl and fled into the gym, forgetting that he was only in his underwear until he found himself face-to-face with the entire cheerleading squad.

Unfortunately, the snake tipped my hand. I'd kept my identity as the prankster secret until that point, but I was well-known at school for being good with animals. My mother was a world-famous primatologist, my father was a world-famous wildlife photographer, and I lived with both of them at FunJungle, the world's largest zoo. Vance quickly deduced that I'd planted the snake and came looking for payback.

He found me in the cafeteria on Monday, having lunch with Xavier Gonzalez. Xavier was my best friend at school. In fact he was my only friend at school. He was an outsider too, a smart kid who'd once made the terrible social error of admitting that he actually enjoyed his classes. Before I'd come along, Xavier had been Vance's favorite target.

There was a distinct hierarchy to the seating in the school cafeteria. The coolest kids, known as the Royals, sat in the center, where they could be seen and admired. These were the eighth-grade jocks and cheerleaders, plus a few rich kids. They were surrounded by the Lower Royals: the younger jocks, cheerleaders, and rich kids who would assume the throne someday. Then came almost everyone else: the normal kids who hoped to be popular someday, but knew it would probably never happen. At the very corners sat the lowest of the low, whom even the normal kids looked down on: the losers, loners, and freaks who hadn't mastered how to fit in.

I had spent every lunch so far in one of the corners with Xavier. So it wasn't hard for Vance to find me.

As usual, Xavier and I were talking about FunJungle. Most of my fellow students liked FunJungle—after all, it was the biggest tourist attraction in all of South Texas—but Xavier was a FunJungle fanatic. He had more than twenty different FunJungle T-shirts (not to mention sweatshirts, caps, pins, and other assorted merchandise) and claimed that the day the park had opened was the greatest day of his life. He wanted to be a field biologist when he grew up and idolized my mother the way other kids revered rock stars. He'd read everything he could find about her, so he knew all about me before I'd even set foot in the school. He'd sought me out on my first day at Lyndon B. Johnson, wanting to know if I could introduce him to Mom.

Xavier generally spent every lunch peppering me with questions about FunJungle. The day that Vance came after me, we happened to be talking about Shark Odyssey, which was one of the more popular exhibits. It was a huge aquarium with a glass tunnel running through it, from which guests could watch sharks swimming all around them.

"Doesn't that drive the sharks crazy?" Xavier wanted to know. "It must be like waving red meat in front of a lion."

"Sharks don't really eat humans," I told him. "In fact, most attacks seem to be accidents. The sharks usually spit the humans back out after biting them."

"I know," Xavier said. "But still, they're hunters, right? And now all these humans are moving right through their habitat. It must trigger some sort of primal instinct."

I shook my head. "No. In the first place, the glass tunnel is lined with some kind of reflective surface, so the sharks can't see the humans from inside. And even if they could, sharks don't really hunt by sight. They hunt by smell— and by sensing vibrations in the water. You could drop a whole mannequin in the shark tank and the sharks probably wouldn't even give it a second look."

"I bet it'd freak the guests out, though," Xavier laughed.

"Yeah," I agreed. "It would be pretty funny."

Xavier stopped laughing at that point, which I should have taken as a sign that something was wrong, but I was too caught up thinking about the prank. I kept rambling on, unaware that Vance Jessup was bearing down on me. "Know what would *really* freak the guests out? If you only put *part* of a mannequin in the tank. Like just an arm. So it'd look like the sharks had already eaten the rest. *That* would be hilarious."

Now, Vance decided to make his presence known. He

grabbed my chair and spun me around to face him. "What would be hilarious?" he demanded. "Are you planning another prank on me?"

I gulped, terrified, and did my best to lie to Vance's face. "What are you talking about? I've never played *any* pranks on you."

"I know you put that snake in my gym bag, Monkey Boy. And you're gonna pay for it." Vance held up a clenched fist the size of a grapefruit.

I recoiled, aware this wasn't an idle threat. Vance got in fights almost every day—and usually won. He was covered with bruises, scratches and scrapes, though his opponents generally looked far worse. He was currently sporting a half dozen Band Aids dappled with blood that was probably someone else's.

Meanwhile, I'd never been in a fight in my life. I wouldn't stand a chance against Vance.

"Teddy wasn't talking about playing a prank on *you*," Xavier said quickly, trying to bail me out. "He was talking about playing a prank at FunJungle. Dropping a fake human arm into the shark tank to make all the guests freak out."

Vance lowered his fist. His sneer faded and he made a strange noise. At first I thought he was choking—but then realized he was laughing. "That *would* be funny," he said. "When are you going to do it?"

"Er . . . never," I said. "I only meant it would be funny *in theory*. I would never really do something like that. It might start a panic—"

"Exactly," Vance said, and then laughed again. "Let's do it after school tomorrow."

I shook my head and tried to come up with a believable excuse. "Sorry, but it's not possible. There's a ton of security at FunJungle. They'd catch us if we tried to sneak the arm inside."

"No, they'd catch *me* if I tried to sneak the arm inside," Vance corrected. "Not you. You don't have to go through the main entrance."

I winced. I hadn't expected Vance to know that. I struggled to come up with something else. "We don't have a fake arm, either . . ."

"Leave that to me," Vance said. "I can steal one from the department store in town."

"You know, now that I think about it," I said, "I don't think this would be that good a prank at all. But I'll tell you what might be a lot more fun. Maybe I could get you a backstage tour of the shark exhibit. It's pretty fascinating. . . ."

Vance's eyes narrowed in anger. "I don't want a tour of some dumb shark tank."

"Oh, it's not dumb," Xavier put in, trying to be helpful. "It's actually quite amazing. In fact, it's the largest shark tank in the world, housing over thirty different species—"

"Shut up," Vance told him.

"Okay," Xavier said, backing down.

Vance clamped a hand on my shoulder. "I want to play this prank," he informed me. "And I need your help to do it. So you're going to help me, right?"

I wished I'd had the nerve to stand up to Vance right then and there and tell him what I really thought of him. But my shoulder was already in terrible pain, and Vance wasn't even squeezing that hard yet. I got the sense that if he wanted to, he could snap me like a twig. And yet I still hesitated before giving Vance an answer.

That didn't please him at all. "Trust me on this," he said. "You don't want to be my enemy. Before I heard about this shark-tank thing, I was about to pound your face in. I'd still be happy to do that."

"No!" I said desperately, wanting to keep my face the way it was. "I'll do it!"

"Okay, then." Vance released me and flashed a cruel smile. "See you tomorrow afternoon."

So that's how I ended up dropping fake body parts into Shark Odyssey.

Vance cornered me right after school the next day. True to his word, he'd obtained the arm of a mannequin—and a foot as well. "The more body parts the better," he explained.

Just in case I'd managed to work up the nerve to say no to him—which I'd been working on for the past twenty-four hours—he'd brought along two bullies-in-training: Jim and Tim Barksdale. The Barksdales were identical twins in the eighth grade. They were so dumb and mean that everyone, even their parents, had trouble telling them apart. Since they were rarely without each other, everyone simply called them TimJim.

Vance had hidden the mannequin parts in a large backpack, which he insisted I take with me on the school bus. "Don't even go home," he threatened. "Take it right to the sharks. We'll be waiting for you there. If you try to chicken out—or tip off security—we'll come find you."

"And then maybe we'll feed *you* to the sharks," either Tim or Jim said.

The boys all laughed at this.

I felt like throwing up, but I didn't really see that I had a choice. So I left my regular backpack in my locker, took my homework and Vance's backpack and hopped onto the school bus. Xavier, who rode the same bus as me, volunteered to come to Shark Odyssey as moral support—although I suspected he was actually more interested in getting to sneak into FunJungle the back way with me. "Thanks," I told him, "but I should probably do this alone. Maybe I can trick Vance into doing it himself and get him busted for it."

"I wouldn't do that," Xavier warned. "If Vance catches on, it'll only make him angrier at you."

"He won't catch on," I said. "He's a moron. The guy's flunked eighth grade twice."

Xavier shook his head. "Vance didn't flunk because he's stupid. He flunked because he's lazy. In fact, Vance is smarter than most people realize. If he put as much thought into studying as he does into being cruel and mean, he'd be graduating college by now."

I thought back to my many nasty encounters with Vance and realized Xavier was right. Vance was actually quite clever; he just used his gifts for evil. For example, he knew how to make his own cherry bombs with chemicals he'd pilfered from the science lab. "So what should I do?" I asked.

"Pull the prank as fast as possible," Xavier advised, "and pray you don't get busted."

My bus stop was the last one, as FunJungle was located several miles from town. Technically it wasn't located in *any* school district; a special exemption had been made for me, the only child living there, to attend Lyndon B. Johnson.

FunJungle was so big it actually qualified as its own city. The park had been built by J.J. McCracken, a local billionaire. He claimed he'd done it for his daughter, Summer—but the fact that 175 million people visited zoos in America every year had certainly influenced him as well. FunJungle was officially a zoo—the world's biggest, by far—though, to attract tourists, it was also part theme park. There were thrill rides, stage shows, themed hotels, and plenty of innovative exhibits, like a massive African habitat where you could go on a safari and several pools where you could swim with dolphins. Despite the gimmicks, however, FunJungle was committed to providing top-quality care for its animals. J.J. had hired lots of distinguished biologists (like my mother) and had shelled out big bucks to make the animal exhibits state-of-the-art. The whole park was nearly ten miles square, with its own police department, fire station, and hospital. (Technically it was an animal hospital, but it was nicer than most human hospitals and had a physician on staff for any FunJungle employees who got sick.)

I didn't really live at FunJungle per se. There was a trailer park behind the safari area that served as free housing for the distinguished biologists and their families. As Vance had ordered, I didn't go home once the bus dropped me off. But then I never did. There was no point in sitting in our trailer all by myself. Not when Mom's office was nice and cozy and had windows that looked into the gorilla exhibit. Many days I went straight there to do my homework, but if anything interesting was happening at FunJungle—and there often was—I'd go there instead. Thus Mom didn't really expect me to show up at any specific time. And as for Dad, he was generally roaming the park taking pictures—if he was even at the park. His contract allowed him to accept freelance jobs as well. He'd just returned from photographing anacondas in the Amazon for *National Geographic* a few days earlier.

I entered the park through the rear employee entry booth, which was next to the employee parking lot and the trailer park. Darlene, the guard posted inside, barely gave me a glance as I entered. She was watching a downloaded movie on her iPhone, which was probably a violation of sixteen different security directives, but on that day I didn't care. I didn't want any scrutiny. The entry booth wasn't much bigger than a storage closet. On one side a door led in from employee parking. On the other side a door led into Fun-Jungle. Darlene sat between them next to a metal detector. "Hey, Teddy, how was school?" she asked.

"Same as usual." I set the backpack down by Darlene, passed through the metal detector, and grabbed the pack again without giving her the chance to rifle through it. Not that she tried. Darlene hadn't examined my things once in the last six months. However, she did stare at the pack a little bit longer than usual.

"That new?" she asked.

"Yeah. Mom just got it for me."

"It's awful big."

"They give lots of homework at my school," I explained.

"Yuck." Darlene made a face of disgust, then returned to her movie.

I exited into FunJungle and made a beeline for Shark Odyssey.

The rear employee entrance was on the opposite side of the park from the main gates, hidden behind a thicket of trees so that tourists wouldn't notice it. A narrow path brought me out onto Adventure Road, the main route through the park, right between Carnivore Canyon and the Land Down Under.

The park was eerily empty. During the summer, capacity crowds had come every day and Adventure Road had been as crowded as a Manhattan sidewalk. But now the tourists were few and far between. The reason, everyone claimed, was the weather, which had been far worse that year than anyone had expected.

The main reason J.J. McCracken had built FunJungle in the Texas Hill Country was that it was supposed to be warm all the time. This would be good for the animals, most of which came from warm climates, and better for the tourists, who would theoretically flock there year-round. (This was the same reason that Disney and Universal Studios had built their theme parks in Southern California and Florida.) Unfortunately, this particular winter had been the nastiest anyone could remember. Ever since mid-November, a freak cold front had stalled over the Hill Country, pelting the park with an incredible array of horrible weather. There had been hail, freezing rain, record cold temperatures, and even a few tornadoes. (Thankfully, these had all been quite small and done little damage, although one had uprooted a jungle gym in the Play Zone and flung it into World of Reptiles.)

Thousands of guests who'd booked for Thanksgiving and the Christmas holidays had canceled their FunJungle travel plans. This was terrible luck for the park, which had finally rebounded from its previous crisis, the murder of its mascot, Henry the Hippo, that summer. If anything, this was worse. Henry's death had at least sparked interest in the park; tourists had streamed in to see the notorious murder site. But few people had any interest in spending their vacations shivering in a sleet storm, staring at animal paddocks that were empty because the animals themselves had had the sense to go inside.

The stretch between Thanksgiving and Christmas should have been a low-tourism time anyhow, but now it was far worse than expected. So J.J. McCracken had resorted to a few desperate moves to lure people to the park. The first was to drastically slash ticket prices.

The biggest deal FunJungle now offered was on annual passes. For only five dollars more than the cost of one visit, people could upgrade their FunJungle FunPass and come for free all year-round. McCracken's idea was that the park could make back the money by gouging repeat visitors for expensive food and park merchandise—although most people quickly caught on to this and started smuggling in their own lunches. However, virtually everyone within a fifty-mile radius had bought the passes. FunJungle, no matter what the weather, was still the most exciting thing to happen in that area in decades, and the discount deal was simply too good to pass up.

Vance Jessup and TimJim had annual passes. And at fifteen, Vance had his learner's driving permit. This meant he was only supposed to drive with an adult in the car, but he drove himself all the time anyhow—and since he looked like an adult, the police never stopped him. The boys had all come to FunJungle directly from school and were waiting inside Shark Odyssey for me.

Normally, Shark Odyssey was one of the most crowded exhibits at FunJungle. In the summer there had often been hour-long waits to get inside. Now almost no one was there. It wasn't hard to spot Vance and TimJim in the sparse crowd.

Shark Odyssey was designed to present its inhabitants from many different angles. You began at the top of the massive three-story tank, from which you could look down into the water and watch the sharks from above. From there you moved down a long ramp that spiraled around the tank, allowing you to see the sharks from the side. And finally you ended up in the big glass tube with sharks swimming all around you.

Vance and TimJim were at the first viewpoint, above the surface of the tank. Vance checked his watch as I approached. "Took you long enough," he groused. "I figured you'd chickened out. We were about to come looking for you."

"I got here as fast as I could," I said. "The bus has a lot of stops to make before mine."

"Whatever," Vance said dismissively, as if this explanation didn't make sense. "We've waited long enough. Security's already started to pay attention to us."

"How so?" I asked, trying to hide my concern.

"Some big woman guard with a ton of attitude's been giving us the stink eye," Vance explained.

Large Marge, I thought. *Of course.* Marge had been a constant thorn in my side since I'd come to FunJungle; she'd always been far more concerned with busting me rather than catching any park guests disobeying the rules. Originally this had been a mere annoyance, as Marge was only a grunt in the security force, but after she'd helped catch Henry the Hippo's murderer, she'd been promoted to head of park security. In truth, *I'd* done almost all the work catching the killer, with some help from Summer McCracken. I'd found all the leads, taken all the risks, and finally solved the crime. All

Marge had done was punch the bad guy as he was trying to escape. But she'd done that right in front of J.J. McCracken, who'd been impressed and promoted her. Now Marge had an entire security force she could order to keep an eye on me—although she still preferred to try to catch me red-handed herself.

"Where is she now?" I asked.

"I don't know," Vance admitted. "She came over a few minutes ago and warned us not to cause any trouble, but then someone called her on her radio and she took off."

"Why'd she think you were going to cause trouble?" I asked.

"What do I look like, a mind reader?" Vance demanded. "She was just being a jerk."

"Yeah," either Tim or Jim muttered. "All we did was spit in the shark tank."

I turned on Vance, unable to control my annoyance. "You spit in the shark tank?"

"What's it matter?" Vance asked. "It's not like it'll hurt the sharks or anything. They live in water—and that's all spit is."

I tamped down the urge to tell Vince what a jerk he was. Spit *isn't* just water. It carries all sorts of diseases, which could be spread to the sharks, for which reason there were dozens of signs posted around the shark tank telling people not to spit into it. The boys had blatantly broken park rules, getting Marge's attention.

"We can't do the prank now," I said. "I know Marge. She wouldn't just let you guys off with a warning. She's probably still lurking around here somewhere."

I started for the doors, but Vance seized my arm and squeezed it hard. Even through my heavy winter jacket it hurt. "You're not weaseling out of this," he told me.

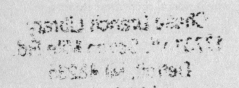